House Arrest

HOUSE ARREST

a novel

Ellen Meeropol

RED HEN PRESS | *Pasadena, CA*

Book layout by Kathrine Davidson
Book design by Mark E. Cull

Library of Congress Cataloging-in-Publication Data

Meeropol, Ellen.
House Arrest : a novel / Ellen Meeropol.—1st ed.
p. cm.
ISBN 978-1-59709-499-3 (alk. paper)
1. Nurses—Fiction. 2. Pregnant women—Fiction. 3. Home detention—Fiction. 4. Cult members—Fiction. 5. Domestic fiction. I. Title.
PS3613.E375H68 2011
813'.6—dc22
2010040787

The Los Angeles County Arts Commission, the National Endowment for the Arts, the California Arts Council and Los Angeles Department of Cultural Affairs partially support Red Hen Press.

First Edition

Published by Red Hen Press
Pasadena, CA
www.redhen.org

ACKNOWLEDGEMENTS

The women in my manuscript group read these chapters more than once, with patience and insight. My deep appreciation to Lydia Kann, Kris Holloway, Jacqueline Sheehan, Rita Marks, Marianne Banks, Dori Ostermiller, and Brenda Marsian.

I am grateful for the support, friendship, and mentorship I received from the Stonecoast MFA community. Thank you Lee Hope, A. Manette Ansay, Michael C. White, Alan Davis, Lesléa Newman, Ann Hood, Meriah Crawford, David Page, and especially the Vanettes: Sarah Stromeyer, Ginnie Gavrin, Sharon Doucet, and Perky Alsop.

Thank you to those who generously shared their expertise and knowledge with me—Amy Romanczuk, Liz and Jim Goldman, Jane Bobowicz, Juanita Martínez, Jane Frey, Ruth and Sam Small, Rabbi Amita Jarmon, Rhoda Boughton, Hermine Levey Weston, Susan Galvin, Frances Goldin, Joan Grenier, Jon Weissman, and Bill Newman. Many thanks also to publicist Mary Bisbee-Beek, agent Roger S. Williams, and to Kate Gale and all the staff at Red Hen Press.

This book owes a great debt to my former patients at Shriners Hospital and their families, who taught me about spina bifida, about latex allergy, and about perseverance.

My daughters graciously invited these characters into our family, allowing them to monopolize many visits and conversations. Thank you, Jenn and Rachel.

Finally and always, thank you, Robby. For everything.

For Robby, life partner in everything

House Arrest

1 ~ *Emily*

I tried to get out of the assignment. Prenatal visits to a prisoner? Okay, house arrest, same difference. I couldn't believe that I was supposed to take care of a woman whose child died in a cult ritual. What kind of mother could get so involved in an oddball religion that she'd let her baby freeze to death? And what kind of name was Pippa?

Don't get me wrong. Every patient deserves expert and compassionate care. Even the most despicable criminal. I learned that in nursing school and I believe it, really. Still, this assignment gave me the creeps.

Driving to her house that mid-November morning, I knew precious little about Pippa Glenning or her cult. Just that she was under house arrest, which is why I had to visit her every week for routine prenatal monitoring. I knew that her daughter and another kid had died during a religious ceremony in Forest Park last December, their bodies discovered months later. I hadn't paid much attention to the hype of the newspaper articles, but I remembered the headlines: the Frozen Babies Case.

From the assignment sheet, I knew she was twenty-one. Not awfully young to have a baby. A second baby, I reminded myself. No medical records. That did not bode well. Neither did the scrawled sentence in the space for primary care provider: We don't believe in your medicine. Under Religion was written Family of Isis. Ditto for Household Composition: Family of Isis.

Okay, so Ms. Glenning lived in a cult. Nurses meet lots of oddballs. How different could a cult be from a commune? I'd had patients in communal households before. It always gave me a twinge, because my parents lived in a commune in Ann Arbor before I was born, and that ended badly. And some people thought my own living situation was weird; I shared the bottom half of a duplex a few blocks away with my cousin Anna and her disabled daughter, and Anna's ex-husband Sam lived upstairs.

I am good at this work, I reminded myself as I turned onto the block where the Family of Isis lived. Pioneer Street was new to me. Crowded with triple-decker houses, it sat on the boundary line of the historic Forest Park neighborhood, far removed from the elegant homes along the park and from the duplexes like Anna's, neatly painted to emulate the park-side style. Pioneer Street didn't even try. Pippa Glenning's house was an anomaly, set back from the cracked sidewalk with a single front door. No rusty bikes chained to the downspout at the corner of the house. No broken flowerpots on the stoop or piled scrap lumber from an unfinished porch repair. No tire swing dangling from the low branch of the single oak in the front yard. How many people lived inside and why didn't their lives spill out into the yard the way their neighbors' did? Didn't their children have bikes or red wagons? I parked, took my supplies from the trunk, and rang the doorbell.

I am always excited on the first visit. I think I'm at my best with my patients. And I'm curious. Okay, nosy. I like seeing how regular people live. But I already knew that Pippa Glenning wasn't regular. I rang the doorbell again and listened to the silence.

The young woman who opened the heavy front door was short and round. Stocky, but not fat, not at all. Spiky yellow hair framed a circular face like the crayoned rays around a child's drawing of a sun. Her eyeglasses were shaped like a pair of wings, set with sparkles. Eyes such a dark blue they were almost black, with puffiness around them. Losing sleep?

"You from the nursing agency?" Her voice had a trace of a southern accent. Her mouth was round, just like her body. I might have called it generous, except that it didn't smile. She held her head to the side in the same graceful tilt as the orange cat at her feet. I felt tall and gawky.

"Yes," I said. "I'm Emily Klein."

"Well, I'm Pippa. Come on in." She turned away into the dim hallway.

My heart hammered. This is just another patient, part of the job, I reminded myself. I took a slow breath, bumped my rolling backpack over the threshold step, and entered Pippa Glenning's home. I followed her through the dining room, past the commune-sized table covered with a relief map of Massachusetts. Fresh green paint glistened on the Berkshires. My father helped me make a map like that in third grade. Would I ever have a child, to help make paper maché projects for school? Anyway, in a few years Zoe would have assignments like that, and I knew my cousin Anna would let me help.

So there must be kids living here. School-age kids. I hoped the Department of Social Services was keeping a close eye, given what happened to their little brother and sister, or whatever relation those poor babies were.

"How many children live here?" I asked Pippa.

"Two." She kept walking. "We can talk in the living room."

Our footsteps echoed on the wood floor. The kids must be in school. I thought about the other adults, tried to imagine cult members working nine-to-five jobs.

At the arched entrance to the living room, I forgot my musings about relief maps and cult employment. The painting stretched eight, ten feet long, covering the entire wall over the fireplace. The artist had applied thick pigment liberally so the intense color exploded from the canvas. The half-woman, half-bird creature watched me, an expression of suspicion on her exotic features. Her massive wings were outstretched. She nursed a baby against one breast and embraced a large black cat against the other.

"Isis," Pippa said.

I might have imagined the mockery in her tone.

Pippa sat on the sofa and pointed to an easy chair. "Have a seat."

I thought about asking if we could talk in the kitchen, away from this painting, but that would give voice to my discomfort. My job was to accept all my patients as they were, with respect. No matter what my personal feelings were about New Age Goddess-worship or oddball households. No matter how I felt about people who let their children freeze to death in the snow, and then got pregnant again when other people had no children at all, I would do my professional best to help Pippa Glenning have a healthy pregnancy and a strong baby. So I sat down on the edge of the chair, angled my back towards the painting, and took my laptop from the backpack.

Other than the painting, the living room was ordinary. The furniture was mismatched, like bargains from second-hand shops, except for the pair of button-back chairs upholstered in mustard yellow brocade and facing each other in front of the bay windows. On one chair, a sleek black cat slept curled up in bands of sunlight sliced by the Venetian blinds. The orange cat jumped onto the other one and began purring, harsh and sputtering like a tractor.

"Are those chairs Victorian?" I asked.

Pippa shrugged.

"They could be valuable, if there's a manufacturer's mark on the bottom. Somebody and Sons." My Aunt Ruth said that symbol made her button-back chair her nest egg for old age. But Aunt Ruth would never have allowed cats on her nest egg. "Check under the seat sometime." I let my voice trail off into silence. Why was I babbling about antique chairs?

Pippa poured from a round-bellied clay teapot. "It's red raspberry leaf tea."

I might have frowned, because Pippa put her cup down, sip untaken.

"Thank you," I said quickly.

"We make it ourselves. It's a favorite at the Tea Room," Pippa said. "It's good for pregnancy, to tone the womb and prevent miscarriage."

I bit my lip. Raspberry tea was fine in the last few weeks of pregnancy to prepare the uterus for labor, but this early it could trigger a miscarriage. Once Pippa trusted me, we would talk about herbal teas, but now she probably wouldn't listen.

"Tea Room?" I asked.

"Our family business, the House of Isis Tea Room at the X. Homegrown organic teas served in hand-thrown teapots and cups. Fresh baked cookies, too."

I had driven by that oddly painted storefront a dozen times, barely noticing. I'd have to pay more attention, but now there was a lot to cover. I took two paper towels from my pack and spread them on the coffee table. Put the laptop on one and supplies on the other. Stethoscope. Waterless hand wash. Blood pressure cuff. Urine test strips. Pamphlets on healthy pregnancy.

"Excuse me." Pippa pointed at the table. "But what's that for?"

"What's what for?"

"Paper towels. You think the table will contaminate your stuff? Our house is clean."

"No, no. It's to protect you. So I don't bring germs from another patient into your home." I felt myself flush and hoped it didn't show. Rules are fine, but I despise the paper towel policy. My boss Marge was fierce about it, though. Infection control regulations. Rumor had it that Marge fired a nurse once for not following protocol. I looked at Pippa's round face. "It's a dumb rule. Insulting. I'm sorry."

"Don't worry about it," Pippa said with a gracious wave of her hand. "Let's get on with this. Don't you have questions or something?"

While I logged on the computer and opened the Intake file in the Glenning folder, I explained the health interview, blood pressure and weight checks, the urine tests for protein, sugar and bacteria. Then I started the questions. "Marital status?"

"Single." The orange cat deserted the button-back chair and jumped onto Pippa's lap, burrowing into her armpit.

"Your baby's father? How do you pronounce his name?"

"Tee-in." Pippa put the emphasis on the first syllable.

"Tian," I repeated slowly, postponing the next question. "Other children?"

"Abigail died last December. That's why you're here, isn't it?"

I nodded. "I'm sorry. Do you want to tell me about her?"

"No." Pippa stroked the cat's deep fur with both hands.

I looked back at the screen. "Who lives in the household?"

"My family."

"Who's in your family?" The big house felt empty. If anyone else was home, they were staying out of sight.

Pippa bristled, her spiky hair quivering. "None of your beeswax."

Okay, I could understand her protecting her privacy. I certainly had my own secrets. But I was trying to help.

The black cat stretched, jumped down from his chair. He ignored the fingers I wiggled at him and strutted out of the room. His exit was a snub. Not that I was thrilled with this interview either. I was twelve years older than Pippa, but clearly she was in charge. I needed to draw her out.

"What are your cats' names?" I asked.

"That was Bast, who just left."

"I've never heard that name."

Pippa pointed at the black cat in the painting. "An ancient Egyptian cat-deity."

I smiled. "He's beautiful."

"She. And this is Newark." The orange cat arched as Pippa stroked the curve of his back.

"Another god?"

Pippa threw me an odd look. "Like, New Jersey? Tian is from Newark." The orange cat settled again in Pippa's lap, the diesel purr loud.

I rummaged in the backpack, pretending to look for something. Usually I liked the intimacy of visiting patients in their homes. Especially the elderly, who were often lonely and eager to talk. Sometimes Marge assigned me the kids, because once I mentioned I help my cousin Anna at home with her daughter's procedures and therapies. And often I got the women with high-risk pregnancies at home on bed rest, because I worked labor and delivery in Portland before I moved down to Massachusetts. Maybe that's why I got stuck with Pippa.

How could I rescue this interview? I rubbed my index finger along my nose. A nervous habit, Anna says. My nose changes directions halfway down, and there's a bump at the crooked part. I'm sure that's the first thing people notice about me. Sometimes when I feel people staring, I explain that birth forceps squished my nose and that I might go back to school and become a midwife. If I do, I'll never use forceps. I'll bet Pippa's cult doesn't believe in forceps deliveries either.

Any early swelling of pregnancy was hidden by her spring-green jumper, where lush wildflowers grew across the meadow of fabric hanging to her ankles. Something about the serene way she sat, hands resting lightly on the cat, suggested a southern lady. Then I remembered about house arrest and the monitoring device. I tried to sneak a peek at Pippa's feet among the fabric folds.

Pippa stuck her right foot out, lifting her skirt to display a black beeper-sized box strapped snugly to her ankle. "Is this what you're looking for?" Then she grinned and her mouth did look generous for a moment.

"Does it bother you?"

"Not if I wear a sock." Pippa slid her index finger between the rubber strap and the white cotton. "After my shower I get big red welts that itch like crazy. When I put a sock on, the blotches and itching fade away."

"How does it work?"

"The ankle thingy sends electronic signals to that box." Pippa pointed to a black plastic cube on the mantel between a vase of dried cattails and a telephone. It looked more like a video game console than part of a surveillance system. "The box transmits the signals through the telephone line to the police station. All done by computer. If I leave the house without permission, it has a conniption fit and they send in Sherman's army, or whatever you have up here."

"Up here? Where're you from?" Good. She was opening up a little.

"Georgia, a long time ago."

"I'm from Maine, a long time ago." I was surprised to hear myself offer that information and steered the subject back. "So the monitor keeps track of everything you do?"

"Supposedly. I haven't put it to the test, yet." Pippa's smile was peculiar, as if she meant something else entirely.

I picked up the blood pressure equipment, and moved next to her on the sofa. Fastening the velcro cuff, I positioned the stethoscope ear tips and diaphragm, inflated the bulb. Together we watched the jerk of the dial. "That's good, 112 over 62." I held out a plastic cup. "Could you manage a urine sample?"

Twenty minutes later I had recorded the urine test results and Pippa's weight, and reviewed the pamphlets on pregnancy health. Then I asked about her diet.

"We don't eat anything that ever had a face."

Lofty sentiments from a woman who let her baby freeze to death. I handed Pippa the diet recommendations for vegetarians and the list of foods and herbs to avoid during her pregnancy. "I think we've covered everything for today. Remember to let someone else clean the litter box. Any questions?"

"Nope. I've been through this before." Pippa spoke towards her lap, where her hands were still.

"Abigail."

"Abby. She was fourteen months old."

I looked down at my own lap. "I'm so sorry."

"The judge believes I'm responsible for Abby's death. He thinks I'm not a fit mother and Tian's not a fit father and this isn't a good home." Pippa scowled. "They sent you to check up on me. If you say the wrong thing, I go to jail."

I wanted to tell Pippa that I didn't trust judges either. But I never talked about that, and certainly not to a patient. I couldn't trust my voice. I just shook my head and started packing. The pamphlets and packets seemed huge, engorged. My fingers fumbled with the supplies, but they refused to fit in the backpack.

Pippa bent down to retrieve a packet of gloves that had slipped off the coffee table to the floor. "Do you have kids of your own?"

I jammed the stethoscope into my jacket pocket and forced the backpack zipper closed. That was none of her business, but for some reason I answered. "No. But I live with my cousin and her daughter Zoe. She's five."

"That's not the same. If you don't have children, how do you expect to empathize, or whatever it is that nurses are supposed to do?"

"Zoe's like a daughter. She has spina bifida and I take care of her a lot." I shook my head. "But this isn't about her, or me. I'm here to help you have a healthy baby."

"I felt her move yesterday." Pippa's hands cupped the small bulge of her belly. "What I really need is help getting out of this mess."

I leaned forward. "Out of the cult?"

Pippa's response was halfway between a snort and a sob. "Hell's bells, no. They're my family. I could leave any time, if I wanted to. Out of this." Pippa pointed to the box strapped to her ankle.

"I don't know anything about that." I stood up and started towards the front door. "I'll be here Friday morning to take you to your obstetrician appointment."

❧

Like I said, I tried to get out of the assignment.

I just found out about Pippa that morning. I had been listening to my voice mail at my desk in the far corner of the staff nurse room. With the phone scrunched between my shoulder and ear, I was constructing a house of cards on my desktop with leftover supplies from the day before. Two-inch gauze packages formed the walls. A pair of upended bandage scissors outlined the doorway. It was a delicate moment—balancing two sterile dressing packets, one in each hand, along the slope of the scissors for the peaked roof—when my boss appeared. Marge, the owner-manager of the Hampden County Home Care Agency. She slapped a Form 44a, a new patient assignment sheet, on my desk. My hands jerked and the fragile shelter collapsed.

"New intake this morning, Emily. A prisoner. Prenatal visits." She swiveled on her alligator heels and headed towards her private office.

I thought I must have heard wrong. I hung up, swept the dressings into a neat pile, and called to Marge's back. "A prisoner?"

"Not exactly." At her office door, Marge stopped to examine her reflection in the window glass. "She's under house arrest until her trial. Wears some kind of ankle monitor."

"She's pregnant?" A stupid question, since she said "prenatal," but my brain froze at "prisoner." The panic in my voice must have snagged her attention, because she turned around.

"Early second trimester. Her name is Pippa Glenning. Priority intake this morning." Marge licked her finger, pressed it against a stubby eyebrow hair that stood straight up, trying to flee her face. Marge's eyebrows often appeared to operate independently of each other. But this morning they moved in perfect agreement, except for that one escaping hair.

I forced my attention back to her words.

"You'll report every week to her probation officer," Marge was saying, "to let them know she's cooperating with the medical program."

"Why the house arrest?" I tried to strike the right balance of curiosity and respect. You had to be careful with Marge.

"Her first baby died under suspicious circumstances. Cult ritual in the park. Her fetus is under protective custody." Marge's mouth puckered like the words tasted nasty.

That's when I remembered the Frozen Babies case. It had been in all the papers two, three months ago. "That woman?" I stared at Marge. "You've got to be kidding."

Marge's eyebrows arched and leapt as she turned away and entered her office. This time I followed her to the doorway. No one entered Marge's private space without an invitation. I counted under my breath, to compose myself before speaking. One nonviolence, two nonviolence, three nonviolence, like my father taught me when I was seven years old and furious at the neighborhood boys for teasing fat Marta next door.

"Can't you assign her to someone else?" I grasped both sides of the doorframe, hoping I didn't sound as desperate as I felt. "I'm not comfortable with this kind of situation, with courts and cops."

"Miss Glenning is your assignment." Marge thumbed through the pink message slips on her desk. "If you have a problem with it, perhaps you'd prefer to find another job." She looked at me and smirked.

Marge would have loved any excuse to sack me. And while there were plenty of nursing positions available, not many would allow me to start at the crack of dawn and be home by mid-afternoon when the Special Ed van delivered Zoe home from kindergarten. That way, Anna could finish work knowing that her daughter was safe, snacking on milk and fig newtons at the kitchen table and getting a head start on her afternoon therapy.

Marge had a lot of rules and regulations. Some don't make much sense, like the paper towels. But breaking the rules was what got my father into so much trouble. I didn't know Pippa well, but I already suspected she wasn't much on toeing the line either.

Me? I follow the rules.

2 ~ *Pippa*

Pippa hurried into the living room to pick up on the second ring, hoping it was Tian. Hoping the sympathetic guard was on duty down at the jail, the bald guy who Tian said looked like a pro wrestler. The guard had told Tian the first night that most folks thought his church was pretty weird too, but that didn't bother him none. He let Tian call home whenever no one else was around. Of course her telephone itself was a bother, all hooked up to the cuff around her ankle, a high-tech snoop. It didn't feel private, but nothing she could do about that.

"Hello?"

"You okay, Babe?"

Even from jail, even over the spooky phone, Tian's voice was so deep and fluid that Pippa dove into it and didn't need to come up for air. "I'm good, don't you worry. The nurse just left. She took my blood pressure and tested my pee and said I'm doing just fine."

"Baby too?"

"Baby too." Pippa sank into the cushions of the easy chair, still warm from Emily. "Have you seen Murphy?"

"Nah. They keep us separated, men to the north and women to the south. But my guard buddy brought a message from her this morning and she's hanging in there. Her lawyer says they'll try for bail again at the hearing."

The hearing was set for the Tuesday after Thanksgiving, less than two weeks away. New bail motions and something about trying them separately or together. The lawyers predicted that Tian would go to prison. "What about you?" she whispered into the tainted phone. "Will they let you out on bail?"

"Fat chance. They need a scapegoat and I'm it, the big bad leader of a bizarre cult that kills babies. Then there's my juvy record, the one that was supposed to be sealed."

"I miss you." She paused to let her throat settle, but she had to tell him. "I have an appointment with the doctor on Friday."

"Aw, Pippa." Tian's voice splintered. "I hate to think of you having to put up with all that crap."

Pippa pictured him at the other end of the phone line, cradling the receiver against his midnight skin, his cheekbones asserting long dynasties, his lips full of secrets. Tian was bigger than life. He was worth everything she went through, even her father, even the nasty weeks on Lyman Street.

Except Abby. Was Tian worth losing Abby? Maybe it was wrong thinking, but she couldn't help wondering.

She took a shallow breath, trying to get air past the tight regret in her throat. "Don't you fuss about the doctor, Tian, because the nurse promised to come with me." Pippa wasn't sure how much comfort Emily could offer, with her skinny neck that might be graceful if she didn't hold it so stiff. Still, it was better than going alone. "She'll make sure nothing bad happens. I'll just open my legs and close my eyes. I'll chant to Isis and pretend I'm not there."

"When I sleep-chant, Babe, I add something new at the end." He spoke so softly Pippa had to listen hard. "I chant your name and it becomes a mantra." Tian began to croon, "Pippa Pippa Pippa Pippa," and it sang out like a prayer.

How astonishing that Tian would make a hymn out of her name, which Pippa had hated since kindergarten. That was the first time she was around other children, except for her brother Stanley, and Charley and Martha from the next farm. Now those were regular names, sturdy and normal, not foolish like Pippa. At recess the kids in the schoolyard teased and chanted different rhymes. Pippa peepee, Pippa poopy.

Sally Ann moved to town in second grade and her desk was next to Pippa in the front row because they both had weak eyes. Sally Ann came from Pippa Passes, Kentucky, and she said it was the most beautiful place on earth. Pippa once asked Ma if she was named for that pretty town in the Kentucky mountains, but Ma said no, she read the name in a book when she was a girl. Pippa was so grateful that Sally Ann liked her name that they became best friends, her first friend really, because a brother didn't count. But in fourth grade Sally Ann grew boobs and Ma said she had turned into a slut and Pippa couldn't play with her anymore.

Tian's singsong chanting of the Pippa hymn ended abruptly, cutting off her daydreaming. "Lunch call, Babe," he said. "Got to go." Before the click severed the connection, Pippa could hear him complain. "Back off, man. I'm coming. I don't eat most of the crap they serve here anyway."

Pippa stroked the receiver, as if her touch could sizzle along the phone lines to Tian. She wished she could be like him, confident and tough even in jail, instead of worrying about everything, like the dumb phone shuttling secrets from her ankle to the computer downtown. There had to be a way to get around that flimsy little circle of rubber and microchip.

She could be strong until Tian returned, Pippa promised herself as she walked into the kitchen. Then, everything would be okay. She held the refrigerator door open with her foot while she piled fixings for lunch on the counter: leftover soup, lettuce and cukes, bean sprouts, pears and apples.

She stirred the soup, then counted out seven forks, seven spoons. Before Abby and Terrence died, before Tian and Murphy were taken away, they all ate lunch together in the dining room and Tian led them in chanting before the meal. Now, it was just the seven of them at noontime—Marshall and the twins, Francie if she woke up in time, Liz or Adele if they weren't scheduled at the Tea Room. And Pippa. Now they ate in the kitchen and skipped the chants.

Pippa had tried to be a good mother. Everyone said that she had done a wonderful job. She used to nurse Abby on the sofa under the gaze of Isis feeding baby Horus, whispering stories all mixed up from Tian's teaching fables and vague memories of south Georgia. She thought about her bloodline mingled with Tian's, mixed together like those stories, and there was nothing her father could do about it. In the eleven months since it happened, she ached for Abby every day. But Nan Malloy, the probation officer, had fastened the house arrest monitor around her ankle and warned her that the judge could take this new baby away too.

"Your fetus is under protective custody," Nan had said.

"But I would never hurt this baby."

"Follow the rules. Ours and the doctor's. That's your best chance to keep your baby."

Pippa covered the soup and turned down the flame. She had a few minutes to herself before it was time to wake Francie for lunch.

Her bedroom was tiny, nestled under the sloped roof, with one window round and thick like a ship's porthole. She pulled the Indian bedspread curtain across the doorway, although her housemates rarely climbed the creaking stairs to the attic. She sat on her mattress and pulled Abby's favorite picture book from under her pillow. The glossy cover illustration of the sunshine-haired princess in her father's castle transformed to last December's snowstorm.

They had all worn white. Silent and almost invisible in the blowing snow, they slipped under the massive bronze arch into the park. They walked single file, even the twins, following the narrow path through skeleton trees. They didn't need flashlights. All day, fat flakes had melted on the city streets, covered branches and decaying leaves and pine needles. Although the solstice moon was shrouded, the snow crystals absorbed and mirrored its weak light. Pippa's head barely reached Tian's shoulder, but she stretched into his footprints, rocking Abby who slept cradled in a blanket heavy across her breasts.

At the granite boulder whose profile resembled a stern face, they turned right, deeper into the forest. The trail led between diseased hemlocks, up a frozen hill, then dead-ended at the rhododendron hedge. It looked impenetrable, but they slipped one by one through the hidden passageway. On the other side the trail widened and Pippa skipped forward next to Tian. He shifted the mound of extra blankets and quilts to his other arm, then pulled her close.

When they got to the circle, Tian and the twins lit the fire. That afternoon, they had arranged the logs and chanted the blessings. In honor of the occasion, Marshall wore his white bandana. Pippa wondered again why he always covered his neck, but then he lit the solstice candles and the outer circle glowed and she forgot to ask. The ritual manual said to use torches, but they substituted hand-dipped candles with a likeness of the goddess. The feathered shield of her wings dried perfectly in the soft wax. It didn't feel second-best. In the ring between the blaze of the bonfire and the gleaming of the candles, their robes shimmered.

In a small clearing at the edge of the circle, Pippa and Murphy got the little ones ready. They spread the tarp over the snow, covered it with sleeping bags to make a nest under the thick canopy of trees. Sitting thigh to thigh with blankets tented over their shoulders, they nursed Abby and Terrence. Pippa checked Abby's diaper, opening the zipper just enough to slide her hand under two layers of pajama sleeper.

From the clearing Pippa watched the final preparations. Liz and Francie mixed the libation in heavy clay jugs, stirring diluted honey into the red wine to balance the bitterness of the peyote buttons. Judging by their eyes, they had done some heavy tasting. Liz stopped to wipe the snow from her wire-rimmed glasses with the edge of her robe. Adele stood alone on the fertility stone, massaged her belly, and prepared to dance.

Someday I will be pregnant for this ceremony, Pippa thought. I will perform the mother-dance. She stroked Abby's face, the only skin exposed, slightly chapped and rosy in the cold night air, wishing her daughter was old enough to appreciate this moment.

Murphy settled the sleeping Terrence under the blankets, then stood. "Come dance."

But at fourteen months, Abby still nursed greedily, with total dedication. Pippa felt so full, even as her breasts were emptied. Proud too, to give her daughter a family who loved her and kept her safe, connected her to the earth and the ages.

Abby was finally sated, sleeping. A milk pearl balanced on her lower lip, glistening in the flickering light from the bonfire. Pippa laid her down next to Terrence and tucked the quilts snug around both babies. She paused to watch Abby's mouth making empty sucking motions. Then she stepped through two inches of new snow to the fire-lit circle and joined the celebration. It snowed harder.

They should be cold, but were on fire. White and hot and holy, they danced. Separate and together. Arms extended and robes billowing. Moths drawn to each other in the swirling moonlit snow. The twins had been practicing on the clay Darbouka drum and took turns playing the heartbeat rhythm. Murphy slipped the slim wooden recorder from her pocket and played soprano harmony, the notes light enough to hover between the snowflakes.

Just before midnight, Pippa checked on the sleeping babies in the clearing, then spun back to the group. She was ignited by the drumbeat, the fire pumping through her veins, the rapture of the dancing, and by Tian.

At midnight, Tian stepped into the center of the circle and they stopped. He was the tallest of the dancers, his bare chest dark against the eddying whiteness of snow and muslin. Watching him, Pippa hugged herself. He made her feel small and protected on the outside, big and hopeful on the inside. When he summoned the Goddess, she would listen.

"Isis," Tian thundered, lifting his arms to the sky. Snow crowned his thick hair. "Your family is gathered. In these days of deepest dark, of profound evil in the world, we worship your light. Give us spring and new life."

Adele joined him in the center of the circle and stepped onto the fertility stone. Tian parted her robe, lifting both panels and folding them back over her shoulders. He knelt and laid both hands on her belly.

"We do our part and bring new life into your world."

Then it was Adele's turn. Pippa studied every perfect move of her mother-dance, each stylized movement executed precisely as choreographed. The manual described the steps and the women taught one another to transform the moves into prayer. Adele's body swayed and twisted on the flat dancing stone, her bare feet the same color as the granite. She rippled with the simulated waves of childbirth. Her long arms undulated in the firelight, weaving together the centuries-old stories and their hopes for the future.

When she finished, Adele smiled and opened her arms wide to invite the others into the inner circle. Alive and electric, they danced as one entity with eighteen swirling arms, eighteen stomping feet. Their shadows spiraled with the flames and their lusty songs and the whirling snow, and the fiery drink, and rose with the smoke into the sky.

Finally exhausted, Pippa led Tian to the small clearing and pulled him close. After their lovemaking, wrapped in each other and their blankets, they curled around Abby and Terrence, cupping their small shapes, and fell into sleep.

Pippa woke at first light, her breasts tight with milk. She and Tian were half buried in snowdrift. She reached for Abby. Her hand patted the blanket. Grabbed at the sleeping bags. Pawed the quilts. There was only nylon and wool and snow.

❧

Tears flooded Pippa's cheeks and pooled in the corner of her mouth. She dried her face on the crimson fleece sleeper, then slipped it back under her pillow with Abby's book. She paused outside Francie's bedroom to let her breathing calm, then knocked on the doorframe. No secrets in the family, that's what Tian taught, so they took all the doors off their hinges and lined them up like defeated soldiers in the basement, each leaning on the one ahead.

"Wake up, Francie." Pippa pushed aside the tie-dyed curtain hung across the doorway. "Lunchtime."

The quilt-covered form on the mattress shifted. "Five minutes."

Bast jumped off the bed and followed Pippa downstairs, rubbing her ears against the edge of the ankle monitor. Marshall and the twins would be home any minute and they'd be hungry. Wednesday was field trip morning, to the museums and library downtown, the highlight of their home school week. She would have to hurry to get everyone fed and the kitchen cleaned before work. The ankle device allowed her five hours out of the house, not a minute more, Nan had warned. When Pippa got to the Tea Room, Adele could head home to the drying porch, so they didn't run out of organic spearmint tea. Along with Francie's trust fund, spearmint paid the rent.

Pippa stirred the soup and lowered the flame. Tian expected her to keep things together in his absence. She leaned over and scratched under the rubber ankle strap with the handle of the long wooden spoon. Even though she was the newest member of the family, being his woman carried certain responsibilities, and she wasn't going to let him down.

A volley of kick-thuds brought Pippa to the back door. Marshall kept promising to fix it. Just needs a quarter-inch shaved off the top, he said whenever anyone complained how badly it stuck. This time it was Marshall trying to kick the door open with an armload of library books resting against his protruding middle. The twins carried more books and they squeezed through the doorway at the same time.

"We went to the planetarium." Timothy started talking as soon as he saw Pippa. "Did you know that the planets are named for ancient gods and that olden people thought the planet-gods in heaven controlled everything on earth?"

Jeremy dropped his canvas bag of library books on the linoleum floor. "Uh huh and Mars was named for this fierce dude and Mercury was the fastest runner and Saturn was cruel."

"It was way cool," Timothy said, grabbing a slice of pear. "You lean way back and look up at the stars and planets on the dome and it looks realer than real."

Pippa took the pear from Timothy and nudged him towards the kitchen sink. "That's great, but wash your hands first. You too, Jeremy."

She still sometimes mixed them up. Two minutes older, Jeremy was a tad taller than his twin brother. When Pippa first joined the family, the boys were only five and she couldn't tell them apart at all. Back then she was confused about all the relationships in the household, who loved who, whose kids were whose. But now Pippa could see that the twins were a perfect blend of Tian's dark beauty and Francie's light hair. Her curls reminded Pippa of creamsicles from the ice cream truck that jingled on the street every afternoon in the summer, but was gone now. Now she could see behind their identical faces to the softness that Jeremy tried to hide from his brother and his dad. And that Timothy's ears were big and stuck out. Back home, those ears would have earned him the nickname of Dumbo, but here nobody teased Timothy.

The brothers splashed each other at the sink, hips and elbows jostling, and raced for their favorite corner seat in the breakfast nook.

"What's for lunch?" Marshall frowned at the platter of sliced fruit, the bowl of greens and sprouts, and the round loaf of dark bread with sunflower seeds poking through the crust. He fingered the turquoise bandana knotted around his neck. It might have looked jaunty, if he washed it once in a while. "Anything besides rabbit food?" Marshall had known Tian in Newark. He had been with the family from the beginning, but he still didn't accept Tian's rules about junk food. "Don't put that crap into your sacred body," Tian liked to say. Marshall's response was automatic too. "Shit comes out, no matter what goes in." His fingers drummed on his belly and Pippa looked away from the soft ripples under his shirt.

"Leftover lentils." Pippa ladled the soup into pottery bowls, each one stamped with the House of Isis logo of Bast's paw print.

"Ugh." Timothy mock-gagged. The twins made it clear that they were in Marshall's camp on food. The three of them probably snuck off together for hamburgers, but she wouldn't rat on them. It amazed her that the boys, just turned nine, were confident enough to joke about meals, and that the adults didn't punish them for speaking their minds.

At nine years old Pippa wouldn't have dreamed of complaining about food that Ma put on the table. Even Stanley, full-grown at eighteen, wouldn't. Father's calloused hand would have connected with the side of his head faster than heat lightning on a June evening. So Stanley kept quiet, even when Ma served up chicken livers fried with collard greens. He would close his eyes, force down a few bites, and hold the rest under the table for the Doberman who replaced the German Shepherd that Father shot.

The Family of Isis children weren't timid at all, and that was good. That meant they were growing up healthy and strong, not warped like the District Attorney claimed at the arraignment. "Can you imagine the unhealthy, perverted environment these poor children suffer?" the D.A.'s voice had trumpeted across the courtroom.

Pippa banished the D.A. from her thoughts and listened to Jeremy talk about the homeless guy they met that morning hanging around the library, his frizzy white beard decorated with dribbles of green stuff. He had told the twins a story about Saturn while they waited for the bus.

"He said Saturn was named after Cronus, this god who wanted to be king," Jeremy said. "But his daddy wouldn't give up the throne, so Cronus cut off his daddy's privates."

Timothy burst into giggles and goosed Jeremy in his privates and they wrestled on the bench, sending Newark dashing from the room and spilling Timothy's soymilk.

Pippa mopped it up, then grinned at the twins. "That sounds like Lettuce Man. He scrounges for discarded salads in the dumpsters behind the downtown restaurants." Pippa remembered him from the days before Francie found her. Lettuce Man liked to hang out with the street kids, shoving wilted greens into his mouth and telling dirty stories to make them laugh. Timothy said that he and Jeremy bought Lettuce Man a bus token so they could hear the end of the story about how Cronus worried that his kids would overthrow him.

"Cronus swallowed his kids when they were born," Jeremy said. "Whole."

"Then he barfed them up," Timothy added.

"Morning, everyone," Francie called from the hallway. She pulled her terrycloth bathrobe snug around her shoulders and stopped to turn up the thermostat before entering the kitchen. With her blue eyes and hair like carrot curls tangled over her white robe, Francie looked just like the drawing of the princess in Abby's book.

"It's afternoon." Jeremy pointed to the clock on the wall.

"Why don't you get dressed," Marshall asked, "instead of cranking up the furnace and sending dollar bills up the chimney?"

"Give it a break." Francie sat down next to Timothy on the bench and both cats jumped onto her lap. Francie kissed Timothy's cheek and pouted when he wiped it off with the back of his fist. Then she kissed her pointer finger and reached over to touch first the tip of Jeremy's nose and then Marshall's stubbly cheek. Pippa thought Francie hesitated slightly before blowing a kiss to Pippa at the stove.

"Work okay last night?" Marshall asked. It looked like he was staring deep into the vee of Francie's bathrobe, where her skin was even whiter than her face. No one in the family ever wanted to talk about who was sleeping together behind flimsy curtains. No one owns anyone in this family, Tian taught, but Pippa was curious anyway. Francie used to be with Tian, that much was clear from looking at the twins. Pippa carried soup bowls to the table for the boys and then for Marshall.

"Work wasn't bad." Francie reached for a slice of apple. "The E.R. was wild, but the switchboard was quiet. Good thing, since the supervisor called out sick and it was just me."

"I didn't hear you come in," Marshall said.

"It was late." Francie accepted the steaming bowl from Pippa, cradling it with both hands. Bast jumped onto the table and sniffed.

"How can you eat lentils for breakfast?" Timothy asked.

"That's life when you work nights, sweetie." Francie turned to Pippa. "Did that nurse come this morning?"

Pippa emptied the last ladle of soup into her bowl. "Yeah."

"What was she like?"

"Not awful." Pippa pictured Emily's nose that seem to change course in the middle. "Not as bad as I expected."

"What about your ankle device? You figured out how to get it off?"

"How can I do that?" Pippa set down her spoon. "They'll slap me in jail."

Timothy slid down under the table, pulling his brother along. They tugged at the strap around Pippa's ankle. Timothy popped up with a serious expression. "We can figure this out. Marshall's been helping us take things apart and put them back together."

"That monitor is a whole different ballgame than clocks and toaster ovens," Marshall said. "Electronics are in next year's curriculum."

Francie shrugged her shoulders, extending the opening of her robe. She looked at Pippa. "It's your turn this year. Don't let us down."

Francie was right. This was Pippa's year, her turn to dance in the center of the circle. Since the moment she joined the Family of Isis four years ago, she had been waiting for this. Except everything was different now. Now, there was a hunk of plastic strapped to her ankle. Now, Abby and Terrence were dead.

The morning after last year's solstice, the family had searched for the toddlers in the blowing, drifting snow. All day they hunted and the next and the next, taking turns staying with the twins. Timothy wanted to help in the search, but Jeremy couldn't stop crying, and Tian decided they should both stay home. On the third day, the wind got fiercer and everything froze. The snow grew a crust that gave way with each step, hacking bruises on Pippa's legs above the top of her hiking shoes. That evening, Tian called them together at the goddess stone and announced that Isis had called Abby and Terrence home to her.

"No." Pippa shook her head back and forth, back and forth. Tian pulled her close and held her head tight against his chest to stop the shaking.

In bed that night, Pippa couldn't stop weeping. "If Isis has the power to bring back the sun and resurrect the dead," she asked Tian over and over, "why didn't she save our babies?" Pippa would never understand, no matter how many times Tian tried to explain that just because Isis could, didn't mean she would. Finally he gave up, and turned away. Leaning her wet cheek against his back, Pippa felt his solitary shudders slow into sleep.

Pippa took another spoonful of lentil soup, but she wasn't hungry. Recently Francie had been so mean. Maybe she wished she and Tian were still together. Marshall was a nice enough guy, and he was great with the twins, but his belly was gross. He sure wasn't Tian.

The telephone in the hallway rang. Pippa ignored it and looked at Francie. "I know it's my turn and I don't want to let everyone down. What can I do?"

"Don't ask me." Francie got up from the table. "You're the wise Mother this year."

Pippa stared at Francie's white terrycloth back leaving the kitchen. How could the woman who had rescued her have changed so drastically? Never mind Francie, Pippa told herself. Tian is counting on you to keep the family together until he comes home. But in the meantime they didn't feel much like a family at all. More like a few people stuck together, with nothing much in common except being different from the folks outside. A lot like her family back home, the one she'd left.

❧

Pippa knew early that there was something wrong with her family. People treated her father as if he might bite, like the German Shepherd they had when she was little, who growled and snapped and finally took a chunk out of Stanley's leg, so Father put him down behind the barn with one rifle shot. When she and Stanley were late with their chores, or left the basket of eggs on the grass to play with a garter snake or a barn kitty, their father would clench his eyebrows and aim his searchlight stare at them. They would drop the snake wiggling into the grass and run to the house, careful not to drop the eggs.

Mostly, her father ignored her, and when he noticed at all, he treated her like a small farmhand. She couldn't do heavy work, but she fed the chickens and gathered eggs, weeded the vegetable patch, milked the goats and finally, when she was five, she started mucking out the stinky stalls with Stanley.

One afternoon her father was haying the front field when the yellow bus spat the four of them out at the mouth of their dirt driveway. Charley and Martha headed home and Stanley ran straight to the barn, but Pippa walked slowly toward the milk and cookies set out on the kitchen table. Her father leaned on the tractor instead of driving it, smoking a cigarette and staring at her. Later, she was setting the table when he came in the house. She was trying to remember which side the fork went on. She couldn't tell left from right, but she had a birthmark on her right hand, just where the thumb and pointer finger met, and she always tried to remember by that. "B" for birthmark. "B" for butter knife. Knife on the birthmark side. Problem was she had to look at her hands and think about it and that took time. That's what she was doing when her father came in and watched her. He looked like he wanted to say something, but Ma shooed him right out of the kitchen. "George," she grumbled, "you take that filthy cigarette outside."

Being cut off from their relatives was the other reason Pippa knew that something was wrong with her father. Stanley told her that they had two uncles and a passel of cousins living about ten miles south. Years before, after a big argument, the uncles sold off a piece of the family farm and gave her father the money to buy his own place. They never saw their kin, not even at Christmas or Easter. At holidays it was just the four of them; the cold feeling around the dinner table seeped into the walls of the parlor. Ma loved her and Stanley, but Ma was insubstantial, like someone who could walk through walls. Her hugs were thin and the safe feeling evaporated right after she let go.

When Pippa left Georgia, the night she followed her father and saw what he did, she had never heard of Springfield, Massachusetts, but it seemed as good a destination as any. Alone in the Springfield bus station with no more money, no plan, no place to go, she hid in the end toilet stall in the ladies' room. When she ran out of sobs and came out to the sink, a tall woman in a sky-blue wool coat handed her a paper towel to dry her face, and introduced herself as Mrs. Carney. She offered a hot meal and a place to sleep. Pippa might be a hick but she wasn't stupid. She recognized the roughness in the woman's face, but what choice did she have? She stayed a few nights, before running away again. The streets were frightening, but safer than in Mrs. Carney's house.

Francie found her hanging with some kids behind a restaurant. At first Pippa ignored her, but there was a shining in Francie's face, radiant and homey at the same time. Four nights in a row, Francie stopped by on her way to work, even though Pippa told her to get lost. Francie talked about Isis, how she was the mother of everyone, wise and forgiving. She described Tian as Isis' great great many-greats grandson and the head of the family. Tian helped people find the comfort of believing in ancient ideas like the solstice and the sun's return, following traditions as old as civilization. Tian was especially on the lookout for lost girls, raw and ready to belong to something good, because no one had helped his sister when she needed it. Pippa came to see Francie as an angel, dressed all in white. Later she found out that wearing white clothes for ceremonies was part of being pure for Isis. Francie was the only one who wore white all the time, even to work, even though no one could see her on the hospital switchboard.

Pippa got up to clear the dishes. No matter what else anyone might say about Francie—about her being bossy, or trying to get Tian back, or anything—she was one persuasive lady. After four nights of urging, Pippa agreed. She was so weary trying to take care of herself. Francie's family sounded way better than being a hooker or a runaway. She followed Francie into the family's feeble old van that smelled of dried thyme and spearmint. A few months later, Pippa dressed in white too and danced at her first solstice celebration in a remote section of Forest Park. That night, four years ago next month, Pippa joined the Family of Isis.

Francie's face was paler than usual when she returned to the kitchen.

"What's wrong?" Marshall asked.

"That was Liz on the phone. There's a problem at the Tea Room." Francie turned to Pippa. "Wait for me to get dressed. I'm going down there with you."

3 ~ *Emily*

I had to swing by the office after leaving Pippa. Anticipating our first meeting had flustered me so badly that I forgot to restock my supply bag. Marge despised poor planning but luckily her office was dark. I opened my backpack on the table in the empty supply closet, glad that no one could see the jumbled mess I made in Pippa's living room.

When I started working at the agency, the nurses all carried blue canvas bags. After we switched from paper charts to laptops, my shoulders ached every night. So I bought a wheeled backpack. At first the other nurses made jokes and rolled their eyes. Andy drew a cartoon on the message board of a geeky nurse with a giraffe neck pulling a humongous rolling bag. Everyone could tell it was me, but he was Marge's snitch, so no one liked him much. Besides, the comfort tradeoff was worth the occasional snide comment. Since then, other nurses had started using rolling packs. My friend Gina was the first.

"Nurses on a roll." Gina's musical Jamaican accent perked up even an offhand comment. When Andy snickered, Gina turned her back on him.

I emptied the clutter from my bag, and repacked the standard items: waterless hand wash, stethoscope and blood pressure cuff, alcohol wipes, sterile gauze pads, disposable dressing sets, sterile saline, syringes. The red bag with blood-drawing equipment and the needle disposal box fit neatly into the bottom corner between the portable scale and the laptop. If you took the time, everything would fit just so, even the roll of paper towels. That made me think about Marge's rules and Pippa's comment. My cheeks burned.

Marge had never liked me. It had gotten much worse the week before when I found Mrs. Newman in the hallway of her apartment building, naked except for a wide-brimmed straw sunhat, searching for her key in non-existent pockets. I reported to Marge that the old woman wasn't safe living on her own anymore, even with maximum hours of nursing and homemaker support. Marge snapped at me, said those were administrative decisions. Her job, not mine. But yesterday I saw Mrs. Newman again and Marge hadn't done anything. So I gave Gina a statement; she was our union steward. When Marge heard about that, she would really be pissed off at me.

I collected the supplies for my regular Wednesday patients. Suture removal kit and sterile gloves for Mrs. Grover's post-op incision. Absorbent dressing made from seaweed for Mr. Stanisewski's foot ulcer. Sterile swabs and hydrogen peroxide for Josué's pin site care. Thinking about the little guy made me smile. I slipped the tiny yellow school bus from my pocket, and scratched off the price tag with my fingernail. The toy tucked perfectly into the front zipper pocket of the pack. Once a week I tried to bring Josué some small gift, even though Marge had a strict policy about not getting personally involved with our patients. I knew I wasn't the only one who brought a toy, a piece of sugar-free candy, a bunch of grocery-store flowers to brighten a kitchen table.

Before leaving the office, I checked my phone for messages and found a Post-it note in Gina's looping scrawl stuck to the receiver. "Late lunch? Two-ish?" I checked my watch; if I hurried I could see my three patients, meet Gina for a late lunch, and still get home to meet Zoe's bus.

The moment I handed Josué the toy bus, I cringed. How could I have forgotten that it was a school bus that clobbered him? On the second day of kindergarten, right in the crosswalk while the guard in her orange apron stretched her hand out for the driver to stop. But Josué grinned and stuck the tip of his tongue through the double gap in his front teeth. He didn't remember anything before waking up with stainless-steel pins sticking through his leg, pins attached to circular metal rods that held the bones while they healed. I first met Josué at the children's hospital, two days after his accident. He taught me how to pronounce his name.

"Hoe-sway," he enunciated carefully. "Remember that."

I remembered, and Josué had gotten used to me cleaning the pin sites with sterile swabs, but it still hurt. We sang his favorite songs while he banged the tambourine against the mattress with one hand and made the toy school bus dance with the other. While I fit the spongy dressings between his skin and the metal rods, he steered the bus over his pillow and blanket between lines of small plastic soldiers. Soon the pins and rings would be ready to come off, Carmen told me, and Josué could return to school.

"But you'll still visit." Josué drove the school bus up my right arm, parallel parking in the crook of my elbow. "Right?"

"Yup, even when I'm no longer your nurse." Sometimes I thought about introducing him to Zoe. Would they be friends?

Across town, Mr. Stanisewksi hobbled to meet me at the apartment door, refusing his crutches. When we first met, he didn't bother teaching me to pronounce his name. "Call me Mr. S," he had said.

He smiled as widely as Josué at his favorite treat, a sugar-free lime lollipop. "I know it's funny for a grown man to suck on a pop." His mouth puckered at the first taste of tart. "Don't you tell me that old age is a second childhood, young lady. I'm not a violent man, but that idea makes me want to smack someone."

"It's not for the young and inexperienced," I agreed, then gloved up and removed the old seaweed dressing from the diabetic ulcer on his big toe. "Looks much better today."

While I cleaned and repacked the shrinking ulcer, he described the science fair experiment his eleven-year-old granddaughter in Amherst was conducting. My mind flashed to the project on Pippa's dining room table. I wondered who was making that relief map, and if there were adults like Mr. S. to keep track of the progress.

"She plays two hours a day of Beethoven to the first group of seedlings." I could hear the pride in his voice. "Folk songs to the second group, rock and roll to the third, and nothing at all to the control group. At the end of the month she'll measure them all and see which plants grew the tallest."

"I'd choose the folk songs," I said. "What about you?"

"There's no polka music, so they'll all be pipsqueaks." He laughed at his own joke.

I wondered what kind of music Pippa liked. Did she sing lullabies to Abby, and to the new baby in her womb? What exactly had happened to Abby? What kind of man was Tian? And who else lived in that big house? The health interview hadn't answered any of those questions. Usually I was good at drawing out my patients, eliciting their secret worries while building a therapeutic relationship. But most of my patients weren't Pippa.

"See you on Friday?" Mr. S. asked.

I pulled my thoughts back from Pioneer Street. "Same time, same place."

I'd been at this job for almost four years, but I was still touched by my patients. I pretty much fell into nursing in the first place. The morning after my high school graduation I took the ferry off the island, then the bus down to Portland. I knew what I was leaving, but not what I was looking for, except that I wanted to fade into the background. The city had changed in the eight years I'd been away. Perhaps I could have found some childhood friends if I'd looked, but I wanted to start over.

The nursing home job was advertised on the bulletin board at the Food Coop. It turned out that I loved the physicality of taking care of people. People who didn't know about my past. Who only cared that my hands were gentle when I washed their feet and I listened to their stories while I rubbed their backs. That I didn't make a face when I helped them off the bedpan, or when they didn't make it on in time. They didn't pity me and I didn't pity them. Sometimes, we were so short-staffed that patients were left in their wheelchairs for hours, before anyone could change their diapers. Incontinence briefs, we were supposed to say. For dignity, as if there was dignity in sitting around in your mess, no matter what you called it. But the nursing home wasn't all grim. I loved the moments when a child would come running into the sunroom and call "Grandma!" and thirty gray heads would turn smiling toward the voice. Even if they had no grandchildren, or couldn't remember them, or their grandchildren lived in California and never visited.

Mrs. Grover lived just a few blocks away. While I cleaned the railroad track incision across her vast brown abdomen, she brought me up to date on her son's custody battle for his three children. My mind wandered back to Pippa. Who would get custody of her baby if she and Tian both went to prison?

"Terrell needs me," Mrs. Grover grabbed my hand. "I have to get well so I can help when he gets the kids back."

I moved her hand away from the sterile dressing and patted it. "The incision is still a bit red and puffy," I said, removing the final skin sutures. "But it looks less angry, and your fever is down."

While the antibiotic infusion dripped through the tube tunneled into her chest, I half-listened to Mrs. Grover describe her daughter-in-law's demands, and half-worried about Pippa's appointment Friday morning at the obstetrician's office. If she didn't believe in our medicine, would she refuse the pelvic exam? What did Isis teach about childbirth?

Outside Mrs. Grover's apartment building, I checked my watch, stashed the pack in the trunk and transferred my lunch bag to the front seat. I was late to meet Gina. The Forest Park road twisted down the hill to the duck pond. Any day now it would be too cold to sit outside, for even fifteen minutes.

Gina waved from our favorite bench, facing the gray water choked with shriveled lily pads and the dark forest beyond. Her red lipstick and fur-trimmed emerald green jacket were the only splashes of color visible. Everything else was a wan shade of beige or gray or muted brown. The woods, the ground, the sky, even me. Marveling for the thousandth time that such opposite people could be so compatible, I grabbed my lunch bag, and hurried towards her. I was eager to talk about the situation with Mrs. Newman. And about Pippa Glenning. Next to Anna, Gina was my closest friend. She knew about my work in Portland, even a little bit about Chad. But I had never told her about my father. Or about the island where my mother and I were sent when he went to prison.

I hadn't told Gina about the phone call either. Aunt Ruth, my mother's sister, had called last weekend to tell me that my grandfather had a stroke, a serious one. If he died, I might have to return to the island for his funeral. I hadn't been back since the morning after graduation. Fourteen years. My parents were dead and there was nothing left for me there except bad memories. Gina knew nothing about those either.

Sometimes, like now, I was tempted to tell her. But Gina had strong feelings about what was right and what was wrong. And, much as we liked each other, I wasn't at all sure how she would feel about being friends with a jailbird's daughter.

4 ~ *Gina*

Gina watched Emily pick her way towards their bench, skirting shallow brown puddles glazed with ice. That girl could use some color. Rouge, maybe? A purple scarf?

Emily sat down and opened her lunch bag. "Okay morning?"

"Max is failing. Even sedated, he's such a professor. Today he lectured me on the political significance of his Bar Mitzvah Torah passage. He claims he remembers every Hebrew word, seventy years later." Gina peeled her orange, trying to keep the skin intact in one long strip. That made her think about Granny Teisha, and Granny brought the sadness full circle back to Max. She hoped Emily wasn't tired of hearing so much about the old guy. "You're Jewish, right? Did you have a Bar Mitzvah, or the one that girls do?

"A Bat Mitzvah? No."

Gina waited for more, arranging the snake of orange peel back into the whole round shape. Granny used to do that, then she would fool the kids, offering them an empty piece of fruit, throwing back her head and laughing as it fell apart. When Emily didn't elaborate, Gina asked, "What about your morning?"

"New patient," Emily said. "The pregnant woman from the Frozen Babies case."

"No kidding? How did it go?"

"I'm not sure. You know anything about her?"

"Just what I read in the paper," Gina said. "A religious cult, wasn't it? They worship the solstice, all-night bonfires, like that. Some kids died and I think her husband's in jail." Gina popped an orange segment into her mouth. "What's she like?"

"She's okay. It's a bizarre situation. I'd like to help her, and her baby. But I don't know how to act. I have to meet with her probation officer. I'm a nurse, not a cop." Emily frowned. "You should have gotten this assignment. You're better at the complicated stuff."

"No, thanks." But Emily might be right, Gina thought. Emily was a good nurse, smart and compassionate. But sometimes she seemed frozen herself. Gina had once asked if there had been someone special in her life. Emily had mumbled about someone named Chad, her supervisor at the nursing home in Portland. He had urged her to apply to nursing school and helped her get a scholarship. When Gina asked what happened, Emily said it didn't work out, then started describing how Chad quizzed her for exams by making up funny ways to memorize the bones of the wrist or the Krebs cycle. Well, she would probably never know what happened with Chad, because that girl certainly liked her privacy.

Gina offered Emily the perfect husk of orange on the palm of her hand.

Emily laughed. "Your hand skills are wasted in this job. You ever think about going back to the OR?"

"Nah. I love these hours, spending time with my boys. And guess what? I like my patients awake." Gina drank from her thermos. "What about you? Do you ever want to go back to labor and delivery?"

Emily seemed to search the dark pond surface for an answer. "I miss the births. Sometimes I think about becoming a midwife. But I'm not sure about going back to school." She turned to face Gina. "So what do you think about Mrs. Newman. When I saw her again yesterday, nothing had changed. She refuses to bathe, doesn't eat unless she's fed." Emily shook her head. "She needs residential care, but Marge won't do anything about it."

"It's tricky. She's the supervisor."

"All she cares about is losing the business. I'm thinking of calling Mrs. Newman's doc on my own."

"Have you documented everything?"

Emily nodded. "You bet. Every detail of Mrs. Newman's behavior and every word of my conversation with Marge. You're the union rep. Can't you do something?"

"Not really. The union can bargain for benefits and safety issues, file a grievance if you're treated unjustly. But this is a professional issue."

Emily rubbed her nose hard, like Gina had seen her do before when she was worried, but then she grinned. "So, you mean if I call Mrs. Newman's internist and tell him the situation and Marge fires me, then the union can help?"

"Sure." Gina laughed, then got serious. "Is that your plan?"

"Do I have a choice? Marge already said to drop it, and you know how strict she is about getting her permission before notifying a patient's attending."

"Well, there's rules and there's rules," Gina said.

Emily looked at her. "What do you mean?"

Honestly, sometimes that girl was so naïve. "You know. If the rule is bad, and you've got to break it for the patient's sake, sometimes you go ahead."

Like Granny Teisha's illness last year. The tiny hospital in Ocho Rios sent her home with vials of narcotics and no hope of recovery. Granny Teisha threw the pills away and spent her last weeks surrounded by four generations of family, comfortable in a cloud of ganja. It was illegal, but it was right. The only hard part for Gina had been trying to explain that distinction to her sons.

Emily sighed. "Between Mrs. Newman and Pippa Glenning, I'm not sure about anything. I just like to take care of my patients, not deal with all this administrative stuff."

Gina didn't much like workplace politics either, but that was life. "The two cases seem totally different to me," she said. "Mrs. Newman needs your advocacy. So you do what's right, and the union will back you up. This other thing, this cult and dead babies and house arrest, I don't know about that. You probably don't want to get too involved with that girl."

"But Pippa's my patient too."

"True," Gina said. "But like I said, there's rules and there's rules. You be careful."

5 ~*Pippa*

The city bus bumped against the curb in front of Forest Park. Pippa stroked a soft spiral under the rough wool of her pea coat. "It's okay," she whispered to her belly.

Francie didn't react to the jolt or the whisper. She had refused to explain what was happening at the Tea Room, but it must be pretty bad to get her out of her bathrobe after working all night. Pippa leaned her cheek against the window and watched the green and red holiday decorations on the elementary school flapping in the wind. She was glad to be out of the house, even heading towards something ugly at the Tea Room. Passing Forest Park, she turned her face away. She hadn't set foot in the park since it happened. She had begged off participating in the June Teardrop ritual, unable to return to that sacred, awful place. After the bodies were found in late August, she wanted to see the deep gully their own search had missed. Twice she got as far as the bronze arch, but she couldn't walk under it.

Pippa snuck a glance at Francie. Did she mourn their babies every day too?

At the "X," where three main streets intersected at the commercial heart of the neighborhood, Francie tugged on the stop cord. Pippa followed her down the steps, plucking the clingy fabric of her skirt so the hem hung over her ankles. She had borrowed a pair of Tian's rag wool socks to cover the bulge at her the ankle. On the sidewalk, Pippa forgot all about hiding her house arrest monitor.

The House of Isis sign stretched across the top third of the storefront. Murphy and Adele had painted the huge wings of the Egyptian goddess sheltering her baby and the cat-god Bast. It matched the painting inside the Tea Room, hung on the brick wall shared with the barbershop next door, and the one over the fireplace at home.

Tar splattered Isis. The viscous, black liquid dripped from her face into the crevice between her breasts and onto the beige stucco wall. Bundled in Marshall's oversized sweatshirt and perched on a ladder, Liz scrubbed at the mess. The part she had already scoured was still veiled by a gray film.

"Great, huh?" Liz removed her glasses and wiped her glistening face with her sleeve.

"Tar," Francie muttered. "Terrific. Where are the feathers?"

Pippa remembered talk back home about tar and feather parties. There was a blackened tree stump behind the five-and-dime; kids said that's where the night-riders brought the men who needed to be taught a lesson. Her teachers said those days were over.

"I'm glad you guys are finally here. Adele couldn't take it and she split." Liz looked down at Pippa. "Get the cookies, will you? The timer just buzzed." She tossed the rag down into the bucket on the sidewalk. "I'll be right in."

Turning away from the filthy bucket, Pippa pushed open the heavy glass door and stepped into the aroma of baking molasses. She pulled out two trays of cookies, dark with carob and plump with cranberries, and set them on the butcher block counter to cool. Usually at one-thirty, late lunchers and neighborhood shoppers were still enjoying tea and cookies. That afternoon the Tea Room was empty.

Liz pushed through the front door, soiled rags in one hand and bucket in the other. "I've had enough," she said. "I'm going home."

"Why today?" Pippa asked. "Was there another story in the paper?"

"Who knows? Maybe they spent weeks planning this. There was a spray-painted message too—*Keep devil cults out of Forest Park*." Liz dumped the dirty water into the sink and ran the faucets full blast. "Francie went next door to see if Mario heard anything.

The baking smell reminded Pippa that she had only eaten half a bowl of soup for lunch. She tested the cookies with a spatula, but they were still too soft.

Liz soaped her hands. "For some reason, the defaced sign made our loyal customers decide they didn't want tea today."

"What did you do when you found it?"

"We didn't call the cops, if that's what you mean. They'd be worse than graffiti." Liz pushed her round glasses back up the slant of her nose, leaving a perfect circle of soapsuds on the nosepiece. "I baked cookies. Adele scrubbed the sign and graffiti. She was pretty freaked out, you know how she's been since the miscarriage. When she left, I called Francie. I knew you'd get here sooner or later, but I didn't want to be here alone."

Pippa shook her head. "If I leave the house a minute before one o'clock, the monitor will turn me in."

"Well, some of us don't rate shortened work days, just for being pregnant," Liz said.

That wasn't fair. One minute her pregnant body was a sacred vessel, a crucible for the solstice ceremony. The next minute it was her fault the court said her baby was at risk.

Liz flung Marshall's soiled sweatshirt on the floor. "I'm out of here."

After she left, the room was too quiet. Pippa switched on the stereo, turned the sweatshirt right side out, and hung it on the empty hook between the potter's wheel and the music stool. Before her arrest, Murphy used to sit on the stool and play odd medleys of Celtic tunes and Yiddish melodies on the psaltery, which she insisted was as old as Isis. Customers loved to watch Murphy dance the bow over the strange-looking instrument and often ordered another pot of tea or plate of cookies just to sit longer and listen.

Pippa climbed onto Murphy's stool. Where was the psaltery now?

She breathed in the steamy carob aroma, remembering the first time Francie brought her to the Tea Room four years earlier. Liz had been baking cookies that day, too. The morning sunlight had shimmered through the plate glass window and the scent from the oven smelled like home.

After that first day, Pippa lived at the Tea Room for almost a month, visiting Pioneer Street for meals and showers. Daytimes, she worked with Liz and Murphy and Adele, baking cookies and serving tea in Francie's handmade mugs, selling organic teas and herbs, homegrown and slow-dried hanging upside down. In the long evenings, Francie pulled the shades closed and held class about their Isis beliefs and traditions, and all the major world religions.

"Why do I need to know this stuff?" Pippa had once asked.

Francie looked up from measuring spearmint tea leaves into plastic bags. "Most people are born into a faith and never question it. Tian researched religions and utopian societies. Then, he chose Isis and she chose him. If you want to live in our family, you have to choose her too."

"Why utopian? That means perfect, doesn't it?" Pippa tied a green ribbon around the last bag of tea leaves.

"Nothing's perfect," Francie said. "But Tian wanted to avoid the biggest mistakes that other groups have made."

When Francie left for the graveyard shift at the hospital, Pippa slept in the back room on a cot between shelves of restaurant-sized mayonnaise jars filled with herbs and teas and spices. Her feet were warmed by the small kiln, where they fired the earthenware teapots and cups glazed with images of Isis and Bast.

What would they do if the customers stayed away?

Pippa slipped off the stool and checked the cookies. They were cool enough to transfer into a wide glass bowl. She brushed the crumbs from the cookie sheets and dropped small balls of raw dough in even lines. She imagined Tian sitting in the hush of a public library studying old religions and utopias. What kinds of mistakes did other people make?

But their community hadn't worked for everyone, either. Soon after Pippa joined, Meg and Enoch left with their three kids. No one would tell her what all their arguments with Tian were about, but they didn't find the family so perfect.

Francie brought a whiff of burnt tar into the room. "Mario said the sign was already vandalized when he opened at seven," she said. "I doubt if any customers will come today, but we should stay open, just to show them we're not intimidated."

Pippa wondered if Francie was really as brave as her words. Maybe a brick through the window would be next.

"When the cookies are done, why don't you work on the sign," Francie said. "I'll get started on the next batch of teapots. If business stays slow, we may have to sell our pots and tea through other stores."

Francie scooped two large handfuls of clay from the barrel next to the potter's wheel and slapped them onto the kneading board. Pippa watched her body move into the rhythm of working the clay. Lubricating the particles, Francie had explained, so the clay will dance. After a few minutes, Francie seemed satisfied and placed a handful on the throwing head. Positioning herself on the plastic seat, she kicked the concrete wheel hard five or six times until it spun and hummed. She dipped her hands in the water bucket, pulled the spinning gray clump into a tall column, then squashed it down.

Pippa washed the empty bowl at the sink, still smarting from Liz's comment. Her probation officer said that the judge had an insane soft spot for motherhood, and her pregnancy was the only reason Pippa wasn't in jail too. She turned to Francie, trying to keep the whine out of her voice.

"Liz was really mean to me just now, about only working afternoons. That's not fair. If I weren't pregnant, I'd be in jail. Then you would really be short-staffed."

Francie lifted her hands from the wheel, displaying the glistening clay gloves extending past her delicate wrists. "Fix my hair, Pippa? It's in my eyes."

Pippa chose a pink scrunchy from the teacup on the window sill and gathered Francie's hair. Touching the silky curls made her throat thicken. Pippa's first month in the family, when she and Francie spent so much time together, Francie would let Pippa brush and braid her hair, like the sister she always wanted. She fastened the scrunchy around the ponytail, and turned back to the oven.

"It's more than the part-time work." While she spoke, Francie focused on the gray shape that was growing curved walls. "People are upset that ever since you joined, you've gotten special treatment. Like having Tian mostly to yourself."

Pippa took the last batch of cookies from the oven, holding the hot tray with a dishtowel. What did Francie mean by mostly?

"It's been tough on everyone." Francie flared the spinning walls out and then drew them in to form the neck. "With Tian and Murphy in jail and Marshall doing the home schooling and Adele still upset about the miscarriage, and me working nights, and you with short hours." She paused for a breath before continuing. "Plus we're all nervous about the hearing coming up. And then you bring that nurse home to spy on us."

That wasn't fair, blaming her for the nurse. "I didn't ask for her to come. I'm the one who has to put up with her nosiness, and her stupid advice. How do you think I feel?"

"How do you feel?" Francie looked up from the pregnant teapot shape emerging between her hands.

Francie's fingers looked so competent, so certain. Pippa longed to make those buoyant shapes out of clay. One day during Pippa's first winter, Francie started to teach her to throw pots, but Pippa had been impossibly clumsy. They laughed so hard during the first lesson and had so much fun that Pippa thought maybe they would become real friends.

"I'm not sure," she said to the back of Francie's head. Mostly she still felt numb. "I'm worried about this thing on my ankle, and how I can dance at the solstice. About keeping my baby. And I'm lonely, I guess."

"Lonely? We're your family."

"No one in this so-called family has tried to help me with this house arrest. No one will even talk about Abby." Pippa wished she felt better, getting that off her chest. Instead, now she felt lonely and scared. She scooped a still-soft cookie off the metal sheet with the spatula, pulling it into two pieces. She held half out to Francie.

Francie opened her mouth for the cookie, then touched Pippa's hand, leaving two earth-colored fingerprints.

"Thanks," Francie said. "We make the best cookies in town." She let the wheel slow, then used the wire with small wooden handles at both ends to separate the teapot from the metal surface.

"And the healthiest. Would you believe that nurse this morning tried to teach me about wholesome eating? She probably scarfs down meat and all sorts of processed crap and calls it a healthy diet."

"Makes sense they'd send a carnivore. But what do you expect from a nurse working for the cops?" Francie smoothed the rim of the teapot with a wet chamois cloth, then lifted the glistening pot onto the drying shelf.

"She's not that bad, doesn't actually work for the cops. She kind of got under my skin." Pippa grinned. "Like a chigger." Francie looked blank, started centering a small lump of clay for the teapot spout. Right, they didn't have chiggers in Massachusetts.

At least Liz grew up in Virginia, and knew about things like chiggers and sweetshrub and copperheads hiding in autumn leaves. They didn't talk much on Pioneer Street about where they came from. Pippa knew few details about Tian's old life, except that he and Marshall had been in opposing gangs in Newark until something awful happened, something to do with Tian's little sister and the bandana Marshall always wore. But occasionally, when it was just her and Liz in the storefront and business was slow, they would trade crazy stories, remembering the good parts of growing up in the south. Or the simple parts, like chiggers.

"The nurse wasn't too bad," Pippa said again. "Besides." She stopped talking and concentrated on transferring the fragile cookies to the bowl.

"Besides what?"

"None of you guys seem interested in helping me get out of this shackle for the solstice." Pippa placed the spatula carefully on the counter, lining it up next to the cookie bowl, and finally looked right at Francie. "Much as the idea makes me queasy, I think I'm going to need her help."

"Be careful." Francie removed her hands and let the clay spin alone. "I didn't rescue your sorry butt from Lyman Street so you could cozy up to some nurse spy. Don't you forget it, Pippa. She's not one of us."

6 ~ Sam

Sam only half-heard the first beep of the Special Ed bus. He had spent all afternoon trying to breech the cyber-defenses of a university admissions office for a client who suspected racial bias in his law school rejection. Sam was supposed to prove discrimination, but the firewall was tougher than he expected.

When the horn sounded a second time, louder and longer, he scooted his desk chair over the pine floorboards to the second floor window. Most days, Emily zipped out the front door to meet Zoe before Mr. Gonzalez had the flashers on, but Sam didn't see her or her car. At the third insistent honk, Sam grabbed his jacket and hurried downstairs. The bus driver was helping Zoe maneuver down the steps with her crutches. Her rhinestone headband sparkled, even though the afternoon had turned cloudy and it looked like snow.

"Papa, I'm going to marry Señor Gonzalez," Zoe said. She turned to wave goodbye to the silver-haired driver. "Right?"

"Si, si," the driver said, handing Zoe's backpack to Sam. "Hasta mañana, Missy."

Zoe scampered ahead to the front door, her sticks clacking on the sidewalk. "I want a snack. Can we cake bookies?"

"Sounds dunky hory to me," Sam said, following his daughter onto the front porch. He had started talking to Zoe in spoonerisms when she was an infant, even though it drove Anna crazy. By the time she was four, Zoe had figured out how to switch the first sound of words by herself. It was their secret language.

As he dug into his jeans pocket for his emergency key to Anna's half of the house, Emily's car sputtered to the curb.

"Sorry I'm late." Emily slammed the car door and caught up to Sam and Zoe in the doorway. "Thanks, Sam."

"No problem."

"We're going to bake cookies." Zoe headed for the kitchen.

Emily tapped Zoe's shoulder to get her attention, and pointed to the bathroom. "First your cath," she said. "Then your snack."

"I'm too hungry to wait." Zoe turned back towards the kitchen.

"You know your mother's rules. Hurry up. Your papa will wait for you."

Sam hadn't moved from the front door, uncertain if he should come in, or go back to his apartment.

"Right?" Emily looked at him.

Sam nodded. When Zoe closed the bathroom door, he followed Emily into the kitchen. Emily went right to the computer and pushed the power button. While it powered up, she started pulling food containers from the refrigerator and cupboards.

"Thanks again." Emily opened the jar of peanut butter and sniffed.

"No problem." Sam pointed at the computer, still loading. "When are you and Anna going to let me update that dinosaur for you?"

Emily didn't answer. Sam had been making that offer for years. When Anna had first discovered that she was pregnant with Zoe, she and Sam had carefully planned the kitchen desk space. Sam would be able to work on the computer while watching the baby play on the kitchen floor, and Anna could return to her teaching job. That was before the ultrasound.

Emily plunked the armful of snacks on the table, leaned over the desk, and typed, then waited. Sam could hear the dial-up tones. So slow. Finally, she typed again and hit enter with a small flourish.

"Ready," Zoe called.

Emily hurried towards the bathroom. Sam could picture the scene inside. Emily would inspect Zoe's hands, making sure that she had washed them carefully. She would watch the girl lubricate the small plastic catheter and insert it until the yellow stream splashed into the toilet.

He scooted the kitchen chair closer to the monitor and saw a Google search for "Frozen Babies." He clicked on the first entry and read a front page story in the city newspaper from August 24, almost three months earlier.

The partially decomposed bodies of two very young children were discovered yesterday by hikers in a remote section of Forest Park. Springfield Chief Detective Marshall Mahon revealed today that the bodies were hidden in a deep gully in the rarely-used southeastern section of the park. He theorized that they were frozen there over the winter and promised a full investigation, with prompt arrest of those responsible.

Why was Emily interested in this stuff? He heard the flush of the toilet, clicked on the Back arrow, and then on the second search entry, dated October 29.

Chief Mahon announced this afternoon that the frozen babies have been traced to a cult in the Forest Park neighborhood called the Family of Isis. Three adults have been arrested and will be arraigned tomorrow morning—the mothers of the two dead children, and a man allegedly the father of both. Law enforcement consultants from Boston deny any known association between Isis cults and child abuse or ritual sacrifice.

But Mahon warned that "any cult must be approached with extreme caution and the expectation of bizarre behavior."

Zoe rushed into the kitchen, her stuffed purple rhino gripped under her chin. "I cathed myself again, first try."

Sam scooted his chair back to the table. "Good work, Poose." He rescued the rhino and kissed the top of her head, letting her sandy curls mix with his own. Poose was her old nickname from the days before she mastered the crutches, when her preferred means of transportation was the papoose carrier on Sam's back.

Zoe grabbed one waxed tip of Sam's mustache and tugged. "Papa, I walk now."

"You're still my papoose." Sam opened the bag of carrot sticks and dumped them into the bowl on the table while Emily scooped peanut butter onto Zoe's plate.

"That's three times in a row, all by myself. So I get a treat. Right?" She looked at her plate. "Hey, what about baking cookies?"

"No time to bake today." Emily poured grape juice into Zoe's plastic cup. "But, you're right about the treat. I bet you've earned a trip to the Toy Palace this weekend."

It had taken months of patience to teach his daughter to catheterize herself. Sam suspected Emily had done most of the work. Having Emily live there had turned out pretty well. He had been dubious when Anna's Aunt Ruth called to say that Emily was moving from Portland down to Springfield, and could use some family. Just for a few months, while she got settled. That was four years ago. By the time Emily arrived, he had already moved into the upstairs apartment, so he didn't have any say in the decision. He admired how the cousins arranged their work schedules so that Zoe always had supervision. Sometimes, he wished they needed his help more often.

"I'd rather have a kitty." Zoe clasped her hands behind her back, leaned over her plate and licked the peanut butter off a carrot stick. "Meow."

Emily rescued the rhinestone headband slipping down over Zoe's nose. "Don't push your luck. Finish eating, so we can do your stretching exercises, okay?" She sat at the computer and leaned towards the screen.

Sam stood up. That was probably his cue to leave. But he couldn't help looking over her shoulder. "Why are you interested in this stuff?"

"It's work-related. Confidential."

She took those rules awfully seriously. Always saying she couldn't talk about her patients because of the new federal HIPAA privacy regulations. Sam couldn't help teasing.

"I get it," he said. "Top secret."

"Sop tecret." Zoe echoed, and then slapped her hands over her mouth, looking at Sam.

Emily didn't seem to notice. Sam brought his index finger to his lips. He wasn't exactly sure why he insisted that the spoonerisms be their private language, but he liked it that way.

"Do you know anything about this Isis group?" Emily asked.

Sam shook his head. "I just remember reading the stories when the bodies were found, and then they arrested some cult members. But that was a few months ago, right?"

"Uh huh. It says that they found the bodies on August 23." Emily clicked on the next entry. "But it took the cops a couple of months to track down the family."

"Wasn't there something about an orgy, dancing around a bonfire on the winter solstice? Isn't that when the kids died, in that big snowstorm last December?"

Zoe twisted to look at her father and the carrot missed her mouth, landing a splotch of peanut butter on her cheek. "What kids died?"

Emily rubbed the peanut butter off with a napkin, kissed the cleaned spot on Zoe's cheek, her lips pressing there until the girl squirmed. "Never mind, Zoe," she said. "Those kids were different from you."

Even so, Sam didn't want to think about kids dying. He worried about Zoe every single day, mostly about her shunt. He looked at Emily. "How about if I do Zoe's stretching? You can keep reading that stuff."

"Okay." Emily was already moving towards the computer. "Thanks."

"Let me be your burst of beaden," Sam whispered, squatting in front of Zoe's chair. She and Rufus the rhino climbed onto his back and they trotted into the living room.

Whatever it was that was going on with Emily and her top secret work situation, it bought him an extra hour with Zoe. He never had enough time with his kid. He couldn't blame Anna; he had been the one who couldn't hack it and left. Anna was fair about custody, making sure he got exactly what was stated in the divorce agreement—every other weekend and holiday, plus one weekday evening. Unless Zoe was sick and couldn't go to school, then she stayed upstairs with him while he worked. Most Sundays he was invited downstairs for dinner. Anna wanted Zoe to feel that even though her parents were divorced, she still had a family.

Zoe grabbed the television remote. "I get to chip the flannels."

"Good one." Sam helped Zoe position herself on the rug with a throw pillow under her head so she could see the screen, with Rufus snuggled against her neck. "You find Sesame Street and I'll shake off your twos." Zoe giggled, and he removed her shoes and socks and leg braces, checking the skin underneath for red pressure areas. Then he stretched the tight muscles behind her right knee to the count of ten, while on the television screen a blue giraffe danced the polka with the letter H.

Watching his daughter's face, Sam thought about Emily in the kitchen researching the frozen babies. He didn't really get it, her living like a maiden aunt in Anna's home, helping with the household work and childcare. One Sunday dinner about a year earlier—they were having lasagna—Emily had mentioned a guy.

"Chad called this morning," Emily said. "He wants to visit."

"Who's Chad?" Sam's forkful hovered, mozzarella strings dangling.

Anna threw Sam a warning look. "Emily lived with Chad in Portland." She smiled at Emily. "When's he coming?"

Emily got up from the table, even though her lasagna was untouched. "I told him no."

Sam didn't learn any more about Chad after Emily left the room. Anna said it was none of his business. She would never talk about when she and Emily were kids on the island. Sam knew there had been some kind of tragedy with Emily's parents, something about prison and family members taking sides, but apparently none of that was his business either. Whatever happened, it was a long time ago. Emily was grown up now. Didn't she want a family of her own?

Zoe laughed and tugged on Sam's sleeve. She pointed at the cartoon giraffe, now trying to do a headstand and balance his awkward body on his long skinny neck. "Watch with me, Papa."

Sam switched to the left leg, flexing Zoe's hip to ninety degrees, then slowly straightening the knee. On impulse, he grabbed Rufus and skipped the rhino across Zoe's belly, burying his plastic nose in her armpit. That brought on a waterfall of giggles that banished all thoughts of Emily and her frozen babies.

7 ~ *Emily*

I could hear their sing-song voices counting hamstring stretches. Afternoons were my special time with Zoe, just the two of us, until Anna got home from school. Then all the business of making dinner and eating and getting Zoe ready for bed took over. Normally, I liked to do Zoe's afternoon stretches myself, but today I was glad when Sam squatted down in front of Zoe's chair so she could climb on for a piggyback ride. He whispered something, and she giggled, and for a minute I wanted to send Sam upstairs and keep Zoe to myself.

But that would be selfish. Anyway, I needed the time to learn more about Pippa. Glancing at the thickening clouds outside, I flipped on the kitchen light and concentrated on the computer.

If I ignored the diatribes against freezing embryos, most of the search results on "frozen babies" were from the local daily paper—news stories, feature articles, editorials. When I read about late summer hikers finding the bodies, I couldn't help imagining Pippa opening the newspaper the next day. Did anyone warn her? Was she sitting on that yellow brocade chair, with the diesel-purring cat on her lap? Did she read that headline under the harsh gaze of the bird woman?

In early October, the newspaper reported three arrests.

Two suspects remain in custody: the male leader of the cult, identified only as Sebastian, and Murphy Barnett, the mother of the boy who died. Because of her pregnancy, Pippa Glenning, the mother of the dead girl, is released under house arrest on electronic monitoring and her unborn child has been placed under protective custody. Two older children remain in the household with their mother, Francine Beaujolais, under close supervision by the Department of Social Services.

On autopsy, the cause of death was determined to be exposure. The children were apparently in good health before the incident leading to their demise. The deceased were racially mixed, according to the medical examiner's office.

What difference did their race make? And how could they tell? After eight months, frozen and then thawed, wouldn't the bodies be decomposed? Wouldn't they haven been bothered by animals? What would the bodies look like, after all that time? With a jolt, I remembered that one of those bodies was Pippa's Abby.

In early November, the tone of the newspaper articles grew more hostile.

Chief Mahon urged the citizens of Western Massachusetts to be vigilant as the winter solstice approaches. "There may be substantial public risk," he stated. "The potential for harm in the practices of cults must not be ignored. We have no credible information about what they do in their bizarre rituals secluded in the woods."

Not everyone agreed with the Chief of Police about the public risk. One woman from Amherst wrote:

Isis worshippers revere all life, work to save the environment, and expressly forbid any sacrifice, either ritual or actual. Everyone is accepted in that so-called cult. All religions are welcome. How can this be dangerous?

Fierce arguments raged on the pages of the editorial section in early November. The angry words made me feel prickly and I switched off the computer. None of this seemed remotely connected to the poised young woman I met that morning. But then, the Pippa Glenning I met didn't strike me as a person who would let her baby freeze to death.

Maybe it was those articles, or the snow outside, but that evening I couldn't settle down. I rearranged the shelf of library books by due date, straightened the newspapers on the coffee table into a perfect stack, rescued a balled-up purple sock from under the couch. And I worried about Zoe, who had been unusually quiet at dinner.

"Do you feel sick?" I had asked her. "Headache?" I would never forget the time Zoe got quiet, and then muted, and then tearful, and finally was rushed to the hospital in the middle of the night for surgery to replace the malfunctioning shunt in her brain.

"I'm not sick," Zoe insisted.

"She's fine." Anna smiled at me. "Don't be such a worrywart."

When the dinner dishes were done, Anna and Zoe cuddled on the sofa with Rufus and Babar. I grabbed a heavy sweater and took my cup of tea to the porch.

The sun porch was my favorite room. With windows on three sides, it hugged the eastern wall of Anna's three-story house. In summer, sunlight baked the air and faded the fabric cushions. But that night, wind gusts rattled their way inside and a thin coat of snow collected in the corners of the windowpanes.

Sam's heavy footsteps thumped upstairs. I wondered exactly what kind of computer work he did to make a living, when he rarely left the house. That was his concern, I'd always told myself, even if it might be dicey. He was an odd duck, sporting a retro handlebar mustache with waxed tips. But I believed in people minding their own business.

Except I was grateful that Aunt Ruth liked to butt in on everyone else's affairs. Living with Anna had been her suggestion. Aunt Ruth was my mother's only sister and she took us in when my father went to prison. She was the social director, keeping track of every relative who ever lived on Saperstein Neck. When I left the island after high school, she wrote me newsy letters, even though I rarely answered. I telephoned her when I realized it was no good with Chad, to let her know I was moving down to Massachusetts. She reminded me that my cousin Anna lived in Springfield. My strongest memory of Anna was as a forlorn teenager at her parents' funeral, after they drowned when their sailboat overturned in Penobscot Bay. We had never been close, even though her mother was my dad's sister. Anna's mom had disapproved of my parents and discouraged our friendship as kids, but that didn't prevent Aunt Ruth from producing Anna's phone number, and insisting that I get in touch.

"You two will get along great," Aunt Ruth predicted. "You even look like kin, both so tall and slim."

I stared at the snowy night sky, chopped into small squares by the windows. Aunt Ruth couldn't have predicted how much I would love Zoe.

Before Zoe, I had never known a person with spina bifida. Oh, I had studied the condition in nursing school. And one night, working labor and delivery in Portland, I assisted at the delivery of a baby with a glistening red sack at the base of his spine. A riptide of silence rushed through the delivery rooms and spilled out into the sad blue hallway. There was a defeated look on that mother's face as she listened to the obstetrician explain that her son had a birth defect and would never walk. Anna said they told her and Sam the same thing when Zoe was born. Anna still ranted and fumed about it sometimes.

Anna never told me the whole story of Zoe's birth. Just that when the ultrasound showed the hole in Zoe's spine, Sam wanted an abortion and she wanted the baby. Anna won. Turned out she didn't entirely win because Sam couldn't handle it. He moved to the upstairs flat on Zoe's first birthday. In his own way, Sam was a good father. His work schedule seemed infinitely flexible, and he was always available. The arrangement worked for everyone. Especially for me. I loved Zoe, and Anna was like a sister. Only I never had a sister and neither did Anna, so what did we know? Maybe this was even better.

☙

Once Zoe was asleep, Anna joined me on the wicker loveseat.

"She okay?" I asked.

"Fine." Anna wrapped a ratty quilt around her shoulders. "Some girls at school were mean to her, wouldn't let her join their club."

I sat up straight. "What happened?"

Anna waved her hand in the air. "That's the way kids are. She'll forget about it by tomorrow."

"Aren't you going to say something to her teacher?"

"Kids can be brutal. I see it every day. Zoe has to get tough."

She was probably right to ignore the classroom malice. But I kept picturing Zoe standing alone on the playground. I did a lot of that as the new kid at the island school.

Anna held out an envelope.

"What's that?" I left it fluttering in the air between us.

"From Aunt Ruth, to both of us. Your grandfather is still in a coma." Anna turned to face me and I saw Aunt Ruth's pale yellow notepaper peeking under the ripped flap. "If he dies, we'll drive back for his funeral."

"No."

"We have to," she said. "We'll go together."

Who made her boss? Ivan was my grandfather, Anna's great uncle. I pushed the envelope back toward her. "We can't both go. I'll stay here with Zoe."

"She can stay with Sam."

I heard the exasperation in my cousin's voice, but I couldn't stop. "She'll starve. How can you leave your daughter with someone who never cooks?"

"He cooks."

"Yeah, he puts things in the microwave and presses 'start.'" I stood up. "Come on, the guy drinks instant coffee."

"So what? Zoe's too young for coffee." Anna stood too. "Why are we arguing about Sam? Maybe Ivan will recover. Let's see what happens."

"We'll see," I said. No way, I promised myself.

"I have papers to grade." She sighed and left the porch.

Standing alone, I took several slow breaths to blow away my worries. I was sorry about Grandpa Ivan, but I barely knew my mother's father. Certainly not well enough to get me back there. My true family was in Springfield, with Anna and Zoe and my patients.

I looked around for something that needed doing. As I plucked dead leaves from the ficus tree, my hand brushed a thick web. A fat brown spider cozy in the perfect center of her web, a captive fly tucked below her. Safe and snug, with a full pantry. I sat down and wrapped myself in the quilt, still warm from Anna's body.

All that talk about Grandpa Ivan and returning to the island. I tried to control myself, to imagine my childhood refuge, the leafy sanctuary of Aunt Ruth's tree house. But I couldn't help it. My thoughts tumbled backwards instead to my parents' kitchen when I was ten. We were eating granola for breakfast.

❧

The granola has raisins and pecans in it. My favorite. So I take a bite, even though my stomach is jumpy because we're having auditions today, for the last play of fourth grade. I'm trying out for E.T.

"Just look at this eggplant." Momma holds up the purple-black shape for our approval.

"Nice," Daddy says without looking.

She cuts it into chunks and dumps them in the crock pot with the onions and zucchini and yellow squash and barley and broth. Momma gives after-school piano lessons at the Jewish Community Center. This way dinner will be ready when we all get home.

Daddy's spoon taps against the edge of his coffee cup to emphasize each point as he reads the lesson plan about Vietnam that he revised last night. It made him and Momma argue in the living room when they thought I was asleep. It made him wheeze too, until he had to go find his inhaler. "They want me to teach what colonial families ate for dinner," he had said, "as if turnips and sweet potatoes will create good citizens." I covered my ears with my pillow.

I arrange my raisins in a row along the narrow rim of the cereal bowl and try to ignore his spoon-tapping. I imagine myself as a wrinkled brown extraterrestrial far from home. Does E.T. like granola?

The knock at the apartment door is loud. Momma answers it and steps back to let the two men in suits into the kitchen. They show their policeman badges. They mumble some words I don't understand. They put handcuffs on my father.

"You have to come with us now," the short officer says to my father. The cop doesn't look at us. Momma hands my father his inhaler, then pulls me close. My spine is hard against her chest. I sniff her peach blossom shampoo from the food coop, mixed with a sharp smell that makes me shiver and cross my arms on my chest. Momma puts her arms on top of mine, like double seat belts.

Daddy says two words to Momma as the men lead him away. "Call Abe," he says and Momma nods.

She and I stand still like that for a few moments. Then she drops her arms. And mine. I turn around so I can see her face. She must have bitten herself. A spot of blood hangs, suspended, on her bottom lip. Then it tumbles in a wavy line down her chin and falls onto her yellow Boycott Grapes t-shirt. She doesn't go right to the sink and flush it out with cold water so the stain won't set. She goes to the telephone.

I clear the breakfast table, but I leave my father's bowl. His granola gets soggy and the milk turns grey.

That afternoon, Momma drives me up the coast to Rockland. We're going to take the ferry to the island where she grew up. Her sister still lives there. Momma tells me I'm going to stay with Aunt Ruth for a few weeks. I start to cry. I don't know Aunt Ruth very well and barely remember my cousins, even though we're about the same age. We don't visit them often. Daddy says we don't see eye to eye.

"Just for a couple of weeks," Momma promises. "So I can take care of your Daddy."

What about me, I think. Take care of me.

We leave the car in the parking lot and walk onto the boat with one suitcase for the two of us. We stand in front, holding onto the metal chain. When the ferry passes the jetty lighthouse and picks up speed, the wind gets fierce. Momma puts her arm around me and steers me inside. We sit at an orange table. I pick pieces of rust off my fingers.

"Do you remember our photo album, from when Daddy and I lived in the commune?" Momma begins that way.

I nod. With those raggedy clothes, it was hard to tell who was a boy and who was a girl. We had laughed together, my parents and me, over those pictures.

"And remember the war in Vietnam? Your Daddy and I were against that war, and so were our friends in the commune."

I know all about their war. My third grade class studied Vietnam. We made care packages of pencils and crayons and notebooks, mailed them across the world to children whose schoolyards had trees that still wouldn't grow leaves.

"It was wrong to draft young men into that evil war, to kill and be killed. We wanted to stop the bombing." Momma puts her finger on my chin and lifts it up, so I have to look at her. "We set a fire in the draft board where all the records were kept. So they couldn't process any more soldiers, at least for a while."

Momma set a fire?

"Afterwards, your father and I decided not to do that kind of protest any more."

"You mean fires?"

She nods "Fires and other things that could hurt people. We moved to Portland, and the next year you were born. Last month one of our old friends from the commune was arrested. He was in a lot of trouble." Momma's lips get so skinny they almost disappear. "He told them Daddy set the fire. That's why those men came this morning."

The ferry slows down and turns into the island harbor. We go outside again to stand in the wind. Aunt Ruth is waiting on the pier and drives us to a white house across from the harbor. Momma and Aunt Ruth huddle together for a few minutes in the kitchen while I stand close to the doorway and pretend to look out the window at the boats. I cannot quite hear their whispers, except one thing.

"Mitchell is very nervous," Aunt Ruth says. "Our business depends on our customers' trust."

"Good grief," Momma whispers back. "She's ten years old. Joe McCarthy is dead."

Aunt Ruth makes coffee. Mine is mostly hot milk, with two spoons of coffee and two spoons of sugar. That's the way I like it, but I'm only allowed to drink it on special occasions because coffee stunts your growth.

Momma is in a hurry. She says she has to catch the last ferry back, to be with Daddy in court the next morning.

I whine and plead. "Don't go."

She must be worried about me, because she decides to stay overnight and take the first ferry back in the morning. We share the narrow bed in Aunt Ruth's tiny back bedroom. I sleep with my nose in the peach smell of Momma's hair.

It's way more than a couple of weeks. I miss the tryouts for E.T. and then I miss the play. My Portland teacher sends thick envelopes with schoolwork and my cousin Marilyn plays teacher with me in the evenings. In June, Aunt Ruth asks me to help her with spring planting. I've never had a garden. At home, we get our tomatoes and lettuce and cukes at the food coop. I watch her and copy what she does, pushing my finger into the dirt, up to the second knuckle. Into every hole I plant a seed with a wish for Daddy before sprinkling the dirt back in and patting it down.

Planting hope is my idea.

One early summer afternoon, I help Aunt Ruth weed the garden, using a half-size hoe that belongs to my cousins. The sun warms my back right through my T-shirt. I stop to rest and lean forward on the hoe handle with both hands and look up at the sky. That's when I see the tree house. It's in an old swamp maple that stands alone on the edge of the property, beyond the garden plot.

I use the two wooden slats nailed to the trunk to reach the lowest branches, and then I can climb a few feet to the tree house. Set in a wide fork, it is just a platform, really, with low sides. I part the branches with my hands and watch the ferry pulling away from the dock. Aunt Ruth weeds between the rows of tomatoes. Marilyn and Carla run with their friends along the pebble beach. I am veiled by leaves.

Anna insisted that the sickly avocado plant on the sun porch was just dormant, but it looked dead to me. I pulled off the brown crinkly leaves, crushed them in my hand, and dropped them in the waste basket. I pressed my forehead against the dark window. What happened to my family wasn't my cousins' fault, or Aunt Ruth's, or Momma's, or even Daddy's for that matter. I am thirty-two years old. Why am I still whining about things that happened so long ago? I searched the darkness of the backyard. The garden was all dead stalks, thick with blowing snow and the sparkle of frosted trees. The cold pushed back at me through the glass.

A lonely and icy evening. Pippa's baby died on a night like this.

8 ~ *Pippa*

Pippa had never been to an obstetrician. Too bad she couldn't keep it that way. Friday morning, she sat between the cats on the living room sofa waiting for Emily Klein. From the kitchen drifted the small clinking sounds of Marshall washing the breakfast dishes. At the dining room table, the twins bickered as they mixed paper maché for their relief map.

"That's not enough water," Timothy said.

"It has to be thick, Dummy. So the mountains will stand up."

Pippa cupped her hands over the slight bulge of her middle, hoping for another quivery message from inside. She was fifteen weeks along and two days ago she had felt the first flutter of this baby. When did it start with Abby, that first distant watery tumble? Pippa searched the Goddess's features in the painting over the mantel; they seemed alive in the flickering candle flames.

"How can I dance for you," she asked the painting, "without risking my baby?"

Isis looked back with molten eyes. Pippa couldn't read her expression.

At least she knew what the cats wanted. With one hand she stroked Bast's sleek blue-black fur. With the other she scratched behind Newark's ears, making his guttural purr even louder.

As if he could read her sorrow, Newark opened his eyes, stretched and climbed onto her lap. He didn't have Bast's regal bearing, but Newark always seemed to know when she was mourning Abby. His nose nuzzled along the denim jumper over her breasts, tender already, and into the valley of her neck before curling up. She stroked his back until the lamenting purr returned.

She tried not to think about the doctor's appointment. Ma's voice buzzed inside her head. It don't help one tad to fret about something you can't control, she used to say, so you might as well think about something nice. But Pippa couldn't come up with a single cheerful thought. She tried to remember what Emily said on Wednesday, about the button-back chairs being valuable.

Emily might be book smart, but what did she know about important things, like growing a baby when all the time the court planned to take him away? What could she possibly understand about losing a child? No matter how much she loved her cousin's kid, it just wasn't the same. And no way could Emily get it, how responsible Pippa felt about not letting Isis down, or the family, with Tian in jail. Newark rolled over, presenting his velvet belly to be rubbed. What good was responsibility, when you had no idea about how to fulfill it? The solstice was crucial, and she couldn't figure out how to dance at the ceremony without getting caught. And all this worry had to be bad for her baby.

She looked down at the rug, off-white with a design of grape leaves weaving through a bamboo trellis. The coffee table had been placed slightly off-center covering a pale purple stain. She imagined someone sloshing half a bottle of Chianti across the rug at a party. The blemish hardly showed on the grapes, but on the beige background the splashes stood out like old blood.

Maybe chanting would help. "We grow from your earth; we share your fruits," she sang, her voice growing stronger with each word. "Your wings protect us. Strengthened by your power, we reach for the stars."

She really should be sitting cross-legged on the floor, but even this early in the pregnancy it wasn't easy to get up once she was down. Her center of gravity had already shifted, settled somewhere closer to the earth. The pregnancy had been so different with Abby; how light she had felt even at the end. Her cells remembered the warmth of Abby's infant skin and the memory was unbearable. She looked at Isis, wings luminous in the flickering of the candles on the mantel, imagining herself and this baby safe in the goddess' embrace.

The toot of a horn jerked Pippa's attention to the small green car at the curb. Being a nurse must not pay so well. But Pippa would be happy to own any car. The family had an old van, the roof pockmarked from a hailstorm last year. Most of the time it was parked in the garage waiting for Marshall to fiddle with some little thing not worth paying someone to fix. After settling Newark in her warm spot on the sofa, she blew out the candles, and called goodbye to Marshall and the twins.

Emily unlocked the passenger door and lifted a large paper from the front seat. "Good morning."

"Hi. What's the picture?" The crayoned drawing was crude, a boy in bed with a dark-haired woman dancing behind him. The child's leg was enormous and encircled by a contraption like a cage.

"A present from the patient I just saw."

"Why's the Eiffel tower on his leg?"

Emily signaled to the empty street, then pulled away from the curb. "The metal frame holds the bones together while they heal."

"He drew it for you?"

"Uh huh. A good-bye card. The frame comes off on Monday. How sweet is that?"

Pippa studied the drawing. The metal spikes seemed to go right into his bones. Poor kid. "What happened to him?"

"Hit by a bus. But he's doing well." Emily paused. "I'll miss him."

Pippa twisted around to place the drawing on the back seat. "Do you always get close to your patients?" She rearranged her long skirt around her legs, uncovering the bulge of the small black monitor.

"Sure. Especially if I see them for weeks and months." Emily braked for the red light at Belmont and glanced down at Pippa's ankle. "You mind if we take city streets, instead of the highway?"

"Take your time. I'm in no rush to see this doctor."

"I hate highway driving. When I lived in Portland, I didn't take the interstate for a whole year. I couldn't merge."

Couldn't merge? Pippa glanced sideways at Emily, not sure if it was okay to laugh. But Emily's expression looked serious. Geez, that was pathetic.

"I was wondering," Emily said. "Doesn't a siren go off or something, when you leave the house with that device?"

Pippa shook her head. "It's a monitor, not an alarm. It's programmed, so they know that I go to work every afternoon. They programmed in this doctor's appointment, that I'll be out of the house for a few hours." She studied Emily's profile again, wondering if this was a good time to ask her favor. "I told my probation officer that this appointment would take all morning," she said. "They don't expect me back until noon."

"It won't take that long."

Pippa had called Nan Malloy early that morning, explained that the first doctor's appointment would be extra long. Her plan depended entirely on Emily. She would have to ask, but it was probably too soon. She would wait until after the appointment, when Emily was feeling sorry for the poor pregnant girl having to go through an examination with some old doctor putting his hairy hands where they didn't belong.

"Tell me about your, I don't know what to call your group, your household," Emily said. "Is cult a bad word for you?"

Pippa scratched her ankle, slipping her finger under the rubber strap. "I'm sure you've heard awful things about us. That's what Tian says. He's the head of our religion, but you can only call him Tian if you're in the family. Otherwise, he's Sebastian." Maybe if Emily understood about their family, she would be willing to help. "Tian says if you believe in something, it's true and sacred, like a religion. But if you fear it, if you hate it, then you call it a cult."

"People seem to be pretty scared of you guys. At least, according to the newspapers. I guess that makes you a cult."

"To me, we're a family. Tian's our leader, like the father. He talks with Isis pretty much every day to learn what she wants from us." She tried to search Emily's face for her reaction, but the nurse's face was blank. "Do you think that's weird, hearing voices? That Tian is psychotic, needs medication or something? At least our church doesn't rip people off or screw little boys."

Emily signaled left at the parking garage, but she didn't say anything.

Oops. Maybe she had better change the subject so she didn't offend this stuffy woman. Pippa looked out the window. "This place is huge. I've never been here."

"That's the Children's Hospital, with all the glass. That's where Zoe goes for clinic. The Emergency Room is on the left. We're going to the big building on the right, the medical offices." Emily glanced at Pippa. "Tell me about Isis."

"She's about fertility and healing, about curing the sick and bringing the dead back to life." Pippa still had a hard time with that part. If Isis could bring back the dead, why hadn't she saved Abby and Terrence?

Emily pulled into a parking spot on the top level, under the dishwater-gray sky, and turned off the ignition. "Can I ask you one more question?"

Why was she was so curious about the family? Was that a good sign, or a bad one? "Sure. If I can ask you one."

"Okay," Emily said. "You first."

"Are you Jewish?"

"Yeah. But I'm not observant or anything. Why?"

"I just wondered. Klein, you know?" Pippa shrugged. "If you can be nosy, so can I."

"Fair enough. My turn. What's the big deal with the solstice?"

Pippa looked at Emily's long face, the thin nose bent slightly to the left. Remember who she works for. Don't assume you can trust her, just because she acts interested in you. Pippa thought back to Francie's lesson about the religions of the world, from when she was studying to join the family. "It's kind of like your High Holy Days," she answered, and opened the car door.

There were ten names listed on the plaque next to the door: four doctors and six nurse-midwives. Emily pointed at B. Zabernathy MD. "Your appointment is with him. I've never met him," she said. "Too bad you didn't get one of the midwives."

"Don't I get to choose?" Pippa asked.

Emily left her hand on the doorknob. "Usually they want you to see everyone at least once, since there's no predicting who will be on call when you go into labor. But maybe it's different for you, since the judge ordered these visits."

"It's totally different for me. We have our babies at home. With Miriam. She's a lay midwife from Ashfield. That would be my choice, but my wishes don't count, do they?"

The women of the family gave birth in the greenhouse, the closest place to the forest and to Isis. Their greenhouse was long and narrow and extended across most of the backyard to catch as much southern sun as possible. With Abby, Pippa had labored all night. The flickering light from the ring of candles had been mirrored in a hundred panes of glass, multiplying their prayers and filling the room with anticipation. Her physical memories of labor, of panting and breathing and finally pushing, were all mixed up with the earthy smell of the greenhouse air, wet and ripe with the shoots pushing through dark soil.

The whole family had gathered for the labor and the birth. Pippa lay propped on a mattress and pillows in the warmest corner of the glass room. Tian held the double-handled birthing mug to her lips, offering sips of raspberry tea to strengthen her contractions.

At the potting table, Liz prepared compresses of cool nettle tea to soothe her sore bottom afterwards. "Later, you'll be really glad for these," she said. "Right, Francie?"

Francie nodded. "Liz's medicine really worked for me. After the twins."

"And you were twice as sore." Tian smiled at Francie and touched her shoulder.

The twins sat under the table with their blocks, interrupting their castle-building and catnaps for frequent visits to the baby. Jeremy spoke into Pippa's stretched-out belly button. "Hurry up, baby. When you get here, I'll teach you to draw."

Timothy elbowed his brother out of the way. "I'll teach you to play Frisbee."

Murphy played lullabies on the psaltery, building a musical scaffold for Pippa's rhythmic breathing. She stopped playing only to nurse Terrence when he whimpered, then place him back in his nest of blankets at her feet.

It was late morning the next day before Miriam finally announced, "You can push" and mid-afternoon when Tian led them in chanting the birth prayer. The questions and answers bounced back and forth across the room, bright with autumn sun.

How could something so glorious and profound end so badly? Abby gone and Pippa jolted breathlessly awake most nights by the swirling snowstorm nightmares.

Emily held the office door for Pippa. "I'm sorry you don't get to chose. I guess the court is trying to protect your baby."

"I don't need their protection. We take good care of our children." She pushed into the office.

Forty-five minutes later, Pippa's blood and urine had been collected. Pippa and Emily sat on attached green vinyl chairs in the waiting room. Pippa looked up from the clipboard with the medical history form. "What does this mean, am I allergic to latex?"

"Like medical gloves and balloons. Have you ever had a reaction to them, hives or trouble breathing? Maybe at the dentist?"

"I've never been to a dentist," Pippa said. "I can't remember any problems with balloons."

"Then just check the No box. Anything else?"

"Not about the form." Pippa squeezed her eyes tight. "Just, what's the doctor going to do? Besides shove his fingers up inside me?"

"They'll catch up on all the stuff they usually do earlier in the pregnancy. A pelvic exam to confirm that your baby's growing well. Try to relax and it won't hurt. They'll test your blood and urine for anemia, diabetes. Probably talk about vitamins, diet, avoiding things that could hurt the baby, like kitty litter and hot tubs and medicines. Arranging for the hospital delivery. The usual."

Emily's voice was matter-of-fact. This is so ordinary to her. "None of that is usual to us," Pippa said. "We think having babies is natural, something you do at home with your family. Not a disease that needs doctors and tests and hospitals."

⁂

Dr. Zabernathy was tall and pale. And female.

"Good morning. I'm Barbara Zabernathy." Her voice was gruff.

"Pippa Glenning." Pippa shook the offered hand, trying to gauge its size and roughness, to guess how much it would hurt. The doctor nodded to Emily before sitting at the desk and opening the file. As if she already knew about Emily's role as nurse or babysitter. Or jailer.

The doctor opened the thin manila folder. "Let's see. You're single. First baby was a home birth. Any problems with the labor or delivery?"

Pippa shook her head. "No," she said, grateful that Dr. Zabernathy didn't seem to be surprised or disgusted.

"Your daughter died?" The bad-taste look started to appear around the doctor's mouth, a slight tightening of muscles.

"An accident."

The doctor glanced over at Emily, who was standing out of the way but close enough to count. Maybe her presence in the room reminded the doctor, who nodded and stood up.

"You're fifteen weeks by dates." Dr. Zabernathy handed Pippa a folded paper gown. "We'll confirm that with the exam. You get ready and I'll be back in a few minutes."

"I'll leave while you change." Emily followed the doctor out of the room.

Were they going to talk about her? Pippa undressed quickly and stood next to the door, straining to hear their voices. Nothing. She sat on the hard exam table in the flimsy paper gown, studied the clock on the wall. Ten-fifteen. Would there be time to stop at Forest Park on the way home? Would Emily agree? Worrying made her queasy and she crossed her arms over her belly.

"You ready?" Dr. Zabernathy asked, sticking her head in. Without waiting for an answer, she strode into the room followed by Emily and another nurse. Emily moved close to Pippa, sliding into the narrow space between the exam table and the wall. The office nurse helped Pippa scoot down on the table until her bottom was hanging half off, and position her legs wide open, skin against cold metal troughs.

Not ready at all. The doctor loomed between her knees. Pippa focused on her thick wool socks, glad she didn't have to take them off. If these people didn't look too closely, they might not notice the bulge over her ankle. As the doctor's gloved hand slipped inside, Pippa hugged herself harder, hands tucked into her armpits for comfort.

Filleted open. Like the catfish her father used to catch in the river and bring home for Ma to gut on the back porch and fry up for supper. Remembering the smell made her stomach clench. Or maybe it was the doctor's hand pushing, fingers poking inside and outside, trapping her flesh between the two. She closed her eyes and tried to make her thoughts go blank. But the rolling sick feeling was worse, so she stared at the fetal development poster taped to the ceiling. The drawings of the baby growing in the womb looked pretty fishy too, and her insides somersaulted again.

A row of laminated notices were taped to the wall under the clock: Insurance may not cover the new ThinPrep test. Please tell the nurse if you're latex allergic. Three reasons why all pregnant women should have the Triple Screen.

"What's the Triple Screen?" Pippa asked.

"A blood test." Dr. Zabernathy looked at the ceiling as she prodded.

The doctor's eyebrows joined in the center of her forehead. Wasn't that supposed to mean that she was smart or sexy or something?

"To rule out birth defects," the doctor continued, "like spina bifida and Downs. We'll do it the week after Thanksgiving, same day as the ultrasound."

Spina bifida? Wasn't that what Emily's cousin had? But Pippa couldn't think about that. This doctor's exam was as different from Miriam's approach as Pippa could imagine. Or maybe her hands were just bigger. When the doctor pushed a gloved finger into her ass and pushed halfway to her heart, Pippa thought she'd die of embarrassment. You've had worse, she told herself sternly, but it didn't help. She closed her eyes and heard herself whimper. At the touch of a hand on hers, she looked into Emily's brown eyes.

"Breathe slowly," Emily whispered. "It's almost over."

Pippa looked at Emily and nodded, took a deep full breath and exhaled slowly.

Dr. Zabernathy stripped off the soiled gloves and tossed them into the metal can. "Your blood and urine are fine today. You're a robust young woman and your baby seems healthy. I'll see you again after the ultrasound." She opened the door and turned away. "When you're dressed, my nurse will talk with you about diet."

Outright rudeness would be easier to hate. Emily's crooked smile told Pippa that she felt the same way.

In a windowless office that made her think of Tian in jail, Pippa listened to the office nurse explain the food pyramid, pointing with the eraser of her pencil to brightly colored pictures of meat and vegetables and fruit on a laminated poster.

Pippa cleared her throat. "I think eating flesh is disgusting."

"Your baby needs protein to grow normally." The nurse crossed her arms over her chest. "It is very difficult to get the right balance of amino acids without animal protein."

Pippa crossed her arms too. She could not budge on this issue. Emily sat quietly. Did she disapprove too?

Emily broke the silence. "Pippa is a vegetarian. I'll work with her on diet, if you can't."

The office nurse pulled a pamphlet from the bottom desk drawer. "This is a vegetarian pregnancy diet. Follow it carefully." She handed Pippa the paper and stood up.

They walked back to the parking structure. "I don't think that lady appreciated my opinions about diet," Pippa said.

"That eating flesh was disgusting?" Emily grinned. "We can talk more about diet next Wednesday."

"You come every Wednesday?"

"Yup." They climbed the stairs of the parking structure. "Next week is extra busy because of Thanksgiving, but I'll be at your house around eleven."

Thanksgiving already. It wasn't an Isis holiday, but they had all grown up with it and missed the feast. Last year they created their own harvest celebration with a tofu-bird and Tian wrote special chants for the occasion.

They returned to the car in silence. Pippa scratched at the crook of her elbow and pulled off the Band-Aid from the blood test, rolling it into a small pink ball. She turned sideways in her seat to face Emily. Now was the time, before she started driving.

"Emily."

"Yeah?"

"I need a favor."

Emily looked at her. "What is it?"

"Say yes."

"Tell me what first."

Pippa pushed the words past the tightness in her throat. "Take me to Forest Park?"

Emily didn't answer. She looked down, as if she were searching her lap for advice. Her hair, so dark it was almost black, fell forward to cover her face.

"Why?" Emily asked. Finally.

"I want to tell you about Abby. Where it happened, so you can understand."

Pippa hadn't been back to the park. She wasn't stupid; she had understood right away that Abby was likely dead. She could imagine what probably happened, how the two toddlers must have woken up in the snowy wonderland and wandered off to play. Terrence had loved to take Abby's hand and lead her on adventures. But as long as there were no bodies, she had been able to hope that someone had rescued her daughter and was taking good care of her. Pippa had never seen the place where the bodies were found.

"I'm supposed to take you right back to your house."

"Please. It's been almost a year." Pippa didn't have to act, to make her voice quiver. There was no one else to ask. Maybe if Emily understood how it happened, how it felt, maybe there was a chance she might help. And the only way she could understand would be to go there. To the park, to the deep gully.

Emily had to agree.

9 ~ *Emily*

"Use the back entrance," Pippa told me.

As we approached the purpling shadow of Forest Park, my hands tightened on the steering wheel until the knuckles blanched. I already regretted agreeing to Pippa's cockamamie request.

Lighten up, I tried telling myself, borrowing the voice and inflection from Anna, who often criticized me for being too uptight. This is no big deal, just stopping by the park on the way home from a medical appointment, right? And the probation officer expected Pippa to be late, so at most, I was just bending the rules a little, right?

Then why was I terrified?

Following Pippa's instructions, I parked in front of the last house on the street, just down from the massive arched gate. The park is vast, hundreds of acres bordering the city to the south. As we left the car, I pointed to Pippa's ankle.

"We have to watch the time. So that thing doesn't have a conniption fit."

She threw me a quick look, but I saw it. Pippa was perfectly aware of the time.

"They closed this entrance to cars a few years ago," Pippa said. "Follow me."

We walked under the arch and into the forest, silent and still under heavy clouds. Single file along the path for about ten minutes, until we reached a section of older trees, bereft of undergrowth. Our footsteps crunched on the frozen mix of last year's leaves and pine cones. This was a cold, cold place.

The trail dead-ended at a wall of rhododendron bushes. Now what? The hedge was vast, unbroken, twice our height and stretched as far as I could see in both directions. But Pippa guided me through a narrow cut and we were inside the thick green tangle. We emerged onto a wide track bordered on both sides by the shrubs. The shiny leaves drooped like giant teardrops. Smaller paths forked off, some leading to small clearings.

"I never knew this place existed," I said.

"Francie showed us. It was designed as a nature trail for blind people," Pippa said. "The funds ran out and the project was abandoned, but the bushes kept growing."

"It's a maze. Don't you ever get lost?"

Pippa shook her head. "Francie taught us every inch. She grew up in this neighborhood, worked for a school ecology program that used the park for winter survival classes. If you ever come here with her, you'll see. She'll rattle off the names of plants like striped pipsipsua and winged euonymus."

"That's not too likely," I said.

Pippa looked at me with that feline head tilt.

"Me coming here with Francie."

"I guess not. Watch out here."

We half-slid down a steep hill into a gully with an odd, flat bottom. A perfect circle of flat stones ringed a central fireplace. Around us, the forest formed a natural amphitheater, open to the pewter sky.

"We're here." Pippa sat, brushed the leaves off the flat-topped stone next to her, and patted it, looking at me.

So I sat. "What is this place?"

"It's the Sacred Dingle."

She must be kidding. I wanted to snicker, but locked the laughter inside my cheeks so I wouldn't offend her. "Sacred what?"

Pippa gave me this look, almost a grin, as if she knew exactly how dumb it sounded. "Dingle. It means a gully," she said. "That's what folks around here call it."

"Okay. Dingle." I looked hard at Pippa, but I felt my voice soften. "Tell me. We don't have much time."

Pippa squeezed her eyes tight. "This is our holy place. We have our most important rituals here, like the Night of the Teardrop in June, when we remember the world's pain and yearning. And the winter solstice." She paused. "This is where Abby died."

I touched her arm. I wanted to say something, but she kept talking.

"We try to live in harmony with the natural world. We treat each other well. We harbor no hate, even for those who despise us." Pippa shook her head. "I know it sounds like some simple-minded Sunday school teacher telling first graders about the Golden Rule." Then she looked at me, her face heavy. "I don't know if I can do this."

"Please. Go on." I wanted to hear.

"Okay, last solstice. It snowed hard all day, but in the early evening it let up for a while. We left the van a block away so the Park Police wouldn't be suspicious and come searching for a couple of horny high-school kids."

Probably right where we parked today, I thought.

"When we got here, we lit the bonfire and all the candles and this place became so magical." She turned to me and this time her smile was incandescent. "I wish you could have seen it. It was like every fairy-tale palace you ever imagined. Sparkly and safe. A wild ride, but you knew the ending would be happy."

I tried to smile back. "Go on."

"Liz and Francie finished preparing the libation. We chanted and then drank."

"Libation?"

Pippa pursed her lips. "Red wine and honey," she said. "With ground-up peyote buttons. To transport us from our everyday selves, so we can be fully open to Isis."

I watched the skeleton trees swaying slightly in the wind. I really wished she hadn't told me that part.

"Adele stood alone in the inner circle, preparing to dance. She was five months pregnant, but that night she looked way more than that."

"Wait a minute," I interrupted. "What happens if no one is pregnant?"

"Someone will be pregnant. Someone always is."

I didn't get it. Any of it. "But if someone's pregnant every year, where are all the kids?"

"Three of them were Meg and Enoch's kids. They left the family."

"Because of the deaths?"

Pippa frowned. "No, before that, soon after I joined. I don't know why."

"Where is Adele's baby?"

"She lost it a week later. Miscarried."

Could the libation have triggered a miscarriage? "What happened?"

"They said it was some kind of birth defect." Pippa sighed. "That's it. That's what this ceremony is all about. We have a deal with Isis. Every winter solstice we bring new life and she returns the sun. It's the most important ritual of the year. Last year Adele was pregnant and danced the mother-dance. This year it's my turn."

It sounded to me like Isis didn't meet her part of the bargain last solstice. What did she tell them, I wondered, about why Adele miscarried, and the two toddlers died. Neither one of us spoke for a minute. I had to ask. I tried to keep my voice kind. "What happened with Abby?"

Pippa sighed deeply, as if she was too tired to finish. "Murphy and I nursed the babies and got them all cozy and warm in the nest of blankets. Right over there." she pointed, and then looked at me. "Close by and perfectly safe."

There was a small clearing just off the sacred circle.

"Abby slept. Terrence too. I checked on them. Her mouth made little sucking motions." Pippa hesitated and I wasn't sure if she could continue, but she did. "It snowed hard, but they were fine. We danced for hours. When we danced, it was like we were all one person, all living inside one skin, with one enormous heart, and no loneliness. That's how we honor Isis."

When she described the dancing, how close they felt to each other, like a rapture almost. I can't really explain it but for a split second, I think I got it. My throat ached and I had to swallow hard. At that moment, I envied her.

Then I came back to being me. "You left them there alone? In a snowstorm?"

"We were right there. Sleeping with them. When I woke up at dawn, my breasts hurt with milk. I reached for Abby, to nurse her. She was gone."

Neither one of us said anything, and the wind was silent too.

Finally I asked. "Gone how?"

Pippa buried her face in her hands and spoke slowly, her words pushed out one by one between gloved fingers. "I don't know. They must have woken up, and wandered off and got lost. Abby had just started walking a couple of months before, and Terrence loved to drag her around like a puppy dog."

Could that happen? Could those babies wake up and wonder off? Wouldn't a mother hear them? Maybe not, if that mother was sleeping off a heavy dose of libation.

"By morning the snow was so deep and the blowing was so bad we couldn't see across the Dingle. No footsteps. No trail. We searched until dark and then every day until Tian made us stop. He said our babies were home with Isis."

"Didn't you call the police, to help you look?"

Pippa laughed, a harsh and jaded laugh. "They wouldn't help us." Then she shifted her position on the hard stone, to face me. "So do you understand?"

What was she asking me?

Pippa looked impatient. "Do you understand what I have to do?"

"No," I admitted.

"I have to get out of this Bast-damned ankle device for one night. So I can be here for the solstice. I have to be here. I must dance for Isis."

I shook my head and then I couldn't stop shaking it. "After what happened to Abby?"

"That's why I have to do this. For Abby and this new baby."

"I don't understand. How can breaking the law help them?"

Pippa's voice was stronger now. "I know it sounds so dumb, but I also know this is true. It's keeping our deal with Isis, no matter what I decide to do afterwards. It's following through with my promise, instead of running away again."

Again? I didn't fully understand her thinking, but I did see how much Pippa wanted this. I wasn't frightened, not exactly. But then it came to me. Pippa was telling me this for a reason.

She needed something from me.

10 ~ *Pippa*

Pippa knew the exact moment she and Tian had started this baby.

It happened during the heat spell in August, just before they found Abby's body. Right where she was curled up, on the mattress filling most of her slanty-walled attic room.

Tian believed that every adult should have a space in the house. A room of their own, even if the room had no door. That meant the generous bedrooms of the Pioneer Street house had to be partitioned into smaller ones. As the last person to join, Pippa was given the tiny back room on the third floor. Even when Meg and Enoch and their kids moved out, Tian wouldn't let Pippa take one of their large second-floor bedrooms. They would be back, he promised, even though everyone else had given up on them. No one had ever deserted the family before. Not in six years in Springfield, or before that in Newark.

Early on the Monday morning before Thanksgiving, Pippa's attic nest was comfy and warm. It was tucked under the sloped roof, sheltered from the wind that searched out the cracks in the drafty old house. But, every August there were a couple of sweltering weeks, when stagnant weather patterns in the Connecticut River valley trapped hot air in the city. Most nights, Tian flashed his incendiary smile at her, and she joined him in his first-floor bedroom where triple bay windows wide open to the garden caught every wisp of breeze.

That night last mid-August was roasting. Hoping to sleep downstairs, Pippa smiled at Tian. When he didn't respond, she went upstairs alone. She set the fan blowing stale air across her body. She must have fallen asleep, because she woke to the shiver of Tian's tongue on her belly and the vast undertow of his hands.

Afterwards, resting her cheek against Tian's chest, Pippa eavesdropped on the slowing of their heart rates. She traced the broken shape of his pinky finger, never set and poorly healed, the small blemish that defined his perfection. She inhaled the smell of their mingled sweat. At that moment, soft as a moth's kiss, the cells in her center rearranged themselves. Right then she knew that they had started another baby. She wouldn't say anything to Tian until she missed her period. Maybe not even then, because she didn't know what she felt; elation and sorrow battled inside of her. Tian would not be conflicted; he loved being a father.

She only had one true secret from Tian. One private thing that she could never share. It started when she turned sixteen. She had heard girls at school chatter about birthday parties with cake and balloons and sleepovers, but for her Sweet Sixteen it was just the four of them. Ma made biscuit-fried chicken and a lemon meringue pie. After dinner, in a rare moment of brotherly love, Stanley invited her to tag along with him and their neighbors, Martha and Charley, to the Saturday night dance at Maxy's Place.

No one at Maxy's that evening looked older than twenty-five, but they abided by the time-honored tradition in the county. White folks claimed the front bar, and black people sat at the tables along the rear of the room. Same with the dancing mostly, whites in the front half, blacks towards the back. Pippa sat with Charley and Martha in the shadowy front corner, lit only by the flickering Bud sign. Stanley carried their beers over, hoping nobody would make a stink that Pippa was underage. Not likely, because the Billy Boys were hot that night and the bar was as jam-packed as the dance floor.

"Would ya look at them." Martha elbowed Pippa and pointed back towards the bathrooms. A mixed-race couple danced slow and close, even though the music rocked. The guy's back was towards them, but there was something familiar about the slope of his shoulders. Pippa stared as the couple slowly turned.

"Isn't that Delmar?" Martha squinted. "Who's he with?"

Pippa hadn't seen Delmar since he dropped out of school two years before, the same month her father fired his daddy for drinking whiskey during haying. It had been a decade since the two of them snuck away together to play in the barn on rainy days. Sometimes Delmar's daddy brought him along to work, when his ma took off. That younger Delmar liked to stick hay twigs in the corner of his mouth for whiskers and meow until she rubbed his belly and made him laugh. This Delmar was full-grown, a head taller than his partner.

"Didn't that blondie used to be your friend in school?" Martha asked.

"Sally Ann," Pippa whispered.

"A bit wild, is she?"

Pippa didn't answer. She glanced quickly at Stanley, who looked like his beer tasted sour, then back at the couple. Delmar's square farmboy hands stretched across the tight denim of Sally Ann's bleached mini-skirt. His dark fingers cupping the white cloth of her bottom made Pippa's throat ache.

When Pippa got home later, rosy and sleepy from the dancing and the beer, Ma was waiting up for her. She followed Pippa into her room, sat down on her bed and patted the mattress next to her, smiling.

"Nice birthday?"

"Uh hmm."

It had been a big mistake, telling about Delmar. Ma had never liked Sally Ann, anyways. But that night Pippa was still glowing, and couldn't stop thinking about it. Ma hardly ever asked, so Pippa wasn't used to keeping secrets. She told Ma how they danced so close. She kept to herself how strange she felt watching them together that way, squirrelly and awkward and yearning.

One night two weeks later, Pippa sat on the porch swing. She couldn't sleep. She pushed off with her toes and her thoughts swayed back and forth with Delmar and Sally Ann's slow dance. A pineapple-scented breeze from the sweetshrub bushes rippled her T-shirt. Crickets chirped in the tall grass at the dark edge of the wrap-around porch, their lament loud against a far-off murmur that Pippa couldn't place.

She counted the number of chirps in fifteen seconds like Ma taught her, so she could add thirty-nine to get the temperature, but it was hard without a watch. Footsteps crunched on the gravel driveway, where a tall shape trailed something. Probably Stanley sneaking out with a blanket to meet some girl in the woods. Then she heard the familiar clicking noise her father made to clear his throat. From his smoking, Ma said.

Not knowing why, not really caring, she followed him. She walked barefoot in the grass next to the driveway, so he wouldn't hear her steps. Around the house and along the rutted tractor path up the hill toward the north pasture. The night air was heavy, the moon a chalk thumbprint smudged on the black sky. A shimmery glow outlined the curve of the hilltop against the sky. Too early for dawn, and in the wrong direction.

At the crest of the hill, she stopped. Their pasture was transformed. Pickup trucks lined the county road. A tree trunk with outstretched arms burned in the middle of the field. Among bales of new hay stood hundreds of shapes like Halloween ghosts. In June.

At the bottom of the hill, her father shook out his sheet and pulled it over his head. Next a hood. Then he stepped forward and merged into the crowd. Pippa hesitated for three heartbeats, then followed, staying just beyond the circle of light from the flames.

Pippa wasn't ignorant about the Klan. Everyone knew they were still around in 1999 Georgia, just more secretive. She had never seen any of the good old boys in action, not first-hand, but she recognized their daytime selves manning a booth at the Confederate Memorial Day parade or handing a check to the winner of the "Proud to Be from Dixie" essay contest at a high school assembly. She had not realized they held nighttime rallies in her county, in her father's north pasture.

She did not know they still burned crosses.

The flames flickered across the pale faces of the people milling around, signing petitions on clipboards, looking through stacks of pamphlets, filling sagging paper plates of brownies and cherry pie. Some people wore sheets and some regular clothes. From behind the pie table the sheriff's wife, Mrs. Davis, waved Pippa over. She looked peculiar without her lime-green uniform from the diner on Chestnut Street, her matching muffin cap.

"Glad to see you, honey," Mrs. Davis said. "Don't you want to cover up some?"

Pippa looked down at her cotton T-shirt and sleep shorts, crossed her arms against her chest. She shook her head at the folded fabric Mrs. Davis offered from the cardboard box under the table.

"You seen my father?"

"With the rest of the marshals, I bet." Mrs. Davis pointed past the cross.

White hoods concealed the faces of the sheeted shapes on the makeshift stage, but Pippa heard the raspy sound of him. The shape with her father's voice jabbed his cigarette in the air, like when he wanted her to clean out the barn or weed the garden. He nodded his head hard. The peak of the hood slapped up and down. His eyes were obscured behind black holes cut in the fabric.

The shape with her father's voice lifted his cigarette into the slash in the hood, where a man's mouth should be. The ash flared red. The smoke seeped back out, puffing through the jagged cut in the fabric. Two thin tendrils spiraled out the eyeholes. For several seconds, the haze hung suspended around his tapering hood, before dissolving into the night air.

Pippa turned away. She forced herself to walk until she reached the cusp of the darkness. Then she ran.

She was almost safe, climbing upstairs to her room, when Ma appeared at her bedroom door, her nightgown pearly in the moonlight.

"What's wrong?"

"Nothing."

"Where you been?"

Pippa put her arms around her mother and pulled her close. She was afraid Ma would read the Morse code of her racing heart, but she needed the hug more.

"On the porch. I couldn't sleep."

Ma leaned back and looked at Pippa. She felt the question in her mother's eyes, and did not look away. Ma must know what was going on in the north pasture.

Pippa untangled from her mother's arms. "I'm sleepy now."

She wedged her desk chair under the doorknob. Lying stiff on her back, she studied the landscape of cracks on the ceiling, the canvas for her childhood imaginings of princesses in heavenly mountain palaces. She had never paid much mind to the school lessons about Dixie Forever. Now those slogans ricocheted behind her eyes. She could not imagine ever sleeping again, but maybe she dozed off for a few seconds. She was startled awake by a noise from outside.

It was still dark. The crunching on the gravel was louder. Through her bedroom window she saw a cluster of ghostly shapes enter the barn, shoving a smaller figure in dark clothes. On her way out of the house, she grabbed the yellow flashlight from the hook by the kitchen door.

Pippa crept the long way around the barn to the small side entrance and stood outside listening. A solid, slapping sound. Whimpering. The occasional eruption of the oily laughter men make when they're lubricated with whiskey. She understood that there was danger and that she was not brave, because she did not open the door and walk into the barn. Instead, she crouched in the shadows, resting her arms on the splintery cover of the feedbox. She listened as the smacks grew harsher and the moaning more sorrowful. Then the sounds stopped.

After a long time, she heard the big double doors open and close, then more gravel noises and laughter. Finally the barn was still, the voices silent. She unlatched the small side door and slipped inside. The air smelled used and rusty.

Delmar was sprawled on his side, his skinny arms and legs akimbo. As if they just let him be, however he fell. The rope, still hanging from the beam, was cut. Around Delmar's neck, the noose was off kilter, knotted to the side like a Sunday necktie fastened sloppily, without a mirror. Two by fours leaned up against the goat stalls. The ends were stained with something dark. The dark became deep red in the flashlight beam. Delmar's face and chest were broken.

The harsh grinding of her father's pickup in reverse broke the silence. She returned to her spot behind the feedbox until the voices stopped again and the truck drove off. It was almost dawn when she tiptoed around to the front of the barn.

The double doors stood wide open. Fresh hay had been spread on the floor. The two by fours were missing. The rope was gone. So was Delmar.

Should she call Sheriff Davis? His wife had been in the pasture, but maybe that was part of her job at the diner, maybe she didn't mean it. The sheriff might be out patrolling somewhere on the other side of the county, not even aware of what was going on in the north pasture.

She couldn't ask Ma for help. What happened to Delmar could be Ma's fault. And her own fault too, for telling Ma what she saw at Maxy's. Maybe later that night, Ma had whispered to her husband, "I always knew that Sally Ann was a slut." Or maybe Stanley said something to Pa. Maybe Stanley had been in the field of white shapes. She couldn't stop thinking about Delmar and dancing. But Delmar was gone.

And so was she. Pippa got dressed and emptied the money from the Mason jar Ma kept hidden in the cupboard over the sink. Sorry Ma, she thought. She was on the next bus north, to Massachusetts, as far as Ma's rainy day cash would take her.

❧

Pippa pulled the quilts over her head, muffling the moaning of the wind outside. It was too early to get up. She tried to chant the sleep prayers, but her thoughts were a jumble of images, a stew of regret. The north pasture. Delmar's hands on Sally Ann's bottom. Abby and this new baby. Ma who she missed even though it was more the idea of Ma instead of the person. Tian's broken finger. Smoke puffing out of dark eyeholes in a white hood.

11 ~ *Emily*

I don't know what I expected to find Monday morning at the Hall of Justice, but it wasn't an x-ray security scanner with a conveyer belt, a metal-detector gateway, and two armed guards.

"Empty the contents of your pockets into the blue bucket, ma'am, and place your bag on the belt." One of the security guards spoke to me without taking his eyes from the screen of his shiny machine.

My pockets were empty except for old cough drops, tissue-flecked mittens, four pennies, and two ripped ticket stubs from the matinee of Shrek 2 at the Bing. I dumped the handful of jumble into the blue plastic bowl and watched it disappear into the tunnel, my old pocketbook beside it looking disheveled and discouraged. I pictured the matching gray leather purse and briefcase that Marge carried on Friday afternoon as she prepared for an early start on the weekend. I had asked her what to expect in today's visit with the probation officer.

"You'll find out when you get there," Marge said. "Just tell them what they want to hear."

I walked through the metal detector archway, wondering what kind of radiation scatter these things delivered. Shoving the clutter back into my jacket pocket, I shouldered my pocketbook and turned to the guard.

"Probation department?" I hoped he wouldn't think I was asking for myself. All weekend I had felt like a criminal, worrying that I crossed some line when I took Pippa to the park. All weekend I thought about her story.

"Elevators around the corner to your left." His eyes didn't abandon the display screen. "Third floor. Left turn. First door on the right."

I had the elevator to myself, a quiet moment to worry. I had never met a probation officer. I imagined a bulky man with broad shoulders and a narrow mind, the bulge of a holster over his heart. What questions would he ask? How should I answer them, after feeling the landscape tilt when I sat with Pippa in the dingle and heard her story?

The first door on the right opened into a narrow room crowded with tired-looking people. Alternating green and orange chairs lined three walls. The clerk behind the barred reception window wore a glittery nose ring. I gave her my name. The only empty seat had a large gash in the cushion, bleeding crushed layers of stuffing. I stood awkwardly in the center of the room for a minute, and then sat down on the slashed chair, next to a skinny woman who smelled like low tide. I closed my eyes and tried to take shallow breaths without offending her. Low tide. Maine. Momma did not tell me the whole truth on the ferry trip to the island. She saved the rest for early the next morning, before she left to return to Portland.

☙

Momma and I sit together on the big rock down by the water. Coffee rock, that's what Aunt Ruth calls it. At first Momma is silent. There is just the placid slap of the waves on the rock and the lazy buzzing of a dragonfly skimming the surface of the water.

"About the fire," Momma says. "I haven't told you the worst thing. We set the fire in the middle of the night, so no one would be hurt. But a man was working late, cleaning the offices. He was horribly burned. He almost died."

There is something in my chest that balloons and fills up every bit of space, pushing aside my heart and lungs and stomach and liver, all the parts we color on an outline of the human body in class.

"We felt awful about it," Momma says. "We didn't know how to respond. We never did that kind of protest again. We left Michigan, our commune, our friends. It was a kind of penance, exiling ourselves. Of course we knew it wasn't enough." Momma's voice trails into silence.

The dragonfly hovers above the water, in and out of mist. After a while, my arms and legs feel boneless and I drift with the dragonfly out to sea.

Momma coaxes me back to land with our special game. We touch foreheads, our eyes closed tight. We chant One-Two-Three-Owl, and on the word Owl, we both open our eyes wide and look into each other, deep and close. Momma promises to call me every evening from Portland.

"I have to be there," she says, "for your father."

What about me?

☙

"Emily Klein." The clerk called my name. She buzzed me through the barricade and led me on a snaking pathway through rows of desks to a private office the size of the waiting room.

"Have a seat," the clerk said. "Malloy will be with you in a jiffy."

I sat on the edge of the bench facing the desk. Boxes, binders, dark books with thick spines crammed the floor-to-ceiling shelves climbing the wall to the right. On the opposite wall hung a painting of a razor sharp mountain peak piercing a sky dark with storm clouds. The small bronze label screwed into the frame revealed the title: Final Justice. Such an unforgiving image. A match for Pippa's winged goddess.

Malloy breezed into the room with a handshake and an apology. She wasn't bulky or broad shouldered. Her silky pants suit emphasized her willowy height.

"Call me Nan. Sorry to keep you waiting. Monday mornings are hell around here." She ignored the desk and sat on the other end of the bench, turning to face me. "Thanks for coming in. I know you're busy. We'll make this brief."

I cleared my throat. "I'm not sure why I'm here."

"Because Judge Thomas set Glenning's conditions of bail. She gets to stay at home and work part-time, which is healthier for her and her baby." The probation officer spoke softly, almost as if she cared about Pippa. "She has to wear the monitor and report to me. Your job is to visit her every week and make sure she follows the medical plan."

That I could manage. "I saw her twice last week. At home on Wednesday for the intake. And her initial OB appointment on Friday."

Nan kicked off her high-heeled shoes and pulled a pair of fuzzy yellow bedroom slippers from under the desk. She slipped her right stockinged foot into one, and balanced her left foot on the opposite knee, rubbing her crooked big toe through the sheer nylon. She looked down at her foot, then at me.

"Ugly, isn't it?" she said. "Any problems with Glenning at the doctor's office?"

I shook my head. Why does a woman with a bunion wear pointy shoes? "Pippa has unusual ideas about health and diet, beliefs that don't mesh with mainstream medicine. But that doesn't mean she's irresponsible." I thought briefly about the potential damage from hallucinogenic cactus on a second-trimester fetus. But I couldn't imagine that Pippa planned to drink the libation this year.

Nan Malloy must have read my mind. "Do you have any reason to think her baby is at risk?"

I hesitated a moment, then shook my head.

"Cult members can be extremely manipulative." Nan stopped massaging her bunion and looked at me. "They can be very persuasive. Sometimes they can convince reasonable people, compassionate people, to go along with things they wouldn't normally consider. This Isis group fits the classic profile."

"What do you mean?" I asked.

"Strong, charismatic male leader, probably sexually involved with all the women. More women than men in the group. Some unsavory history, gang violence and prostitution. And then, there's the racial thing here, too."

I opened my mouth to ask about that, but the phone rang. Nan reached across her desk for the receiver.

"Malloy here." She mostly listened, making notes on a yellow note pad shaped like a daisy. I pictured her standing in the oak-paneled room arguing with a judge. I couldn't imagine taking a job that required being in court. Momma had never allowed me to attend any of my father's legal proceedings. Not the arraignment, not the trial, and certainly not the sentencing.

I wondered about Nan's profile of the Family of Isis. Gangs and prostitution? Certainly not Pippa. And what did she mean by the racial thing? The newspaper article had mentioned something about racially mixed children, so I had assumed that Tian was black.

"Sorry about that," Nan said, hanging up the phone. "You and I need to keep in touch about how Glenning is doing. Strict procedure would be for you to come here every week. But now that we've met and established trust, how about we just talk on the phone?"

Was that good, that Nan trusted me? It didn't feel good. I probably didn't deserve it. "You mentioned a racial thing?" I said. "What did you mean?"

Nan shrugged. "The men in the group are black. The women, except the one in jail, are white. The kids are mixed race. That makes ordinary citizens, both black and white, very nervous."

I would think about that later. "Can you explain to me about the ankle monitor?"

"Does Glenning have a problem with it?" Nan's eyes narrowed just a little.

"No, I just don't understand how it works." The truth was that I kept imagining Pippa dressed in white, dancing in the snowy woods, the box on her ankle shackling her bare foot to the earth.

Nan grabbed a carton from the bookcase, took out a small black device and handed it to me. "Here. You want to try it?" She grinned when I shook my head no. "The transmitter is connected to the phone and to an electric outlet. It continuously confirms that the offender is within 100 feet of the box, and triggers a warning signal to the monitor company if he goes beyond the pre-set radius."

Offender? I flinched at that word. I ran my fingers across the polished surface of the monitor, just like the one on Pippa's mantel.

Nan fit the rubber strap into the grooves on the ankle device. "There are tiny wires inside this strap. If the offender meddles with this baby, we'll know about it."

I looked away from Nan, but my eyes found the painting and couldn't stay there either. "What happens if you get a signal that someone has tampered with it, or left their house without permission?"

"Depends. The manufacturer monitors any disruption in the system. Could be a power outage, or telephone service failure, or someone messing with the device. They call the Chief Probation Officer, that's my boss, and he has to decide what to do." Nan shrugged her shoulders. "It's a judgment call. If he's worried about the offender committing another crime, he'll send a squad car. Sometimes, he'll check out the offender's house himself, with the drive-by wand." She pointed to a foot-long tube on the top shelf. "That tells him if the ankle monitor is in the house. Of course, those calls mostly come at two a.m. I wouldn't have his job for anything."

I stood up, anxious to escape this world of drive-by surveillance and the harsh justice of jagged mountains. "Is there anything else?"

"No. Thanks for your help." Nan handed me a business card and walked me back to the security door, still in her fuzzy slippers. "Call me next Monday. Or any time, if you're worried about Glenning. My cell phone number is on the back."

"Okay." I slipped the card in my pocket and shook Nan's hand.

"I'm glad we met." Nan said.

"By the way," I said, pointing at her feet. "If you wear wide-toed shoes, your bunions won't hurt so much."

❧

"You are twenty minutes late, young lady." Mr. Stanisewski tapped his watch with his finger when I arrived at his apartment. "Luckily my schedule is light today and I can fit you in." Then he laughed to let me know he was joking, and I laughed with him.

I was distracted, and I hated that in myself. I'd had to sit in my car in the Hall of Justice parking lot for twenty minutes after the meeting, trying to empty my brain of Pippa and Nan and dragonflies hovering over coffee rock. I pondered the gray November sky until the images of mountains skewering storm clouds and courtrooms and foggy harbors cleared. Until there was just the upscale façade of the court with its bright chrome and sky-colored panels that startled the old brick buildings on State Street.

"My, you are quiet today," Mr. S said. "Lucky I talk enough for the two of us." He was fond of telling me that, and that day it was certainly true. As I changed the dressing on his big toe, he reported on the progress of his granddaughter's experiment with plants and music.

"So far, the plants getting no music at all are a little taller," he said. "That doesn't make sense to me. What does that prove?"

"I have no clue. But I do know that the seaweed dressing is working. Your toe is much better today. I'll call your doctor." I started packing up the supplies. "I think we can switch to a simple dressing, one you can do yourself."

"Then you won't need to visit me any more?"

"Not as often. But I'll still come to check on the ulcer and make sure your sugars are stable."

While I reviewed his blood sugar log and updated his records in the computer, we listened to a record of polka tunes. Mr. S. tapped his good foot in time to the music.

Then I hugged the dear old man goodbye, promising to let him know what his doctor decided.

Josué's vacated time slot in my schedule had not yet been filled with a new patient, which gave me a perfect opportunity to stop by and check on him at the Children's Hospital. His surgery had been scheduled for first case that morning, so he should be back in his room and ready for a visit. Knowing Josué, he'd be hungry.

I first met Josué at Pioneer Valley Children's Hospital after his accident and the surgery to reconstruct his leg. I like visiting my patients in the hospital before discharge, so they recognize me when I show up at their homes for the intake.

Walking into the three-story glass atrium now, I remembered rushing through the lobby in the middle of the night for Zoe's emergency shunt surgery two years ago. Zoe denied any memory of that night. She loved the place, especially the life-sized sculptures of giraffes and elephants stretching their necks and trunks to munch leaves from the trees growing in the light-filled room. At the reception desk I signed in and clipped the green plastic "Visitor" badge to my coat.

Josué's eyes were closed. His mother sat at his bedside, staring at the slow rain of fluid in the drip chamber on the IV pump.

"How's he doing?" I asked Carmen.

"Bien. He woke up after surgery asking for lunch."

"I missed breakfast," Josué opened his eyes and pointed to his leg. "I've got a giant bandage."

Hugging him was tricky, without jostling his leg or the IV in his left hand. I sat on the metal chair next to Carmen. "You feel okay?" I asked, handing him a small green racing car model with a bow around the cellophane wrapping.

"I'm starved. I hate Jello. Can you get me a cheeseburger?" Josué fumbled with the package. "Awesome. I don't have this one."

"Wait a little while for the burger, Josué." I turned to Carmen. "What did the surgeon say?"

"The placa, the x-ray, looked good," Carmen said. "Probably they will send him home tomorrow. You will still come to our house?"

"If I can. A physical therapist might be more useful to him at this point." I touched Carmen's arm and stood. Marge would sack me if she knew I made an unauthorized visit on company time. "Sorry I can't stay. Call me if you need anything."

The afternoon flew by. Mrs. Grover's dressing change and antibiotic infusion, a quick sandwich at my desk, a phone call to report Mr. Stanisewski's healing ulcer to his doc, an intake on a new patient. Then I rushed to get home before Zoe's school bus.

Gina's red station wagon was parked at the curb in front of my house. She sat slumped over the steering wheel, her head buried in her arms.

12 ~ *Gina*

Gina reached into the fur-trimmed sleeve of her coat for her tissue, blew her nose again, and lowered her head into the cradle of her arms on the steering wheel. She looked up at the coughing sound of Emily's engine cutting off.

Two decades of working as a nurse, so why was she so walloped by this patient's death? Sure, she'd been taking care of Max for over a year of chemo. Then there was hospice, with the intense family interactions over the final days of his dying. Like his great-granddaughter from Iowa who wouldn't leave Max's bedside for the last week, and wouldn't stop staring at Gina either. The girl took every small opportunity to touch Gina's arm or hand, like she had never felt dark skin before. So it was doubly odd how comfortable Gina was with the gathering of Max's family. They all talked at the same time, their loud voices peppered with Yiddish phrases. They reminded her of her own family back home in Jamaica, their musical patois just as exuberant and chaotic.

"Gina?" Emily peered into the window. "What's wrong?"

Gina started snuffling again. "Max died this morning."

"I'm so sorry. Come in."

Settled on the loveseat, Gina listened to the comforting sounds of Emily making tea in the kitchen. She had never seen the sun porch, never been deeper inside Emily's home than the living room. She could see why Emily would like this cozy cocoon of a room, even if it was a little nippy for Gina's blood. She adjusted the quilt around her shoulders.

"I have to keep an eye out for Zoe's bus." Emily put a tray with an earthenware teapot and two mugs on the wobbly table by the window. "Tell me about Max."

Gina felt her eyes start to flood. "What's to tell? His family was with him. He was comfortable, dozing mostly, but aware. About an hour before he died, he opened his eyes and looked around and said he was ready to go."

Emily squeezed Gina's hand.

"And then, damned if he didn't get this funny look on his dear shriveled face and told us to all listen up. He announced that he was still a dues-paying member of the American Communist Party and proud of it." Gina made a noise that sounded like half laugh, half choke. "I never knew that. His daughter rolled her eyes, but no one else reacted. Then he closed his eyes and didn't wake up again."

"You really loved him. I'm glad you could be there."

Gina watched her friend's long face dissolve into an unfocused expression and wondered what Emily was thinking about. Gina blew her nose again. "Who would have thought I would cry for an old white Jewish guy with hair sprouting out of his ears." She glanced quickly at Emily, but she didn't look offended. "A commie, no less."

"You've taken care of him a long time."

"That was the only humane thing Marge ever did, to let me continue with him, even when hospice started. Of course, if she had ever noticed how much I liked the guy, she would have changed my assignment just to vex me."

"We're lucky she's so clueless."

"It's crazy, but Max reminds me of my Granny Teisha," Gina said. It was odd that she had never mentioned Granny to Emily. "She pretty much raised me and my brothers."

"What about your parents?" Emily poured tea into their mugs.

"They worked in a resort in Ocho Rios, so we stayed in the village with Granny Teisha. Whenever we left the house, she made us wear thick, ugly sandals cut from old tires. Of course, we immediately took them off, hid them under a bush, and ran off into the woods barefoot." Gina smiled. "Inevitably, one of us would step on broken glass or a sharp stone in the river, and limp home bleeding. Granny Teisha would bandage our wounds, look up at the heavens and wonder out loud how come the sandal wasn't cut, just the foot. We kids would laugh and hug her, before running off again. That's how Max's family treated him. Ignoring his decrees and loving him to pieces."

Emily sounded wistful. "I wish I'd had brothers or sisters."

"You were an only child?"

"Yep."

"Did you always live in Portland?" Gina knew she was pushing, but Emily seemed so forlorn.

"Just until I was ten. Then on an island. With my mother."

"Does she still live there, on the island?"

"She died when I was fifteen."

"What about your father?"

Emily shook her head.

Gina took a sip of the tea, letting the mint steam tickle her nose. She waited for Emily to say more, but she didn't. "How did your meeting go with the cop?"

"Not a cop. Probation officer. She was all right. But I never told you about last Friday." Emily took a slow drink of her tea.

"What happened?"

"Pippa took me to the park, where her daughter and the other kid died."

"I thought when someone was under house arrest they could only go certain places."

"Strictly speaking, that's true. But this was therapeutic. You know, so she could express her feelings about losing Abby."

"You're a nurse, girlfriend. Not a therapist. What happened at the park?"

Emily hesitated.

"Talk." Gina tried to keep her voice calm.

"We went to their sacred place." Emily spoke slowly. "She described the ceremony. Dancing and peyote. A pregnant woman does a special dance, to convince Isis to send back the sun, and spring, all that. It's very important to them." She paused again. "Since Pippa is the pregnant one this year, she has to be there and dance." Emily rubbed her thumb and index finger up and down the bridge of her nose.

"What about the babies?"

"They were close by, sleeping wrapped up in warm blankets. Pippa said they were fine when she and Tian fell asleep right next to them."

"What aren't you telling me, Emily?"

"Pippa plans to somehow get out of her monitor for solstice. To dance."

"You're kidding, right?"

Emily didn't answer.

"She wants to do that again? After her kid died?"

Emily nodded.

"That's child abuse. Leaving those babies wrapped in blankets in a snowstorm while the adults got stoned and danced and screwed all night."

"More like neglect."

"Abuse," Gina insisted. "But even neglect, it's your job to report it. You are going to warn the cops, aren't you? Or at least that probation officer you met today?"

"This stuff freaks me out. I can't think straight about it."

"You've got to." Gina said. "If you don't let someone know, someone in authority, and something bad happens, then you could be an accessory to the crime. You could lose your job. Maybe face charges yourself."

Emily placed her mug on the table, then put her face into both hands. Gina touched her shoulder, but Emily shrugged her off.

Gina leaned closer. "Talk to me, Emily. What is it about Pippa that gets to you so much that you'd take her to the park when you know she's supposed to go right back to her house? That you would consider keeping her secrets, when they're against the law?"

Emily said nothing, just shook her head slightly.

"Okay. I get it that you don't want to talk about growing up, that something bad happened to you. But you got where you are today by your own efforts. Same as me. And there's no way on earth I would risk my nursing license for some runaway who worships an ancient Egyptian goddess. Maybe that's small-minded of me, but it's the truth."

Emily spoke into the cave of her hands. "Pippa isn't a bad person. Her group is not being treated well. I don't know if it's their religion, or race, or just that they're different."

"Is this a race thing, why you want to help Pippa? Who's black in that household?"

"Pippa's white. Tian and the other guy are black. I think Murphy, the mother of the boy who died, is black too. I'm not sure about the rest."

The toot of the school bus startled them both. Emily stood up. "That's Zoe."

Gina watched through the porch window as Emily helped Zoe with her backpack. Was Emily content to take care of other people's children her whole life? Then Zoe burst onto the sun porch, a purple stuffed animal tucked into the basket attached to one crutch. Emily followed holding a box of graham crackers and a jar of peanut butter.

"Don't forget my cath." Zoe put her hands on her hips in a perfect adult mimic. Gina had never seen Emily do that. It must be Zoe's mother's gesture. Anna.

"In just a minute," Emily said, dipping each corner of the graham crackers into the peanut butter and arranging them in a semicircle on Zoe's plate. "We have company. Do you remember meeting Gina and her boys at my office picnic in July?"

"I remember Sammy, 'cause he has the same name as my dad. I want tea too."

"Please?"

"Pretty please."

While Emily was in the kitchen, Gina told Zoe about the trip her boys were planning to visit their cousins in Ocho Rios over Christmas.

"I want to go to Jamaica," Zoe announced, as Emily handed her a Big Bird mug. "It's summertime there at Chanukah."

"Sounds good to me," Emily said, stirring two teaspoons of tea and two of sugar into the warm milk.

Gina looked at the sweet milky liquid, raising her eyebrows.

"My momma used to make me coffee like this, when I was little." Emily turned back to Zoe. "Drink up. You need to cath, then do exercises."

Zoe drained her tea in one long drink. "Can I watch cartoons while I stretch?"

"Okay, but cath first. Call me if you need help. I want to talk with Gina for a few minutes." They watched the girl's progress through the kitchen and into the hallway.

Gina smiled at Emily. "I can see why you love her so much. Wouldn't you like a daughter of your own?"

"You know of any available five-year-olds with sunny dispositions?"

"Ha, you'll just have to make one of your own. But you won't meet anyone, living here and spending all your free time with someone else's family." Not only Anna's family. It was worrisome, the way Emily had gotten so sucked into Pippa's life. "Your living arrangement is pretty bizarre, you know? Both Anna and Sam still both living in this house, owning this place together, even though they've been divorced for ages."

"It works."

"For them. I'm not so sure it works for you. Maybe it's time you moved out and got an apartment of your own. A life of your own."

"You mean a boyfriend?" Emily laughed, but she didn't sound amused.

"Uh huh."

"That hasn't worked out so well in the past."

"You mean that guy in Portland?"

Emily nodded. "Chad."

"Hey, you're the one who left him, right?" Gina didn't know exactly what had happened; Emily wouldn't talk about that either. "One try and you give up? You've got to kiss more frogs than that." Gina could feel her voice was getting into lecture mode and she wasn't the slightest bit surprised when Emily pushed back her chair and stood up.

"I've got to help Zoe."

"I can take a hint." Gina stood too. "I've still got all the charting to do. I'll see you tomorrow." She touched Emily's arm. "Thanks for the shoulder."

Emily held the coat for Gina to put on, then hugged her. "I'm so sorry about Max."

Gina buttoned the silver buttons slowly, trying to think what to say. "I'm worried about this business with Pippa. It's totally different from the Mrs. Newman situation. Is Pippa worth risking your profession? Because if you get in trouble with that cult, the union can't help you. I can't help you. I'm not risking my nursing license for these people."

"I'm not asking you to risk anything, Gina."

Whoa. Gina hadn't thought that through. If Emily didn't tell the authorities about the nasty drugs and sex in the park and Pippa wanting to do it again, that made Emily an accessory to a crime. But now Gina knew that information too. She was a mandated reporter, they all were, required by law to fill out a 51A, to report any potential harm to a child. So did that mean that Gina would have to inform on Pippa? Which would mean implicating Emily, too? Oh, Lord, what a mess.

"Think hard about this, Emily. Because I'm not sure I can keep Pippa's secret. Not if it means maybe hurting another baby. If you help her, you're on your own."

13 ~ *Emily*

At dinner, I tried to forget Gina's parting comment and concentrate on the story Anna was telling about her Family Life class.

"So it was Derek's turn to take a computer-baby home for the weekend." Anna carried the plate of veggie burgers to the table. "I programmed the computer for a cranky Saturday night. To keep the doll from crying, Derek had to carry it back and forth across the lobby of the movie theater while his buddies watched a karate film."

"He missed the movie?" Zoe asked.

Anna nodded. "He was terrific. The computer printout showed no rough handling, no shaking or locking the kid in the trunk of the car. He'll be a great dad." She grinned at Zoe and me. "In at least ten years, I hope."

"Bring a baby home for me next weekend," Zoe begged, holding the ketchup bottle upside down over her plate and thumping the bottom. "I want a baby sister. Hey, this is empty. I need ketchup."

"Those babies are a lot of work." Anna looked through the crusty-rimmed jars of jams and pickles and mustards on the refrigerator door.

"Emily will help me take care of it, won't you?"

Anna was closing the refrigerator when the phone rang.

She covered the mouthpiece with her hand. "Would you find Zoe some ketchup?" She carried the phone into the living room.

I searched the cupboards. "Sorry. We're all out, kiddo."

"Veggie patties are awful without ketchup." Zoe pushed her plate away.

"How about salsa?" I held the jar for Zoe to inspect. "Mexican patties?"

"Only if you talk Spanish to me, okay?"

"Si, señorita. Now eat, por favor." I spooned a pile of salsa onto Zoe's plate, careful not to let it touch the patty or the corn. I strained to hear the murmur of Anna's voice from the next room. It must be important. Anna had a firm rule about no phone conversations during dinner.

"Do you think Mexican people eat veggie patties and salsa?" Zoe tugged on my sleeve until I turned back to her.

"Don't know. What do you think?"

I wondered how Zoe and Josué would get along. Zoe would love his collection of miniature cars and trucks, and he would take her crutches in stride. But in a couple of months, when Josué was finished with therapy and was able to run around normally again, would he forget the time he used crutches? Would he become one of those kids in Zoe's class who snubbed her on the playground, didn't invite her to a birthday party because it was at the skating rink? Maybe I could introduce the two of them, before that happened.

I could hear Chad's voice in my head, the time I invited a lonely co-worker to our apartment for Thanksgiving. "You want to rescue all the misfits," he'd said.

Anna returned to the kitchen and placed the phone back on the charger. She stood between our chairs, put one hand on Zoe's shoulder, the other rubbing along my spine.

"That was Aunt Ruth," she said. "Your grandfather died this afternoon. I'm sorry."

I was surprised at how forlorn I felt. I hadn't seen Grandpa Ivan since high school graduation. Momma was gone by then, and Daddy in prison. My grandfather and Aunt Ruth's family were there to congratulate me. After the ceremony, Grandpa Ivan shook my hand, then seemed to change his mind and gave me a quick hug in the stiff way of old men. His flannel shirt smelled of pipe tobacco and pine forest. His voice was gruff in my hair.

"I'm proud of you, Emily," he'd said.

That was fourteen years ago and I'd left it all behind. I didn't know why I felt bereft. But I knew I didn't want to have the conversation that was coming next. I got up and started clearing the table even though Anna was still eating.

"My grandpas are already dead." Zoe looked at her mother.

"Ivan was Emily's grandpa," Anna said, wiping salsa out of Zoe's hair. "And my great uncle." She put a bite of veggie burger into her mouth and stood behind me, hugging my unyielding shoulders and resting her head against mine. Anna and I are exactly the same height. "Leave the dishes."

I stacked the dishes in the sink, with Anna glommed onto my back.

"The service is Wednesday," Anna said.

"I have to visit Pippa on Wednesday. And Thursday is Thanksgiving."

"Work and Pippa will survive without you for a few days," Anna said, finally letting go of my back to rescue her half-eaten dinner. "I called Sam. He'll be down in a little while, so we can make arrangements." She looked at Zoe. "Guess what, Poose? You get to stay a few extra days with your Papa."

"Eating nuked food," I mumbled under my breath.

"Emily." Anna scolded, but she was trying to hide a smile.

"Sorry," I raised my hands in mock surrender.

"Where are you going, when I stay with Papa?" Zoe put her hands on her hips and looked at her mother.

"Emily and I are going to the island where we used to live when we were little girls. That was Grandpa Ivan's home. We're going to his funeral."

"I want to go. Why can't I go?"

"Because funerals are sad. And you didn't know Grandpa Ivan. You'll stay here with Papa. I'll take you to the island in the summer, for vacation."

"Promise?"

"Promise." Anna hugged Zoe, then positioned her crutches. "Now, you have half an hour to play before bath time. You want to finish your painting from yesterday? Don't forget your smock."

There was silence in the kitchen after Zoe left. I scrubbed the plates. I knew Anna was waiting for me to say something, but I kept my back to her. I had nothing to say.

She doesn't know what's right for me, I told myself. Just because she used to be married and has a child, she thinks she's more mature than I am. I'm two years older and I can take care of myself. I set the last dish in the rack and started scouring the counter.

Anna gave in first. "Sam will be here any minute. Would you please talk to me?"

"Max died today. Gina's patient. She was here this afternoon. Very upset."

"Sounds like she cared more about him than you do about Grandpa Ivan."

"I do care." I abandoned the sponge on the kitchen counter and turned to face Anna. I didn't owe her an explanation. Since leaving the island the morning after graduation, I had never gone back, not even to bury my father. Besides, if I ever returned, no way would it be in late November, when everything was dying and shrinking down for the winter. I had always hated that time of year on the island, when the wind and ice put a stop to my solitary walks. As a teenager, I liked to stand on the rocky ledges and look into the sunset, pretending I could see all the way home to Portland.

"No one's forcing you to deal with anything you don't want to." Anna reached for my hand. "Just go bury your grandfather. Pay your respects. It's the right thing to do."

Anna was right; Momma would have expected me to go. I had never spent much time with Grandpa Ivan, but he was family.

"Hello in there," Sam called as he came through the door. "I'm sorry, Em. I only met the old guy once, at our wedding." He smiled. "And I don't remember much about that weekend except that Anna's clan danced so hard I thought Saperstein Neck would crack off the island and sink into the bay. Remember?"

"I had already left by then."

"Oh," he said. "I knew that."

"Stop blithering, Sam. Go say hello to your daughter. Then, we have arrangements to make."

Sam looked like he wanted to argue, but he went to the living room as instructed.

After he left, Anna looked at me. "Well?"

"Do I have a choice?"

☙

Forty minutes later, I hung up the telephone and crossed the last item off my list. Marge had grudgingly approved my three-day bereavement leave. My regulars were all set. Andy had some extra time and would see Mrs. Grover and check on Josué when he was discharged. Gina agreed to stop in at Mr. S's and do Pippa's home visit on Wednesday. I wished I trusted her to keep her opinions to herself.

I had left a message for Mrs. Newman's physician about my safety concerns. I could get fired for going over Marge's head, but I wasn't really worried. That situation seemed so simple and straightforward compared to my dilemma about Pippa.

I wandered into the living room and flopped down on the sofa next to Sam. He lounged, reading the newspaper and idly twirling the end of his mustache. The soft sounds of Zoe's bedtime preparations tumbled down the hallway.

Sam looked up. "How's the cult business going?"

"I don't have to deal with the cult," Emily said. "Just Pippa."

"Is she weird?"

I thought about that. "No, she's okay. It must be hard to be a prisoner in her own house. Too bad your computer skills can't help with that."

"Who says they can't?" Sam smiled. "I can get into any system in the world."

"What good would it do, to get into their system?"

"What would you want it to do?" Sam let the sports section dangle from his hand.

"Hypothetically," I said with emphasis, "what if someone under house arrest wanted to sneak out. Just overnight, let's say. Without anyone knowing. How would they do that?"

"Hypothetically?" The word had weight in Sam's mouth. "You could hack into the telephone line and disrupt service. Or into the electric grid, and turn off the juice to the house. Better yet the whole section, so they'd think it was a transformer. That would take some time to check it out. But that's a big deal, and could impact many other people—cutting power in December could be rough." Sam shook his head. "I don't know. It's an interesting problem."

"Just out of curiosity," I said.

Sam retrieved the newspaper. "That's a serious crime. Interfering with a house arrest monitor, by any method. You're not getting involved in anything like that, are you?"

"No," I told him and myself. "I'm not getting involved."

14 ~ *Pippa*

The attic stairs groaned, announcing a visitor. It couldn't be Francie because she knew which two stairs complained if you tread in the middle. She was the one who had taught Pippa how to step silently right against the walls, lumbering side to side like a trained bear.

"Pippa," Marshall hollered up the last few steps. "Telephone."

Let it be Tian. He called whenever the bald guard came on duty. Pippa thundered past Marshall down the stairs, smack in the middle of each protesting step, then another flight down to the first floor, banging the ankle monitor into the telephone table in the hallway. She picked up the receiver from the table, ignoring the pain darting into her foot.

"Tian?" Pippa stretched the phone cord into the empty kitchen. She leaned against the wall to let her breathing catch up.

"This is Emily. Are you okay?"

Not Tian. "Yeah, just ran down two flights of stairs."

"Listen, I have to cancel for Wednesday," Emily said. "My grandfather died and I'm going to Maine for his funeral. Another nurse, Gina, will come instead."

Pippa sat down on the bench at the kitchen table. She sighed, exhaling thoughts of Tian. "I'm sorry about your grandfather."

"Thank you. Gina's great. She's my friend. You'll like her."

"Sure. Whatever."

"I'll see you next Monday, for your ultrasound, okay? And you have my beeper number, in case you need me."

Hanging up the phone, Pippa leaned down to rub her throbbing anklebone. Double disappointment. It wasn't Tian, and Emily wasn't coming. The two regrets stuck in her throat. She wanted to ask for Emily's help on the solstice, but she knew it wasn't the right time. Not yet. She couldn't quite figure Emily out. Could she trust her? Did she have the guts to go around the law? Or was she too fearful, too spineless, like the way she slouched to hide her height.

Pippa repositioned the sock under the rubber strap around her ankle and wandered into the dining room, where Marshall and Jeremy were tidying stacks of books and papers into neat piles on the table. Timothy sat at the computer, studying an elaborate maze of squiggles and lines on the screen.

"We're studying electronics," Timothy said without looking up. "So we can help you get out of that device without the cops knowing."

"Is that on your approved home school curriculum?" Pippa poked Marshall lightly on the shoulder.

"It's what they are interested in. So we rearranged the curriculum." Marshall looked at Pippa then, his thick index finger tugging at the faded turquoise bandanna knotted around his neck. "Don't hold your breath, by the way. I've been reading up about these things. They're close to foolproof. Most of the time when people on house arrest escape, they get caught and go to jail."

"Don't worry, Pippa." Jeremy slipped between Marshall's arm and body, resting his head on the man's overstuffed belly. "That won't happen to you. Tim and me will figure this out."

Timothy looked up. "Tian says kids are more creative. Our brains aren't corrupted yet."

"Bedtime." Marshall mussed Jeremy's curls. "Turn off the computer, Tim."

Pippa turned away, but Marshall called after her. "One guy even tried to amputate his foot. Got the monitor off, but he bled to death before he could enjoy his freedom."

"Terrific," Pippa said. "Guess I'll have to cross that option off my list."

In the living room, Pippa sat on the button back chair and put her feet up on the window seat. Newark jumped onto her lap, revolving twice before curling into a soft circle. Pippa ran her fingers through his thick orange fur, two shades darker than the brocade of the chair. Once Marshall and the twins thumped up to the second floor, the evening hushed, leaving the pings and creaks of the old house in the November wind and the cat's guttural purr. It was too quiet without Tian and Murphy. Liz and Adele were probably still crumbling the dried spearmint leaves and packaging them in fifty-gram baggies out on the back porch, where Marshall had stapled heavy plastic over the screens. Francie would be getting ready for her shift at the hospital.

Something about Francie was niggling at Pippa's brain. Something she said, about Tian, when they were arguing that afternoon at the Tea Room.

Yes, she said something about Pippa having Tian mostly to herself.

Nobody in the family owned anyone else. That was Tian's teaching, and Pippa tried to accept it, along with the other rules. Some rules made sense, like being vegetarian and sharing everything. Others were just annoying, like no doors allowed, even on the bathrooms.

"Can't even take a dump in private in this family," Marshall grumbled, and secretly everyone probably agreed, but they all went along with Tian's teachings. Except Marshall, who quietly replaced the door on the second floor bathroom and Tian pretended not to notice.

But no matter what the rule was about sharing love, she and Tian were bound to each other, together and forever. Never mind Isis or family rules about ownership, never mind any of that.

Hooking up with Tian or anyone else had been the farthest thing from Pippa's mind when Francie brought her into the family. For the first four months, she saw Tian only at family meals and rituals. That was another rule, new recruits couldn't sleep at Pioneer Street until they became a full member, and people could only join at a solstice.

She would never forget her first solstice. Meg was hugely, gloriously pregnant. Later, Pippa began to see the tensions erupting between Meg and Enoch and the rest of the family. But that night she saw only the magnificence of Meg's belly, the splendor of the frozen forest, the sanctuary of their rituals. The next morning, when she moved her plastic trash bag of clothes into the attic room on Pioneer Street, Pippa didn't think she could get any happier.

But she did. Late one evening, two months after she joined the family, they were all stripping dried spearmint leaves from the bunched stalks hung drying from the ceiling. Tian stood up, looked at her and blazed his smile. She grinned back, not understanding his signal, even when Liz giggled. After a few minutes he took both her hands and pulled her to stand in front of him. He brought her hand to his face, sniffed the pungency of the spearmint, then licked her fingers, one by one. That's when she understood, and she followed him to his room.

❧

"What are you looking so moony-faced about?" Francie stood in the arch to the living room, spiffy in her white work clothes. At the sound of her voice, Newark arched and stretched, his claws jabbing through her cotton jumper as he deserted Pippa's lap to rub against Francie's ankles.

"Tian." Pippa rubbed her thigh. "I miss him. And I'm worried about the trial. What do you think will happen?"

"Nothing good. They'll probably convict him. Murphy too, though you don't seem too concerned about her. Don't forget, Pippa, you stand trial with them. You may get off, because you're so much younger. But I wouldn't bet on them letting you keep that baby."

When had Francie become so mean?

As if she read Pippa's mind, Francie smiled. The corners of her mouth turned up, and her lips parted to display perfect teeth like a warning. She turned back to the hall and reached into the closet for her coat. "Time to head downtown for my shift." She paused for a minute. "Sometimes, I'm not sure what the point is of keeping everything together."

"Tian says we have to stay strong."

Francie made a sour face. "Maybe it's time we think for ourselves."

"If you want me to think for myself, why won't you tell me what happened with Meg and Enoch? And what happened in Newark?"

Francie's expression softened a little. "I will tell you. But not now or I'll be late for work."

After Francie left, Pippa enticed Newark back to her lap. Francie was just saying those things to get her riled up. She couldn't really believe that they would all go to prison. Or that her baby would be taken away, to live with strangers who tidied up their house for the social worker visit; convincing some judge that they would make better parents than Pippa and Tian. What kind of life would this baby have, away from its family?

What kind of life did Abby have? Pippa cradled Newark against her chest, rocking back and forth, back and forth.

She stood up, unable to sit still with those thoughts. The trial date still wasn't set, though there was the hearing next week. Newark squirmed in her arms growling a protest at the indignity of being held so tight, and jumped to the floor.

Pippa dialed the emergency beeper number on Emily's card, thumb-tacked to the cork board by the hallway phone, and left her callback number. The telephone rang a few minutes later.

Emily sounded sleepy. "Pippa? Is something wrong?"

"Is this too late?"

"No, I'm packing for Maine. We're leaving at five. What's the matter?"

Pippa took a deep breath and then blurted it out. "While you're away, please think about this. I've got to get out of the house for the solstice, just for one night—a few hours is all—and then I'll come right back. I promise. I need your help."

"I can't."

"Don't say anything now. Just think about it? Please?"

15 ~ *Sam*

"Goodnight, Poose." Sam leaned down to kiss her forehead.

"Sit with me, Papa?"

"Just a few minutes."

Anna wouldn't approve. Sam pulled the guest room door mostly closed, letting in just a sliver of light from the hallway. Sitting on the edge of the bed, he rubbed Zoe's back in a figure of eight pattern, the way she liked it. This was Zoe's bedroom, her special place in his apartment, but he had learned not to name it out loud because Anna hated that. Even though Zoe was hardly a guest, and she was the only one who ever slept there. Even though whenever Anna asked if Zoe could stay over he always agreed, like tonight when Anna and Emily wanted to get on the road to Maine before daylight. Even though she slept in this bed, in this room, every other weekend and every other holiday, and sometimes more if she was sick and Anna had to work. Even though he kept the top drawer in the dresser stocked with her neatly folded t-shirts and overalls and catheterization supplies and extra Velcro for her braces. But Anna made it absolutely clear that she was the only parent whose home was allowed to have Zoe's room.

Sam couldn't really blame her. When Zoe was born, he took one look at that shiny red bag of insides sticking out through the skin of her back, and thought he'd puke. Then he felt rotten; how could he react that way to his own kid? The whole first year he was confused, and Anna always seemed to be so damn okay. If only she'd cried just once, if only they could have cried together, maybe things would have turned out differently.

Zoe's breathing slowed and deepened. Sam smoothed the sleep-damp curls away from her forehead, trying to visualize the plastic tubing inside, shunting the extra fluid away from her brain and safely down to her belly. Emily liked to joke about him being a bumbling father, but he paid close attention to his kid. Especially to her shunt.

When Anna brought Zoe upstairs that evening with enough paraphernalia for two weeks instead of four days, she didn't mention anything about how Zoe was talking, but Sam noticed it right away. Zoe was quieter than usual and her speech was slower. But the big thing was the spoonerisms. When Sam started towards the guest bedroom with her duffle, Zoe followed with her backpack, steadying herself with one hand along the wall.

"Sting your bricks," he said. Anna hated that too. They're crutches, not sticks, she insisted.

Zoe didn't even smile, didn't turn back for the crutches.

He dropped her purple duffle on the bed and tried again. "Stump your duff."

Zoe tilted her head slightly to the right, looking perplexed.

"Stump your duff?" he repeated.

No response. His heart forgot to beat.

"Dump your stuff on the bed." he said.

She did.

Her shunt. That was the thing that scared him most about spina bifida.

After the ultrasound when they first found out about Zoe's spine, Sam couldn't talk about it. He had escaped to his mother's apartment, to fix her broken ceiling fan. His mom talked nonstop about spina bifida. "Cousin Millie had a baby like that. Skinny, limp legs. His head was huge, and his shunt kept clogging up and getting infected and Millie would rush him to the hospital for more medicines and surgery. After each operation, he got stupider." Mom was not one to mince words.

Zoe's shunt had failed once, when she was three. Sam had been taking care of her that night too. She had seemed okay before she went to bed. Maybe a little sad and tearful. Looking back, she had been unusually quiet that evening too, but he didn't realize it then. In the middle of the night she started throwing up and she didn't seem to recognize Sam at all. That was the scariest part. Luckily Anna and Emily were downstairs and came right up when he called and they all went to the hospital and sat together in the family lounge while she had the CT scan and then surgery. And she wasn't any stupider afterwards. Still, Sam paid a lot of attention to Zoe's shunt.

Zoe mumbled something in her sleep. Sam leaned down to listen, then pulled the blankets to cover her shoulders and stood up. He didn't think he could concentrate on his mystery novel. He sat instead on the soft cushions of the rocking chair by the window and twisted the stick to open the blinds. Lines of moonlight spilled into the room, painting ghostly bars across Zoe's bed and chest of drawers.

One stripe illuminated the framed photo on the dresser. Sam had handed their camera to a couple from Ohio who they'd met on the trail up Mt. Tom. Anna squinted into the sunlight. Six-month old Zoe was in the baby carrier on Sam's back, peeking over the ledge made by Anna and Sam's shoulders pressed close together. Poose, they had called her.

Deep in his nightstand drawer he had hidden the very first photo of Zoe. Her ultrasound.

☙

Much as he hated hospitals, even Sam had been able to see how much the ultrasound tech loved her job. Her perfect purple fingernails guided the probe in lazy pathways in the gel on Anna's belly. Her left pointer finger traced landmarks on the monitor screen, showing Sam and Anna the kind of details they'd later want to decipher for their friends on the fuzzy photo. "Your baby is so smart," she said. "She's already found her thumb."

The probe froze somewhere along Zoe's spine.

The details of what came next played in slow motion in Sam's memory. The tech halted the guided tour. She stopped joking and punched a green button on the wall. The doc came in and steered the probe around for a few more minutes, staring at the screen.

Finally the doctor spoke. "Sometimes, in the third week of gestation, there is failure of neural tube closure."

Sam didn't understand. He looked where the doctor pointed, at the spot on the back of the fishy thing on a color poster scotch-taped to the wall.

"Your baby's defect is here." The doctor's right index finger touched the ultrasound monitor, tapped the white bumps. A string of pearls. Except the necklace wasn't perfect. Three pearls were misshapen, wrong. The doctor kept talking, protracted sentences that loop-de-looped in the air. When his words finally stalled, Anna dropped Sam's hand and shuffled in the rustling paper gown to the bathroom. She was in there a long time.

His butt felt glued to the metal chair. He stared at the blank monitor and tried to summon back the squiggly gray and black shadows that the tech described as their baby's heart, beating safe inside her rib cage. But he couldn't see very well. Even after blinking his eyes, the room seemed hazy. He couldn't remember what the doctor said. He just knew the probe stopped and the happy talk stopped.

☙

Sam squatted next to Zoe's bed. He slipped his hand under the blankets. The plaid wool one was his favorite when he was a boy. The quilt was from his mom, for Zoe's first birthday, the day Sam moved out. He fingered the delicate row of bumps along his daughter's spine. Her broken necklace. Pearls splayed open, letting her insides spill out.

Before the ultrasound, Sam had never heard of spina bifida.

Anna didn't tell him that she had a friend at work whose son had it. She tricked him into meeting her for a picnic at Forest Park the next afternoon after work. When he got to the playground, the first thing he noticed was the green metal sticks. This little guy, maybe six or seven, used green crutches to propel himself to the end of the line at the slide. The boy coming up behind him hung way back. When it was his turn, the crippled kid climbed the ladder, crutches dangling from the wide metal bracelets circling his wrists. At the top he pushed his sticks down the slide. He waved to a woman sitting at the closest picnic table, then launched himself down the slide after them, then scurried back in line, legs barely keeping up with crutches. Watching him, Sam's heart beat so fiercely it clogged up his throat. He sat next to Anna on the picnic table bench, tugging on his mustache and drinking his beer. He and Anna, each of them sealed in an envelope of their own silence.

The woman from the picnic table had hefted the little boy into a molded bike seat, sized for a toddler. The crutches snapped with a popping sound into plastic clips on the handlebars. The girl at the top of the slide yelled "Bye Noah" before diving headfirst down the chute. Noah grinned, with a grape juice mustache, before he buried his face in his mother's shirt. She pushed off and steered the bike in a slow half moon. She doubled back past the picnic table where Sam sat with Anna.

"Hi, Anna," the woman had said.

"Hi, Susan, Noah. This is my husband. Sam."

Sam said hello. He looked at Noah, trying to see inside him, to his broken necklace of pearls. Then his mother waved and pushed off and pedaled away. Sam watched the sneakers dangling on the boy's thin legs.

"Who's he?"

"Susan and I teach together. Noah's her son."

"You knew they were going to be here?"

Anna nodded.

"You asked them to come?"

"Yes."

That's when Sam had realized that he and Anna were going to have this baby. No matter how uncertain he was. No matter what his mother said. No matter what he wanted, when he figured out what it was that he wanted.

Sam left the bedroom door open behind him. Zoe liked the light from the bathroom down the hall, and Sam wanted to hear her if she woke up. He knew he would be checking on her constantly during the night. He liked it when Zoe stayed over with him. It made him feel like a dad, even though maybe he hadn't been the best one ever. He liked Zoe safe with him, protected and secure, in his apartment. He wished that Anna and Emily were sleeping downstairs though. Just in case.

16 ~ *Emily*

Anna and I bickered all the way to Maine. I picked most of those fights.

"No way I'm driving through Worcester," I said, scowling at the green exit sign. A pre-dawn gloom hovered over the Mass Pike. I knew I was being crabby and contradictory. I wasn't eager to get there, but was in no mood to dawdle either.

Anna rarely challenged my cranky moods. "It's more direct," she said, her voice even. "Quicker too, except at rush hour."

I stared straight ahead, hands at two and ten on the steering wheel.

"It doesn't really matter." Anna's voice softened. "Gorgeous morning, huh?"

It was. Dawn ignited the charcoal horizon. But I wanted daylight already, easier to drive. I wanted to turn north, away from the hopeful sunrise. I wanted to get this trip over and done with. When we brought Zoe upstairs an hour earlier, Anna told Sam we would be home to pick her up by the weekend. That was too long for me.

"Listen," I had insisted. "Today's Tuesday. Tomorrow is the funeral. We can drive home on Thursday and roast a turkey on Friday. Celebrate Thanksgiving with Zoe, just one day late."

"Zoe doesn't care about Thanksgiving. Besides, she'll have a great time with Sam. Let's wait and see what Aunt Ruth has planned before we decide."

Sometimes Anna was so damn stubborn, it drove me crazy. Besides, she was wrong. Zoe was old enough to appreciate Thanksgiving, and even help stuff the turkey this year. Sam would probably take her out for fast food for the holiday dinner.

Speeding past the exit to Worcester, I glanced over at Anna, but neither of us spoke. Guess I won that argument, but the victory gave me little satisfaction. Had she always been so bossy? We never used to argue, when I first moved in.

When Anna had a good idea, not about driving through Worcester, I didn't mind admitting it. Like about cutting my hair. Daddy used to say my hair was the exact color of bittersweet chocolate, and he would make me giggle pretending to munch my braids. Once I mentioned my chocolate hair to Chad, but when he tried chewing my braid, it just seemed pathetic.

"Gorgeous hair," Anna had said on the day I moved in. "Too bad no one can appreciate it," she always added, since I confined it every morning in a thick braid that hung heavy along my spine. Anna was right; the headaches pretty much disappeared after she cut my hair to swing just above my shoulders. We let the long snakes fall onto the newspapers on the kitchen linoleum.

"Beautiful," Anna said, always trying to pump up my confidence, as if I were one of the at-risk teenagers in her Life Skills class. Telling me to go out more, join social groups, meet men. She was persistent. Interfering. She meant well, and I loved living with her and Zoe. But sometimes I wished that my cousin would just butt out.

Somewhere between Lowell and Lawrence, Anna's voice broke the stormy silence in the car. "Let's sing."

No way. Folk songs were a running joke between us, but today it wasn't funny. I could never remember more than six words to any song. Compared to my father, who rarely forgot a phrase. He could recall even dense lyrics like "Violets of Dawn," a song he knew from his college career as an Ann Arbor hybrid of Bob Dylan and Phil Ochs. But that didn't mean it was a genetic trait. My approach was more fluid, like the time I substituted "floating in the breeze" for "blowing in the wind." The folk process. There had been plenty of opportunity to make jokes about my faulty memory, because Zoe begged us to sing in the car, even driving ten minutes to the grocery store. Just like I had done at her age.

Anna didn't push the singing. We rode in silence until she pointed to the bridge. "Maine."

The sun rising over the steering wheel reminded me of Pippa's spiky sunray hair. I wondered if the Family of Isis celebrated Thanksgiving. If I were doing her home visit this week, I would ask her about that, and maybe learn something about her religion. I hoped Gina wouldn't be too hard on Pippa tomorrow. I would miss seeing Josué practice walking with a brace instead of wearing—what did Pippa call his external fixator?—the Eiffel Tower. I started to chuckle, then remembered Anna was sitting next to me and cleared my throat instead.

I tried to banish Pippa from my mind and concentrate on the road. Finally I gave up and pulled off at the Kennebunk service area to let Anna drive. Another long silence, until ten miles after turning north onto coastal Route One, Anna's voice reached into my dark thoughts.

"We'll make the 10:30 ferry easy," she said.

"We could grab an early lunch in Rockland, take the noon boat instead."

"Wouldn't you rather eat at Aunt Ruth's?"

"I'd rather not go to Aunt Ruth's." My voice was sharper than I intended.

Anna smacked the steering wheel. "Stop being a baby. This trip isn't about you. Besides, you're not the only one who lost family."

I felt my face flush, hoping it wouldn't show in the dim morning light. Anna had had her own island tragedy, even if I had been too self-absorbed to be sympathetic at the time.

"Sorry," I said, then added, "How can you bear to go back?"

"I still miss my parents, just like you do. But I don't blame them for dying." Anna paused for a moment before continuing. "If I wanted to blame someone, I guess it would have to be your dad."

That was a stretch, but maybe it made some sense. Anna's mother was my dad's sister. Her father was his friend from college. They met at my parents' wedding.

"If Uncle Arnie hadn't introduced my parents," she said, "they wouldn't have been on that sailboat and they'd still be alive."

Her logic was flawed. "If your mom never met your dad, you wouldn't exist."

Anna pretended to laugh. "True."

"Anyway, it was a storm, an accident. How could you blame them?"

"How can you blame yours? That was an accident too."

I shook my head. "You don't understand. It wasn't only what they did. It was that they didn't tell me anything. Didn't talk to me about it."

"So you repeated the pattern, right? Don't talk about it. Didn't write to your father in prison, or visit?"

Anna just didn't get it. Her parents had been ordinary people, living regular lives. Not fanatics setting fire to draft board records, as if two people could change the world. As if strangers fighting a war half a world away were more important than me, the daughter they would create just a few years later.

"Besides," Anna said. "I love the island, even with all the sad memories."

Maybe living on the island wouldn't have been so bad, if the first ten years of my childhood hadn't been so good. My parents were odd by some people's standards, but we fit right into our Portland neighborhood. Old apartments clustered around my alternative school, which was kept barely solvent with bake sales and spaghetti dinners. I had thought I knew who my parents were—warm and funny folks who would always be there to protect me.

❧

The ferry scraped away from its berth. Anticipating the blast of frosty wind, I pulled the hood of my parka tight around my face and leaned over the rusty front rail. Three seagulls hovered. In the heated passenger cabin, Anna was deep into *Fury*, even though she kept complaining that Rushdie should stick to Indian settings. After one glance at the tables in the cabin—the place we sat when Momma explained why Daddy was arrested—I chose the bitter chill outside.

The ferry pushed into the growing waves past the harbor lighthouse, connected by an umbilical cord of rocky rubble to the land. I inhaled deeply, almost tasting the brine. My knees found the rhythm of the swells. My pores and lungs remembered the sodden wind, its promise of wood smoke mixed with the dregs of rotting shellfish. I pictured the map of Penobscot Bay, with the Three Sisters Islands clustered like poison ivy leaves smack in the middle. Then the cold pushed me back into the small protection of the doorway.

I thought about the phone conversation with Pippa the evening before. When my beeper had gone off, and I saw Pippa's phone number on the display, my stomach clenched with a sick worry. Maybe something was wrong, maybe she was bleeding, losing the baby. What was she supposed to do in an emergency, anyway? Go to the hospital for help, and get arrested at the emergency room door for violating house arrest? I made a mental note to ask Nan about that on Monday.

And what about Pippa wanting me to help her escape for solstice? It was astonishing that she would ask such a thing. And even more astounding that I couldn't stop thinking about it. It was breaking the law. And what about our therapeutic relationship? Would it help Pippa, or land both of us in adjacent jail cells? What would happen to her baby if Pippa went to jail?

For just a moment, before I banned the image, I pictured myself taking care of her baby while Pippa served her sentence.

❧

An hour later, the ferry neared the entrance to the channel between the Sister Islands. Bundled with scarf and hat and heavy winter coat buttoned up against the fierce wind, Anna came out to check on me, frozen in my doorway.

"You okay?"

My shoulders felt heavy with the weight of Anna's concern. As the ferry veered into the narrow passageway between the islands, I turned away from her. The lobster markers were scattered like spent confetti across the tinsel tail of the boat's wake.

"Aunt Ruth said everyone is coming to dinner tonight."

"Hmmm." My reply merged with the deepening engine noise as the ferry slowed for the final approach to the terminal.

The town had changed in fourteen years. There had always been a faded pageantry in the harbor village. The new bright colors crowded along the water took me by surprise. Buildings were stacked like child's blocks every which way, as if the object of the game was to see how many pieces could touch the water without tumbling in.

Anna pointed to the pier. "There she is."

Aunt Ruth waved and called our names as the ferry docked. Her raspy voice hadn't changed at all. I followed Anna down the plank walkway.

"I'm sorry," I murmured into the vicinity of my aunt's shoulder. Aunt Ruth and I had shared so many deaths, but this time the loss was hers and I didn't know how to console her. I could comfort a patient, or Gina mourning Max, but my own family was different. Aunt Ruth ushered us to the old Buick in the ferry parking lot. We all fit across the front bench seat, Anna in the middle and me against the window.

"I'm so glad you're here," Aunt Ruth said. "Thanks for coming."

Driving through down Main Street, Aunt Ruth's left hand greeted each approaching car with the island wave, a spare lifting of fingers off the steering wheel. Uncle Mitchell said that off-islanders never got it quite right, the precise nonchalance of the wrist movement. When Anna asked about Marilyn and Carla, I tried to visualize the holiday cards with family photographs that arrived every Chanukah—a husband and three kids each, stair-step sizes. I leaned forward, across Anna's relaxed talking, to peek at my aunt. When had her cropped hair silvered?

In response to Anna's question, Ruth swung her right arm across the long front seat to display her Grandma bracelet. Each child's picture dangled in a gold-plate frame, connected to the chain with a tiny Star of David. "There's room for Zoe's photo, if you have one to spare," Aunt Ruth said, then turned to me. "Space for your future babies, too."

Aunt Ruth had always been kind. All through high school, she greeted me cheerfully with "So early?" when I came straight home after school, instead of staying with my cousins for basketball team practice or tryouts for the Miss Three Sisters Islands pageant. One year Ruth offered a birthday trip to the mainland for a haircut and makeover. I sensed her yearning, her wish that I would enjoy the social success of her girls. But I could never forget that my father was in prison long enough to focus on my classmates. They left me alone, too.

My chest tightened when we crossed the one-lane bridge onto Saperstein Neck. Then Aunt Ruth turned the Buick into the first driveway on the right. On the rocky hillside stood the old white house, tilting slightly towards the shoreline.

Anna followed Aunt Ruth into the kitchen, but I stalled in front of the piano. My eyes couldn't help it. They went right to the photo in the lopsided terracotta frame I had made in third grade. It was a Mother's Day gift. My father's best friend Abe came over to take the photograph. Daddy with electric curls, grinning so hard his cheeks pushed up and squished his eyes closed. Me cradled inside the armor of his hug. My hair as dark as Daddy's but straight, bowl cut. Everyone in Portland used to say that I looked just like him and that I had his fire, too. I figured they meant his courage. Now I knew I didn't have it and wasn't sure I wanted it anyway.

Momma stood behind us in the photo, leaning over Daddy's shoulder to hug us both. Steel wire-rim glasses framing robin's-egg blue eyes. Freckled cheeks. Right after Abe snapped the picture, Momma took off her glasses and sat me on her lap for a butterfly kiss to say thank you. Her eyelashes brushed my cheek, soft like wings. Barely touching my skin, but the safe feeling danced all the way down to my belly.

❧

Anna opened the door to the back bedroom. "The clan's gathering."

"Who's here?" Would I recognize them?

"Carla and Marilyn are helping Aunt Ruth fix dinner. Which is what we should be doing also, by the way. And the other cousins," Anna ticked off on her fingers, "Sarah's flying up in the morning. Laura came over on the early ferry."

Outside the window, fog wrapped around stunted evergreens.

"She'll be over any minute with her folks. The rest still live here. They'll all be glad to see you, you know."

"I've tried to forget this place, these people. Now I have to make conversation?"

Anna just looked at me.

"Do you keep in touch with them?" I asked.

"Sure, especially Laura," Anna said. "She was my best friend when we were kids. When Zoe was born, when Sam was useless, Laura saved my sanity. She's a physical therapist, so she knew about spina bifida. She took two weeks vacation and stayed with us." Anna stepped closer to the bed and gripped both my hands.

"First," she said, pulling me to stand. "First, we make a salad to feed twenty-five people. Then you can worry about what to say to them."

The large country kitchen was warmed by the wood cook stove. Aunt Ruth leaned over the open oven, basting three dozen cod fillets arranged in crowded rows on foil-lined cookie sheets. Her upper arms hung slack, with empty sleeves of skin.

"Welcome home." Carla's hug was a cloud of garlic and dill.

"About time, Stranger." Marilyn turned from stirring a steaming pot on the stove and opened her arms. I wished I could hide in her soft shoulder for hours, to avoid looking at Carla's freckled face, so much like Momma's.

Aunt Ruth handed me a plastic sack of romaine lettuce. "Start the salad?"

Washing lettuce leaves, remembering to tear them into the bite-sized pieces Aunt Ruth insisted on, felt utterly familiar. When the back door opened, I had no trouble recognizing Laura and her parents.

"Too bad it takes a death to get us together." Laura hugged me hard, and then leaned back and looked into my face. "Here's the plan. A cousins' get-together tomorrow afternoon at my folks' house. If the island gods listened to the Weather Channel, it'll be a nice day and we'll hike to Fox Rocks. Wear boots, okay?"

I nodded. What could we possibly have to say to each other after so many years?

"It'll be great." Laura put her arms around me for another hug. "Our own reunion."

❧

Lying in bed that night in the back room I had once shared with Momma, I couldn't sleep. My nerves felt taut, zingy. I tried to match my breathing to Anna's soft snoring. Sleep never came easy, but my usual methods of tricking my brain into slumber mode failed. Nothing worked, not even the guided self-imagery Chad taught me. He had helped me choose a photo from a travel magazine—a small thatched hut in a seaside Mexican village—the perfect fantasy location, he said, empty of any messy real-life memories. Perfect, except I was still awake.

I might have dozed off for a few hours, but awoke with the weak morning light. I eased the kitchen door closed behind me and walked into the misty yard. The ghost of the early ferry passed and turned into the channel, sounding its forlorn greeting.

Just beyond the garden now desiccated by frost, at the cusp of the rocky slope to the water, stood the old swamp maple tree. The step boards had broken away, leaving rusty nails sticking out from the trunk. Didn't any of Ruth's grandchildren love the tree house? Or was it off limits? I pulled the wheelbarrow to the tree. By climbing on its upturned belly I could reach the thick bottom branch. I put my arms around the old tree, my cheek damp against the bumpy bark, then climbed to the walled wooden platform, wedged firmly in the embrace of the thick branches.

My cousin Marilyn had built the tree house. When I arrived on the island in early spring, the middle-school students were registering for the next year's classes. In her enthusiasm to be a carpenter, Marilyn announced at the dinner table that she had signed up for wood shop instead of home arts. Uncle Mitch lectured her about appropriate activities for a twelve-year-old lady. When Marilyn insisted, her father had the last word. "You want to end up a damn commie like your Uncle Arnie?"

Marilyn abandoned wood shop to the boys and the tree house to me.

The branches now barren, I had to imagine the thick walls of leaves that first summer, followed by the smoldering autumn colors that made my chest swell and burst at the same time. The week my father went to prison, I stared at the rocky coastline and harbor through the bare branches, bereft of all but a few brittle leaves. I had just turned eleven, but I promised myself I would take the ferry off the island for good, the minute I was old enough.

"Emily?" Anna stood at the base of the tree, wrapped in the blanket from her bed. Her swan neck curved back, her face open and sunny in the gray light. "Can I come up?"

"If you dare. I'm not in a cheerful mood."

"Big surprise." Anna struggled a little climbing the tree. But then, she hadn't had my years of practice.

We sat facing each other, our feet propped against the opposite wall and the blanket tenting across both our bodies.

"You thinking about Ivan?" Anna asked.

"Him and everything else." I shifted my bottom carefully on the splintery wood. "The tree house shrunk."

Anna smiled. "This always was your favorite place, wasn't it?"

I nodded.

"I remember you as a kid, squirreled up here in the dying maple leaves," Anna said. "What was so special about this place?"

I couldn't explain it.

But Anna seemed to know. "I think everyone has a place like this. A home place."

"What's yours?"

Anna didn't hesitate. "Wherever Zoe is."

"Let's call, see how she is." I shivered and pulled the blanket higher around my shoulders.

"Later. After the service, after the hike with Laura. Uncle Mitch said today will be warmer, before a storm blows in this evening."

☙

I stood with Anna and Laura among granite gravestones on the sunny slope, swaying back and forth in time to the chanting of the rabbi from Rockland. Islanders usually went to the mainland for services, but Ivan was the last of his generation and everyone agreed he had to be buried on his island. Aunt Ruth wept into her handkerchief and fingered the torn black ribbon pinned to her coat. Grandpa Ivan had two children—Aunt Ruth and my Momma, Jemma. But his three brothers had been more prolific and most of their offspring stayed on the island to populate Saperstein Neck. My Portland friends hadn't believed that Jews lived on the island.

"How did a clan of eastern European Jews end up on a rocky spit on an island in Maine?" Chad once asked me.

I answered him in an unconscious mimic of Grandpa Ivan's accent. "Better we should stay in Poland?"

I couldn't concentrate on the service. As predicted, it was twenty degrees warmer than the day before and I unbuttoned my jacket. My eyes felt scratchy and restless. My gaze jumped back and forth—from the distant view of the bay over the tips of evergreen trees to the small cluster of relatives gathered around the gravesite. To my parents' graves, just a few yards up the hillside.

Then the mourners' Kaddish was over and I took my turn shoveling a small mound of earth onto the pine coffin. Why did tossing some dirt into a hole relieve some of the pressure in my throat? Why should the ritual be comforting, when I never went to synagogue and wasn't sure if I believed any of it?

I did remember the customs. Next we would all walk back to Ruth's house, where the mirrors had been covered with cloth. I would help serve the chicken and lentil soup and dark bread. Ruth and Mitchell would sit shiva for the rest of the week. Family would come every day and visit with them around the long-burning candle, telling stories about Ivan and his brothers and their wives and how life used to be. I could picture their comfort with each other and the easy conversation.

But I wanted to get home, to Zoe and Pippa. The next day was Thanksgiving.

"Emily?" Anna held out her hand. Several round gray pebbles balanced on the palm. "For your parents?"

I had never performed the ritual of placing pebbles on their tombstones. I had never come back to visit their graves. Anna took my hand in hers, cupping my palm into a cradle for the stones, urging my fingers to curl around them.

"They're lucky stones," she said.

I jerked my hand away from hers and stared at the pebbles. When we were kids we all collected lucky stones, each encircled with a perfect ring of a different color embedded in the substance of the rock. These were a light gray with charcoal bands separating each stone into two perfect halves. I rubbed my finger around the ridge of charcoal, a coarse vein of rougher mineral.

"No thanks." I turned away from Anna and walked down the hill alone. I let the pebbles drop into my jacket pocket.

❧

It was mid-afternoon by the time Anna and I finished helping Carla and Marilyn clear and wash the dishes and squeeze leftovers into the refrigerator. The four of us walked down the road to Laura's parents' house. The other cousins were waiting in the kitchen, watching a pot of mulled cider simmering on the stove.

"Ready to hike?" Laura asked.

Sarah looked around. "Where's everyone else?"

"My gang begged off," Bea said. "Jet-lagged."

"I flew in from the west coast too," Sarah said. "I'm beat. Let's sit and talk. It's too cold to hike."

"That's what happens when you move to LaLa Land," Carla said. "You turn into a weather wimp."

"And you forget how to buy boots." Marilyn pointed at Sarah's fashionable suede footwear. "We only have an hour till dusk. Let's take a quick hike up to Fox Rocks to remind the city folks what splendor they left behind. Then we can come back for that hot cider."

"Sounds good to me." I was surprised to hear my voice. Walking sounded better than talking.

It was warm climbing the hill and my brain felt fuzzy with lack of sleep. I unbuttoned my coat. In front of me, Anna took off her jacket and tied the arms around her waist. It swung like a skirt against her legs with every step. Within a few minutes, glimpses of deep blue teased through the bare branches.

I slipped my hand into my pocket. The stones were smooth and hard. As I rubbed them, they grew warm, then inexplicably hot, electric against my fingertips. I wanted to throw them into the bay. Or take them into my mouth. To singe my tongue, to sizzle in saliva. Anything except place them reverently on my parents' graves.

What would it signify, to place the stones? Would it mean forgiving Daddy for firebombing draft board records to save lives? Forgiving myself for never once visiting him in prison? Forgiving Momma for standing by him so completely she dissolved into a shadow when he went to prison? Forgiving my ten-year-old self for begging her to abandon him during the trial, to stay with me on the island instead?

After the trial, Daddy went to prison. Momma returned to the island to share my small back bedroom at Aunt Ruth's. Momma was still young, but she smelled old, a stale sour odor under the peach shampoo. On the first Sunday of every month she and Ruth would take the long trip down to the federal prison in Danbury. They always asked me to go, but I refused and they never insisted. My father wrote me letters, every single week.

His first letter from prison came about a month into fifth grade. I hadn't wanted to go to the dinky island school. I missed my friends in Portland. Aunt Ruth had promised that everyone would've forgotten all about my father's arrest by September. But the postmaster must have said something about the return address to his daughter. She was in my grade. When Carla and I sat down with her at the long table next to the window in the lunchroom that day, the postmaster's daughter stood up, mumbled something to her friends, and they left.

"Ignore them," Carla had said. I glanced at her, leading our hike. Even then she was determined. That day, she had continued chatting about the spelling word she missed on the quiz: collateral. The postmaster's daughter and her friends never taunted me. I almost wished they had. Instead, there was an invisible vacuum around me that no one crossed, except my cousins.

After school that day, when Aunt Ruth handed me my father's first letter from prison, I did not open it. I never opened any of them. In the odd, self-absorbed way children reason, I believed that by not reading his letters, I could protect my Momma. I never understood why she didn't go to prison too. Maybe the cops had forgotten about her. If I wasn't careful, the head cop would smack his head with the back of his hand, in a cartoon gesture of remembering, and stick her in the cell next to Daddy. If I kept silent, if I never opened an envelope, I could keep her safe.

❧

Dusk blurred the outlines of the boats and buildings ringing the harbor, erasing the clear line between shore and sky. Back at Laura's, the cider welcomed us home with the aroma of cinnamon and nutmeg. We lined our boots up along the mud room wall, piled coats onto cast iron hooks, and settled onto the soft cushions of the sofa and easy chairs in the circle of warmth.

Laura looked around the room and raised her cup. "Well, here we are. The clan of the long-necked women."

"Long necks are graceful and refined, like swans," Sarah said.

"You've been in LaLa land too long, cousin," Laura said. "Maine swans are mean."

Carla looked around. "When's the last time we were all together?"

"Annette and Nathan's wedding," Sarah said. "Except you couldn't come, Emily."

"I hate it that we never see each other." Laura jiggled her foot while she talked, just like she did when she was eight. Laura never could sit still.

Marilyn put her face in her hands and leaned against her sister. I think she said, "I really miss Grandpa." I saw her shoulders shake, but it was hard to hear her words because of the buzzing in my ears.

"Are you okay?" Anna touched my arm.

There was no reason to be scared of these people. It wasn't their fault that their home had been my prison. Maybe it was the warm room, or not enough sleep, or the noise of bees in my ears, or how Carla's face looked so much like Momma's. I didn't plan to say anything. But something fizzed open inside me.

"Were my parents wrong?" I blurted. "To break the law, even to stop a war and a draft?" I stared at my cousins, daring them to answer, barely feeling Anna's arms around me.

"I admired your folks, Emily." Carla spoke with Momma's mouth. "I wish they had destroyed the draft board records here, on the island instead of in Michigan. Then maybe Uncle Fred wouldn't have been drafted and blown to bits."

Laura nodded. "Me, too. I've always been in awe of your parents. Your parents died young, but their lives had purpose."

I stood up and thumped my hand on my chest. "Isn't family enough purpose? Besides, did it make any difference? That fire didn't end the war. It just made a bunch of people miserable."

"Maybe sometimes you have to act, in spite of the consequences," Laura said.

I heard her speak, but the words came out in a foreign language, one that I had studied long ago but no longer understood. I whispered to Anna, "I'm going back." She followed me to the mud room, then outside.

Aunt Ruth met us at the front door with a frown. "Call Sam," she said. "It sounded important." As Anna hurried towards the kitchen telephone, Aunt Ruth turned to me. "You're back early. Is something wrong?"

I sidestepped her touch and tried to follow Anna into the kitchen. It had to be Zoe.

Aunt Ruth steered me away from the kitchen door. "What happened?"

"Nothing."

"Just like your father." Ruth's mouth tightened into a thin, discouraged line.

"What do you mean?"

"Stubborn. Blind." Ruth's voice cracked slightly on the last word.

I couldn't believe we were talking like this. "Blind? Seems to me that he was forced to see things pretty clearly, locked up for years. Didn't he see Momma was dying of a broken heart?"

Ruth led me to the sofa and sat herself down at the other end. We faced each other across two feet of green plaid. "Your mother was my baby sister. I loved her. But it wasn't a broken heart. She died of guilt."

"Guilt?"

"Arnie talked big, but he was nothing without Jemma. A zero. He almost caved in, the night they firebombed the draft board. Jemma convinced him not to quit. He was the speechmaker, but she was the strategist, the backbone. Together they were a terrific team."

"Then why?"

"Why did he go to prison alone?" Ruth asked. "Because he was fingered, turned in. He was the speech maker, and too many people knew he was involved. There was no way he could get off. So your parents had a choice: either they both went to prison, or he went alone. They made their decision. He told everyone—the cops, the judge, the newspapers—that he acted alone."

"Why didn't Momma tell the truth?"

"To stay with you."

"But she didn't stay. Not really."

"She tried. She couldn't hack it without him."

"She had me." I stood up, both hands splayed across my chest. "She left me alone."

"You weren't put out on the street, Emily. We took care of you. You had a roof over your head, a family who loved you. Get over it. Stop picking at your past like a giant scab." Then Ruth frowned. "Sit down. There's more to talk about."

"I've had enough." I turned towards the kitchen. Anna stood in the doorway.

"Zoe," she said. "It's her shunt."

17 ~ *Gina*

Well, here goes nothing, Gina thought, peering through the windshield at Pippa's three-story stucco house. It was set way back on its lot compared to the triple-family buildings on either side, aloof from the life of the street. In the yard next door, a white-haired man leaned on the business end of a rake, the handle planted in a pile of snow-frosted leaves. A camera, black against the hunter orange of his parka, hung on a leather strap around his neck.

"Looks like snow," he called across the yard. His words were mild, but something prickly in his voice made Gina turn her head and look at him. He stared back.

Gina nodded, then hurried up the front stairs. She knocked on the door and waited for Pippa. Even though it crowded her day, Gina relished the opportunity to meet the cult girl in person. Maybe then she'd understand why Emily was acting so out of character. The door opened.

"Good morning. I'm—"

"You must be Gina," the young woman interrupted. "I'm Pippa. Emily said you would come." She pulled the heavy door and stood back to let Gina enter. Two cats wove in and out between their legs. Following Pippa into the living room, Gina stared at the thick wool socks below the border of her denim skirt, but couldn't see any evidence of the ankle monitor.

Gina arranged the paper towels and computer on the coffee table. She tried not to gawk at the painting over the fireplace. Soft and round with spiky hair and pointy glasses, Pippa sat cross-legged on the couch flanked by her cats.

"Any problems since last week?" Gina asked. "Cramping? Spotting?"

"I feel fine," Pippa said. "Have you heard from Emily?"

Gina shook her head. "How about digestive problems—heartburn, nausea, constipation?"

"No. Nothing. When do you think she'll be back?"

"The funeral is this morning." Gina read the notes in the computer file. "What about the cat box? Is someone else cleaning it?"

"Liz is doing it."

"And the herb teas? Are you avoiding the ones that can trigger labor too early?"

Pippa looked confused for a moment, then shrugged. "I'm doing everything just like Emily said."

"How's the rash under your ankle monitor?"

Lifting her skirt, Pippa leaned down and pushed the gray wool sock down from her right ankle, exposing the small black device. "It rashes up and itches after my shower," she said. "But as long as I tuck this thin sock under the strap, the blotches and itching go away pretty quick."

Gina nodded and typed Pippa's responses into the file. Looking up, she said, "Let's check your weight, blood pressure, and urine, okay?"

"Emily said she would tell me the results of my blood tests. From last Friday?"

"I don't see them. It takes a few days to show up in the computer record. When Emily comes back, she'll track them down." Gina finished typing, rummaged in the bag, and then held out a small plastic cup. While Pippa was in the bathroom, Gina allowed herself to finally stare at the painting. Why hadn't Emily mentioned that awful bird-woman with her bare breasts and fierce eyes?

Pippa handed the cup to Gina, who took it in a gloved hand and set it on a folded paper towel. She dipped the plastic strip into the urine, and held it against the small squares on the bottle label, matching each color at the precise number of seconds for accurate results. Gina knew that other people weren't as careful, but the details were important to her.

"Everything's normal." She smiled at Pippa.

Pippa's weight and blood pressure were normal too, and Gina folded up the supplies and fit everything neatly into the rolling back pack. That wasn't so bad, and she had plenty of time to check on Mr. Stanisewski before her regular Wednesday morning patients. Then Pippa walked back into the living room carrying a tray with a nut-brown teapot and two mugs.

"Spearmint tea. Specialty of the house."

"I'm not sure I have time."

"Please sit for a spell," Pippa said, her voice slipping into a southern cadence. "I could sure use the company." She poured tea into both cups.

Gina checked her watch. She could spare the time, but didn't like Pippa calling all the shots. The girl wasn't all that strange, just intense. And the house felt pretty ordinary really, like any household with the rest of the family at work and at school. Except for the bare-breasted goddess on the wall.

And, except for the fact that the young woman pouring tea let two babies die while she danced stoned in a blizzard.

"So you haven't heard anything from Emily?" Pippa cupped the mug in both hands.

"Not since she left for Maine."

"I miss her," Pippa said in a small voice. "You think she'll be back tomorrow?"

"Probably not until after Thanksgiving," Gina said. Pippa seemed to genuinely care about Emily. "I bet she'll stay up there with her relatives for a few days. Unless there's trouble with Zoe."

Pippa tilted her head to the side. "The little girl Emily lives with? Didn't she go?"

Gina shook her head. "Just Emily and Anna. Zoe stayed home with her dad. Sam."

"What kind of trouble with Zoe?"

"Sam wasn't sure, but this morning he was worried about her shunt."

"Her shunt?"

"It keeps her brain from swelling, because of her spina bifida. They were on the way to the hospital for a CT scan." Gina put the tea cup down and reached for her pocketbook. She should go. She shouldn't be talking about Emily's private business. She should zip up her big mouth.

Pippa leaned forward and put down her teacup. "What does that mean, if her shunt isn't working? Is that big trouble?"

"*Big chobble*, that's what my Granny Teisha called it." Where did that come from? What was it about Pippa that made Emily abandon her common sense, and now here she was, flapping her mouth without her brain in gear.

Pippa smiled. "So, is a shunt problem *big chobble*?"

Couldn't hurt to answer one more question. "She would need surgery. Right away most likely."

Pippa's face sagged. "Without her mother here? That's awful."

Was Pippa thinking about her own daughter, left alone in the frozen forest?

"Shunt surgery can't wait, not even for a mother. If a shunt fails and revision isn't done in time, Zoe could suffer brain damage or even die." Gina stood up. "Thanks for the tea."

Pippa stood too. "Will you let me know what happens?"

That was an odd request from a patient with *big chobble* of her own. This girl wasn't at all what she expected. "I'm going to stop by the hospital to check on Zoe after work. I could call you, if there's news."

"Emily really loves that little girl, huh? Even though she's only her cousin's kid?"

"Zoe means the world to her."

Gina picked her way down the icy sidewalk, then turned back to wave at Pippa, framed in the doorway with the black cat. She could see why Emily was so taken with Pippa.

❧

"You're not Emily." Mr. Stanisewski's look was accusatory.

Gina placed her sparkly jade wool glove against the closing apartment door. "Wait. I'm from the nursing agency."

"Where's my nurse?"

"Emily is away for a few days. I'm filling in for her. I'm Gina Belinfante." Gina gently pushed against the door. "May I come in?"

Mr. Stanisewski stepped back. "She didn't tell me."

"She didn't have time to call." Gina rolled her backpack into the living room, noting the single crutch leaning against the refrigerator. "Her grandfather passed away, and she had to drive home for his funeral. But she asked me to stop in and check on you."

The old man steadied himself against the back of the brown plaid lounger. "I'm sorry. I didn't know her grandfather was sick. She never talks about her family." He pointed to the sofa. "Emily usually sits there, and puts her computer on the coffee table."

Gina spread the paper towels. "Are you feeling well?"

"Not bad for an old coot," he said. "I've been doing just like Emily said. I take my temperature every day. There's been no fever."

Gina checked the computer notes. "Any more drainage from the ulcer?"

"Not a bit. Perfect sock-checks." He chuckled. "That's what Emily told me to do. Sniff my socks when I take them off. They just smell like old feet, nothing else."

Gina smiled at him. "That's a good way to check for infection. Emily knows all the tricks. May I take a peek at your toe?"

He nodded and reached down to his shoelaces. "Yep. And while you change the dressing, I'll tell you about my granddaughter's plants. You can fill Emily in if you talk to her before I do. She'll want to know how the experiment is going."

Leaving Mr. Stanisewski's home twenty minutes later, Gina wondered if her own patients would miss her as much as Emily's seemed to.

18 ~ *Pippa*

Pippa closed the door behind Gina and leaned against it until the lock clicked.

A hoot, that's what Ma would have called Gina, with her shiny red lipstick and fur collar and *big chobble*. Ma wouldn't have meant any disrespect, just that she was different, in a quirky way. Of course, back home Ma would have never had the opportunity to know Gina as a person, hoot or no.

The deep brown of Gina's skin made Pippa ache for Tian. Gina was darker than him, lighter than Delmar. Isis loved all her children, and they weren't supposed to notice skin color. But she couldn't help wondering what Abby's cocoa skin tone would have grown into as an adult. And worrying that having a white mother and a black father would bring her trouble. Ma used to say that being a mother was nine-tenths worry. Pippa couldn't imagine the worry of having a kid with a shunt.

Gina said she'd let her know what happened with Zoe, but Pippa couldn't just sit around and wait for news. She dumped the tea leaves into the compost bucket on the counter, and rinsed out the teapot. It was probably crazy, but maybe just a quick trip to the hospital, to meet this kid Emily loved and find out for herself what was happening. Perhaps she could even help Sam, keep him company since his family was in Maine.

There was no one around to try to stop her. Francie was sleeping. Marshall and the twins were out on a home school expedition, not expected back until dinnertime. Liz and Adele were working at the Tea Room, where Pippa was supposed to join them in less than an hour. She knew without asking what they all would say. No way could she ask Francie about this, not since she'd turned all ice-princess remote. Pippa shivered with aloneness. She dried her hands on the dishtowel and wandered into the living room. Isis' expression was stern, like she didn't approve either. Maybe in her own way Isis was as rule-bound as Emily.

Tian didn't have any problems with thumbing his nose at authority. He taught them that they didn't have to follow the rules of society that were wrong-headed, or didn't apply to them. But he also taught that they should rely only on each other, didn't need to go looking for anything outside the Pioneer Street family. And look at him, always talking about his new buddy, that bald guard down at the jail. It didn't make sense, trusting a guard that much, but maybe even Tian needed a little help from the outside once in a while.

Rely on yourself, Pippa. Think about this logically. She paced back and forth in front of the Isis painting, stroking soft spirals on her belly. Relax, little one, she whispered. Don't stress out with my worries. The way she understood the house arrest system, nothing bad would happen if she left the house at the regular time, but instead of taking the bus to the X, took the North End route instead. She could safely visit Zoe at the Children's Hospital as long as she got home in time, before the ankle monitor could register anything out of the ordinary. She glanced up at Isis for confirmation, but the half-smile on the goddess's face didn't change. For the first time, Isis's expression looked almost like a smirk.

She scrawled a message on the chalkboard on the wall next to the telephone: Something came up. Home by dinnertime. When she called the Tea Room, she was grateful no one answered; hopefully that meant they were busy. She left the same message on voicemail, adding at the end, "Don't worry. Everything's fine."

Adele would be pissed off; she would probably have to stay and help Liz serve customers. She would sulk for a day or so and then forget all about it. None of them would understand why Pippa wanted to visit some kid she didn't know, why she cared about a court-assigned nurse. Pippa wasn't sure she could explain it either, even if Adele or Liz did want to listen. Was it just because she needed Emily's help, or was the nurse feeling like a friend? Whatever, she was going to visit Zoe.

The afternoon was raw and dreary. Standing at the bus stop, it felt like snow. Pippa zipped her jacket all the way up and twisted her scarf around her neck. Francie always told her to wear a hat, but Pippa hated having anything on her head, any covering at all. The twins laughed at her when they went sledding on Barney Hill, because her short hair stood up in frozen peaks, stiff with ice and snow. In deepest winter, she compromised and wore earmuffs, but never a hat or hood.

☙

No one asked for identification when Pippa signed the guest log as Sally Ann Pike and was given Zoe's room number. She clipped the Visitor Pass to her jacket and watched the giraffes and elephants in the hospital lobby recede from the slow climb of the glass elevator. She peeked into the two-story atrium upstairs at more life-size animals, polar bears and penguins. Multi-colored hot air balloons appeared to float near the skylights, the thin wires visible only if you looked closely.

The Neurosurgery Unit clerk pointed to the far end of the corridor. The door to room 2163 was slightly ajar, with two laminated signs taped to the glass window. One slashed circle forbade medical gloves, NO LATEX RUBBER in bold print at the bottom. The other had drawings of a can of soda and a hamburger and was labeled NPO, nothing to eat or drink.

Pippa heard a low voice singing and peered into the dim room.

A lanky man with sand-colored curls leaned over the slight form on the bed next to the window. He held both hands in front of the child's face, his wiggling fingers decorated with pieces of colored fabric.

"Who's afraid of the big bad wolf?" he sang. His fingers danced, a red-cloaked pinky in jiggling step with a plump blue-dressed thumb.

As Pippa retreated a step into the hallway, her boot clunked into the heavy door. Sam looked up at the sound, brought his bare index finger to his bushy old-fashioned mustache with twisted curly ends, then turned back to finish the miniature song and dance. He leaned over to kiss Zoe's forehead, pushing the elastic cap back up to her hairline. She didn't move. He watched the girl for a few long seconds, then joined Pippa in the hallway.

"I didn't want to wake her." His voice was soft. "Who are you?"

"Pippa Glenning. I'm . . . a friend of Emily's."

"I'm Sam. Zoe's dad. She's sedated for surgery." His voice broke on the last word.

She shouldn't have come, shouldn't have interrupted something so personal between parent and child. She wasn't even related, had never even met these people. "I'm sorry to butt in. I shouldn't be here." She turned to leave.

"Wait. I know who you are." He glanced down towards Pippa's shoes.

Well, that was pretty direct. But what did she expect, barging in like this. Pippa stuck out her right foot, slightly lifting the edge of her denim skirt to display the bulge of the ankle monitor under her thick wool sock. She felt pleased that Emily had mentioned her, even if it was just the awful peculiarity of the house arrest situation.

"Gina told me Zoe was here."

Sam nodded.

"It was stupid to come. But I wanted to help Emily."

"It's okay. Waiting alone is really hard."

"What's wrong with her?"

"Her shunt isn't working. She needs a new one," Sam said.

Pippa shook her head. "I mean in general, what's wrong with her?"

"She was born with spina bifida."

"What's that?"

Sam shrugged. "The bones in her lower back didn't grow right. When she was born, part of her spinal cord and nerves were on the outside of her back, in a big lump."

"Wow."

"They operated right away, to put them back inside. And inserted the shunt."

"But now it's broken?"

"Sometimes the tube breaks or gets plugged. So it can't drain the fluid from her brain." Sam traced an imaginary line from the side of his head, along his neck and chest down to his belly, then noticed his fingers and laughed.

Pippa laughed too. "What are those?"

"Finger puppets. Zoe and I collect old gloves and make puppets from them." He held his fingers up for Pippa's inspection. Short sections of glove fingers were positioned below faces drawn with colored pens, some topped with glove tip hats. "We do puppet shows." He pulled a turquoise tube off his pinky and handed it to Pippa.

She slipped it onto her thumb. A simple hood partially obscured the soft pad of her finger, which could become a puppet's face if she drew features on it. Would Tian ever think of playing a game like that with his babies? She tried to remember how he used to be with Abby. She wiggled her finger at Sam.

"How you doing, young fella?" She made her voice deep and southern.

He smiled, then a nurse pushed a stretcher down the corridor to Zoe's door.

"Is she sleeping?" the nurse asked.

Sam's smile faded. "Yeah."

The nurse maneuvered the stretcher into Zoe's room, right up next to the bed. "I'm going to bring her down to the OR holding room now, OK?"

"We're coming." Sam helped the nurse transfer Zoe onto the stretcher, tucked a purple stuffed animal close to her face, and turned to Pippa. "Okay?"

Pippa nodded.

❧

For a person with no use for doctors or their medicine, Pippa was spending a lot of time in medical waiting rooms. Someone had tried to make this one cheerful. A wicker laundry basket of toys and picture books sat next to the blue oval rug in the corner. On the walls, fist-sized tulips in improbable colors bloomed under dazzling sunlight and brown stick trees grew lush with emerald leaves. The twins would love to paint on a wall. Maybe they could do a mural at Pioneer Street, spiff up the house a little. The bright colors made her feel buoyant and hopeful, until she remembered why she was there, that Zoe was asleep under bright lights with someone mucking around in her brain. She turned to Sam, sprawled on the chair across from her. He bit methodically at the ragged red skin around his right thumbnail.

"Giving Red Ridinghood's grandma a haircut?"

"The show's over," he said, tugging the fabric cylinders off each finger and stuffing them into the pocket of his flannel shirt. "When she gets out of surgery, she'll be so loopy with the medicine that she won't remember she fell asleep in the middle of the story."

"Sounds like you've been through this before."

"Once, when she was three. She was sleeping at my apartment that night too, but Anna was here. Emily too." He looked at his watch. "I left Anna a message at her Aunt Ruth's." He dropped his face into his hands and mumbled, "They'll probably blame me for this."

Pippa nodded. She knew how that felt, being blamed for something horrible. And even worse was blaming yourself. "Did you screw up?"

Sam wiped his eyes with the back of his hand. "I don't think so. Maybe I should have noticed sooner that she wasn't acting normal. It's much better to catch it early."

"Is the operation dangerous?"

"They tell you all these awful things that could go wrong and you have to sign that you understand the risks. But that's just to cover their asses. I think this is pretty safe. I hope. Who knows?" He spit on his fingers and started rubbing the inky grins and cartoon eyes with the tail of his flannel shirt. "Could we talk about something else?"

"Sure. What do you want to talk about?"

"How about your house arrest monitor?" Sam pointed at Pippa's skirt dragging on the floor.

Pippa frowned. This guy was terrific with his daughter, but he could be pushy about things that were none of his business.

Sam leaned back in his chair, hands locked behind his neck. "Explain it to me, how it works?"

How much had Emily told him? Pippa repeated what the probation officer had said in the stuffy courthouse conference room. She stumbled at first, over the electronic hook-up between the ankle device and the telephone, but he asked smart questions that helped her get it right. In the middle of describing how her work hours were programmed into the computer at company headquarters, Sam's cell phone rang.

He pulled the phone from his shirt pocket in a tumble of red and green and sparkly purple tubes. "Anna?"

Pippa only half-listened to his description of Zoe's symptoms. She looked around the windowless room. How odd that a hospital waiting room made her feel safe, protected. What if she had found Abby half-frozen in the snow, the morning after the solstice, and brought her right here to this hospital built especially for kids? Would they have been able to save her? Would Tian have played finger puppet games to help Abby get better? Would they have waited together, sitting for hours on these molded plastic chairs facing a childish mural? And what about this new baby? Who would wait with Pippa, if something went wrong with this baby? Who would keep her company when the judge made her give birth in a hospital instead of at home with the midwife and the family and Isis?

"You okay?"

Her cheeks were wet. This wasn't like her, even with the hormone deluge that came with pregnancy. She nodded. "What did they say?"

"They're leaving now. It'll take six, seven hours for them to get here. Anna said it's supposed to snow."

They both looked at the clock on the green waiting room wall.

"I have to catch my bus at five," Pippa said. "If I'm not home on time, the computer will notify the cops and they'll arrest me."

Sam leaned forward. "Do you have a problem with your monitor?"

"Why do you want to know?"

Sam smiled. "Don't worry. Emily didn't give away any secrets. She just asked me a hypothetical question: How could someone under house arrest sneak out for a few hours, without being caught."

Wow. Emily might be braver than she looked.

Sam wrinkled up his face, as if he was thinking hard. "I assume these few hours can't be during an afternoon scheduled for work, like today?"

"Right."

"I did a little detective work. It's an interesting challenge," Sam admitted. "Like I told Emily, a good computer hacker could get into the electrical grid and turn off the juice to a whole sector. They would go looking for a transformer malfunction. Two problems, though. First, it could be fixed pretty quickly, and then you'd be caught outside the house."

"They'd slap me right in jail. What's the other problem?"

"It's risky. Even with a top-notch hacker, there's a decent chance of being caught. These are felonies."

He's worried about himself, Pippa thought. And Emily. He's worried that she'll decide to help me and we'll all get into trouble. "Have you told Emily about this research?" she asked.

"No," he said. "Not yet."

❧

She could tell by the garlic aroma that Francie had already started making dinner. That was a bad sign. Pippa kicked off her wet boots, left them on the newspapers next to the door, In the kitchen, Francie didn't turn to say hello, kept stirring the soup on the stove.

"Hi," Pippa said. "Pretty nasty out there."

"Where were you?"

Pippa hesitated. She didn't owe Francie an explanation, especially if she was in a crabby mood already. Francie wasn't her mother. But Pippa had never heard that tone of voice from Francie either. Maybe she should just give in and apologize.

"Shall I start the salad?" Pippa asked instead.

"I want to know where you went."

"It's no secret," Pippa said. "I went to Children's Hospital, to visit the little girl my nurse Emily lives with. Her niece, or cousin or something. She had an emergency operation. I kept her father company. Sam. What's the big deal?"

"For that you risked getting caught, and put in jail?" Now Francie looked at her, her expression a mixture of fury and disbelief. "Less than a week before your pre-trial hearing?"

It was a big deal to Francie, Pippa realized, pulling lettuce and vegetables from the refrigerator. But the truth was that Pippa had forgotten about the hearing. Which was weird, considering how much she had been looking forward to seeing Tian, even in a courtroom.

Sure, she had skipped out her afternoon at the Tea Room, but Francie had no right to talk to her that way. "I didn't think it would be a problem, as long as I was gone the same time I'm usually gone for work."

"That's not the point." Francie added a miserly pinch of dried herbs from the bowl on the counter next to the stove, and leaned forward to sniff the steam rising from the simmering liquid.

"What is the point?" Pippa asked.

"The point is why are you socializing with people outside the family?"

Pippa started washing lettuce leaves, ripping them into pieces, and tossing them into the spinner. The noise of the faucet gave her a minute to think. For four years the family had been everything to her. What had changed? Was it Tian being in jail? Abby's death? This new baby?

Pippa turned off the water and looked at Francie. "Lots of reasons. I was lonely. I wanted to help Emily, so she'll help me. Sam was fun. He's got this crazy mustache that twists around at the ends and he played finger puppets with Zoe." Why was she blabbing about mustaches? Francie didn't care about Sam. "Our family is falling apart, isn't it?"

"Out of the mouths of babes." Francie crossed her arms over her chest.

"Stop treating me like a child."

"Stop acting like one. Things are rough now, but if we stick together, if we take care of each other, we'll be okay."

"Without Tian? He's the one Isis talks to."

Francie smiled her chopped-off smile that was gloomy at the corners, and shook her head. "Isis will speak to anyone who listens. Tian doesn't have a private line. Besides, if you ask me, some of his rules are stupid and need changing."

"Now you're the one who's being disloyal to Tian, and disrespectful to Isis." Pippa paused before continuing, her voice soft. "I think if I had real friends in the family, maybe I wouldn't have to look outside."

Maybe she shouldn't talk like that to Francie. But every word was true.

19 ~ *Emily*

Anna's hand clutched the doorframe. "It's her shunt."

"We shouldn't have come," I said.

Aunt Ruth looked from Anna to me. "What does that mean?"

"The shunt tubing could be plugged, or broken," I said. "In either case, her brain swells with the extra fluid." I tried to ignore the memorized illustrations from the pediatric neurology chapter popping into my brain.

Anna rested her forehead against the doorframe. "She's in surgery now."

"Damn. Why didn't Sam notice sooner?" I put my arms around Anna. I knew we shouldn't have trusted him. "What were her symptoms?"

"Oh come on." Anna pushed me away. "We left Zoe with him less than forty-eight hours ago and she was fine."

"Maybe not," I said. "Remember how teary she was last week? We should have suspected something. Tell me exactly what Sam told you."

"That Zoe didn't get his spoonerisms. I thought he gave that up years ago. Doesn't matter. We have to get home." She left the living room.

We followed her towards the bedroom. Ruth whispered to me, "Spoonerisms?"

"Sam and Zoe like to joke that way," I whispered back. "You know, when you switch the first letter of words? It's their secret language." I grabbed the two backpacks from the floor of the closet, nudged the half-flat basketball back in and held it with my foot while I closed the door.

Anna talked while she stuffed shirts and socks into her pack. "Sam said that after I brought her upstairs Monday evening she was quieter than usual. He thought she was just tired and maybe worried about me leaving, and that's why she wasn't picking up on the spoonerisms."

Aunt Ruth brought our bathroom stuff into the room, sorting toothbrushes and combs and shampoos. She handed them to Anna.

"Tuesday after school, it seemed worse. Sam called the pediatrician and got an appointment for today. But early this morning, he spoke with the neurosurgeon's office and they said to bring her to the ER for a CT scan."

Aunt Ruth stood behind Anna, hugging her lightly but not getting in the way. Aunt Ruth had always been good at that.

I knew we shouldn't have come. "So while we were tossing dirt onto Ivan's coffin, Zoe was in shunt failure." The minute those words were out, I wanted to snatch them back. I mumbled "I'm sorry" but they both ignored me.

"The scan showed enlarged ventricles." Anna collapsed back against Aunt Ruth's chest. "Which means the shunt isn't working."

"So what are we waiting for? Let's get down to the ferry." I buckled my pack and grabbed my jacket.

"The last ferry was at 3:15," Ruth said.

Anna turned to me. "Cousin Kevin will take us over to Rockland. He said to hurry, a nor'easter is coming."

❧

Halfway to Rockland, we ran into fierce winds and swirling snow. I couldn't tell if the turmoil in my stomach was caused by the swells or the worries. But Kevin delivered us safely through the tossing and the howling to the calmer waters beyond the harbor lighthouse. I clutched both backpacks while Anna hugged Kevin through his rubber jacket slick with wet snow.

Anna insisted on driving, said she needed something to do. She put Cajun fiddle music in the CD player and seemed to lose herself in the rhythm. I folded my long brown scarf into a pillow and leaned against my door. The defroster made ominous pinging noises but the snowflakes melted on the windshield. My thoughts tumbled and tossed, images rushing at me like the headlights of oncoming traffic. Zoe lying pale and silent on the stretcher the last time her shunt failed, wearing a blue OR cap that covered her eyebrows. Sam drawing puppet faces on the soft tips of his fingers and acting out whispered stories. Aunt Ruth telling me that Daddy went to prison and died there alone, so that Momma could take care of me. Could it have been my fault that my mother felt so impossibly lonely? These flashing memories were jumbled up with images of Pippa in trouble, in premature labor or bleeding, unable to get help because she was tethered to her house by that stupid ankle monitor.

As we passed Portland, Anna turned the music down. "How're you doing?"

"I'm scared. Aren't you?"

"Terrified. But she's probably out of surgery by now, and this is pretty routine, you know. She'll be fine."

I nodded. Anna didn't need to be reminded right now about all the potential complications, about how cerebral swelling or high fever or infection could destroy brain cells. "Do you want me to drive?" I asked.

"Not yet. Talk to me. Distract me."

"What about?"

"How about this afternoon? Are you okay?"

"I don't know." I rested my forehead against the cold windowpane. "I don't know what to think anymore."

"You mean what Laura said? That she admired your parents?"

"That, and what Ruth said. While you were on the phone."

"What?"

"That my mother was the one who planned their crime, their protest, whatever you want to call it. My dad took all the blame so Momma could stay home with me." I rubbed the bump in my nose, but it didn't ease the pain in my head. "Ironic, huh? That she could be so strong as an activist, but gave up on being a mother."

"Does that matter, who was the leader?"

"I don't even know what kind of people they were. How could they risk a janitor's life for some pie-in-the-sky idea?"

"You knew them," Anna said. "What kind of people were they?"

"They were wonderful." I buried my face in my icy hands.

Anna was quiet for a few minutes, then said, "You once told me about the nurses' union you joined in Portland. About the strike at the nursing home, leaving the patients inside while you marched on the picket line carrying signs. What if something awful happened when you were walking the picket line? What if an old guy choked and you weren't there to save him?"

It was to protect our patients that Chad started the union, and I joined it. I hated the negotiating, the demands. Most of all, I hated the strike. I worried all the time that something would go wrong, that a patient would be overlooked and suffer. As I packed my suitcase after a week of striking, I wondered what my father would have thought about his daughter joining a union and striking. What he would have thought about my walking away.

I turned to Anna. "We made all these contingency plans. We did everything we could to keep the patients safe. Anyway, that's different. We had to strike for the patients, for better staffing levels, because it wasn't safe the way it was." I reached forward to the dashboard and turned up the heat.

"Maybe your folks felt the same way." Anna's words tumbled out fast, as if she had held them back for a long time. "Maybe Arnie and Jemma felt like they had to do something too."

"Maybe. And look what happened."

"People can't control everything, Emily." Anna sounded annoyed.

I knew that I was being unreasonable. Even as I spoke, I could feel the edges of my anger unraveling. Those days were over and done with. There was too much to worry about in the present, with Zoe in surgery and Pippa's request.

"I can't think about that now," I said. "Our kid could die."

Anna flashed me a weird look. Our kid. I knew that Zoe was Anna's kid, but she felt like mine too. I glanced sideways at Anna, wondering if I had stepped over some line. But she looked straight ahead, switched off the windshield wipers. The storm was losing power.

I rewrapped my scarf around my neck, and reached into my jacket pocket for my gloves. My fingers touched one of the lucky stones. I rolled it into the palm of my hand and cradled it there.

"Accidents happen." Anna's voice was softer now.

I wished she would just leave this alone. "Yeah," I said. "They do. But people have to take responsibility, don't they? For collateral damage. What about the janitor's family? Did he have a little girl too?"

"Don't go there, Emily. Your dad went to prison. He took responsibility. And your mother suffered too."

"Ruth said she died of guilt." I stared through the windshield into the dark night, thinking about the sour fruity smell I woke up to most mornings in that small room. "But that's not the whole story. I think Momma drank."

"I've heard that."

"What?" I turned to her.

"That she drank, because she couldn't face losing Uncle Arnie."

The first few months Momma told me we'd be moving back to Portland, but pretty soon that talk faded away. On my twelfth birthday, I climbed into Momma's lap, even though I knew I was too old. Wrinkling my nose at her familiar smell, her odd mixture of sour apples and cloying sweet, I leaned my forehead against hers. "One-Two-Three-Owl," I said. She didn't seem to remember the game. Over the next few years, the blue leached from her eyes until they were empty. She died the day after Thanksgiving the year I turned fifteen.

It struck me then. I had never asked about the cause of death.

I glanced at Anna. I didn't want to have this conversation. I didn't want any of this. How did I let myself get talked into returning to the island anyway, when I knew it was a bad idea? And now Zoe was sick.

Anna was back on the strike. "There are laws against striking too, aren't there? Injunctions? Would you have continued the strike, if it was illegal?"

Why didn't Anna can it about the strike? "I don't want to talk about this any more." I opened my hand and let the lucky stone fall back to the bottom of my pocket. "Any of it."

20 ~ *Sam*

By the dim light from the corridor, Sam recorded the urine volume on the Intake/Output clipboard next to the sink. The nurse had offered to do Zoe's midnight cath, but he and Anna always liked to do Zoe's care themselves when she was hospitalized. He scooted the chair close to her bed, tucking the blanket around her small shoulders. Careful not to bump her bandaged head, he checked the ink circle outlining the quarter-sized pink ooze on the dressing. No change. He cradled her hand, the one without the IV, so he would wake up if she moved. Finally he let his eyelids slump.

But it wasn't Zoe who woke him. Anna and Emily stormed into the darkened hospital room, wrapped in frosty air and the thick smell of wet wool. Anna tossed her jacket and backpack on the empty patient bed by the door and made a beeline for Zoe. Sam wiped a bit of drool from his mustache and turned under the blanket edge to hide the dark splotch. He watched Anna lean over to kiss Zoe's forehead. When she stood up, he recognized the granite set of her neck and shoulders, even in the shadow light. He knew that stiff dance. When Anna armored her body like that, watch out. And he was the likely candidate for her anger this time. Even so, he felt himself start to relax now that she was here.

Emily circled around to Sam's side of the bed, squeezing between his chair and the wall unit with its oxygen and suction and Code Blue button. She waited for Anna's kiss to end, then inspected the dressings on Zoe's abdomen and head. She touched the back of her hand to the girl's forehead before glancing at Sam.

"No fever?" she whispered.

Sam shook his head, scooting his chair slightly away to give her room. He glanced at his watch. "How was the driving?"

"Bad," Anna said. "But we're here now." She pulled the other chair to her side of the bed. "Everything went okay?"

"Yeah," he said. "She woke up in Recovery about five, got back here before seven." He shook his head; he had been nagging Anna about a cell phone for times like this. "If you had a cell, I could have kept you in the loop."

"You're right. You win. What did Dr. Fred say?"

"The tubing had broken, up near the valve." Sam felt okay, in control of the medical details. Usually he was the one asking the questions and Anna or Emily with the answers.

"How long does he want to keep her here?"

"Probably Friday, but no promises."

Anna looked exhausted. She collapsed onto the bed, head cradled in her arms next to her sleeping daughter. Driving seven hours from Rockland in a snowstorm. He knew that drive and it was brutal. But, glancing back and forth between her and Emily, he wished she would stay awake long enough to fill him in on what was going on. Last thing in the world he and Zoe needed right now was to get caught up in the middle of those two.

Anna and Emily usually got along fine, but they were both stubborn. When they disagreed, he preferred to be someplace else. Like the year after Emily moved in, when her old boyfriend Chad wanted to get back together. Anna thought Emily should see him, give him another chance. Emily said that she lived with Chad for three years and it never felt right. Neither woman told Sam the whole story, as if a guy couldn't possibly understand these things. He didn't want to be involved in their argument, but he wanted to know what was happening. So he stood outside the kitchen door, in their shared back hallway, and tried to listen in. Anna would say that was snooping, but they were his family.

Even wobbly with fatigue, Emily stood sentry right next to Zoe's bed, between him and the wall. He moved his chair another couple of inches, to make more room. In the dim light from the hallway, her face was stone gray. Was she just going to stand there all night? Or do something nursey, something take-charge? He half expected her to whip a stethoscope out from under her sweater, or pluck a penlight from her sleeve. The last time Zoe had shunt surgery, Emily insisted on flashing that damn light into Zoe's eyes every fifteen minutes, even though the hospital nurse came by and checked her around the clock. But Emily surprised him. She turned away from the bedside and curled up on the reclining sleepchair in the corner by the window, covering herself with her jacket.

Within a few minutes, the hospital room was silent. Zoe murmured something in her sleep and Sam leaned close to listen. But her words became a soft snore that merged with Anna's deep exhalations on the bed next to her, and Emily's slow breaths from the corner. He burrowed his nose into the damp of Zoe's neck and sniffed. When she was an infant, he joked with Anna that their daughter was born with the aroma of autumn in a New England kitchen. The perfume of pumpkin pie, candy corn, and nutmeg lingered, warring with the metallic smell of hospital antiseptic.

Sam never could get used to that hospital odor. Iodine, maybe, or alcohol? It made him remember Zoe's birth with that pulsating thing on her back. She needed surgery right away, and then the shunt, and Intensive Care, the viscous smell of sickness that wouldn't come off no matter how long he stood under the hot shower in the parent lounge. Sometimes it triggered the ancient whiff of his father's dying, of words never spoken.

Anna couldn't understand why it was so hard for him to parent a child like Zoe. He couldn't explain, any more than he could articulate why the medical tasks had finally lost their terror for him. He hadn't even called his mother yesterday, to tell her about Zoe's surgery. What could she do? Maybe she would have stopped by, kept him company while he waited for the CT scan and surgery. But he doubted it. In his family, they turned their faces away and sorrowed alone.

Instead, Pippa had shown up to wait with him. Her face was sunny and bright, with those lemon meringue peaks of hair. He could see why she fascinated Emily, even if she lived in a cult. She seemed like such an odd girl, young and tough at the same time. So spunky that you wanted to help her. Be careful, he told himself. Don't forget that girl was charged with causing her baby's death. Or letting her die. Sam wondered what actually happened. How could you get over something like that? He couldn't imagine how she had summoned up the courage to get pregnant again.

Was Emily really foolhardy enough to help Pippa? That was risky, any way you looked at it. Help her break the law, that's what it came down to. Not that he didn't bend the rules sometimes. He had to, in his business; that's what people paid a computer hacker to do. But as a favor? He wasn't an altruistic kind of guy and there was nothing in this for him. So why did he think of Pippa's dilemma in capital letters, like it was some sort of crusade instead of a sordid bunch of new age hippies living on the wrong side of Forest Park. If it weren't for Emily, he would have never heard about Pippa's problem, would not have to puzzle about what to do. It was hard to believe that nervous-nelly Emily would even consider getting involved with this stuff.

Zoe murmured again in her sleep and this time he understood. "Momma."

"Your momma is right here, Poose," he whispered and guided her bundled IV hand across the blanket to Anna's arm. He watched his daughter's fingers creep up her mother's shoulder to stroke the skin of Anna's neck. In the murky light of the hospital room, he studied their oddly-shaped family portrait. Him on one side of the bed, holding his daughter's hand. Her other hand resting on her mother's neck. Prickly Emily too, sleeping six feet away on the reclining chair by the dark window, making small whistling noises with every breath.

Tomorrow, he would have to find a time to talk with Anna, find out what happened in Maine. They might be odd, but they were his family and he wanted to know. Also tomorrow, he would have to find a private time between hospital routines and turkey day, to take Emily aside and explain about Pippa. That he really appreciated the girl stopping by to visit Zoe. That he liked Pippa, in spite of what she got herself mixed up in. But he would have to decline Emily's request to help her patient break the law.

21 ~ *Emily*

I woke up to the squeak of shoes on the tile floor. The day shift nurse was trying to check Zoe's bandages without disturbing Sam and Anna, both still half-sprawled across the hospital bed. The nurse extricated Zoe's right hand from Anna's clasp to check the IV site, then replaced it. I tried to consider our domestic tableau through her eyes. We probably looked like a typical family: mother, father, and aunt or something. Stop daydreaming, I told myself. Five hours wasn't enough sleep, but it was after ten a.m. and we had a lot to do. I woke Sam and Anna and we took turns driving home for a quick shower and change of clothes before Thanksgiving dinner.

"Look at Dr. Fred." Zoe pointed at her neurosurgeon as we gathered with other patients and families for the holiday meal. "Usually he doesn't wear that silly hat." Instead of the light blue cap that covered his balding head in the operating room, he sported a tall white chef's hat. Instead of a scalpel, he flourished an electric knife to carve the biggest turkey I had ever seen. He balanced each slice of turkey on the flat side of the knife for its brief flight to the huge platters that the staff carried around to the patients and families.

The patient atrium was transformed for the holiday. Wheelchairs and stretchers were crowded around tables positioned among the polar bears and giraffes and lions. Centerpieces of painted cardboard turkeys cut from the outlines of the children's hands jockeyed for space on the white tablecloth with bowls of mashed potatoes and butternut squash and stuffing and green peas dotted with little white onions.

Zoe was still sleepy from the anesthesia. She took miniscule bites of mashed potatoes and pumpkin pie. Mostly she sat in Anna's lap and watched the activity. Sam and I watched Zoe. From time to time, I leaned over to look into her face, to make sure that her pupils were equal and her eyes were bright.

❧

The next morning, I arrived at work earlier than usual. Marge was waiting for me, pacing up and down the staff room.

"I hope you're satisfied. Mrs. Newman was transferred to assisted living." Her voice and eyebrows climbed the fury scale together, exploding on the last two words.

"It's better for her." My voice squeaked a little, but I got the words out. "She wasn't safe at home."

"It's a lot of lost income to this agency. That's what it is." She shook her finger at me. "I don't know exactly what happened, but I'm sure you had something to do with it. The only thing that saved your job is the very nice check her son sent to thank us for taking such good care of his mother." She cleared her throat. "You'd better follow the letter of the law, Ms. Klein. You're on probation."

Trembling, I cradled the telephone receiver between my shoulder and ear, and punched in the code to listen to my voicemail messages. The first one jolted me; it was Marge's voice, presumably before she got the word about Mrs. Newman. After a perfunctory condolence about Grandpa Ivan, she left curt instructions. "I assigned you range of motion exercises on Friday with Josué. I know it's not precisely your job, but I can't get a physical therapist until Monday. No big deal, right? You do it all the time with your niece. Besides," she said, her voice brittle, "his mother asked for you." I clicked on my daily schedule on the computer and saw Josué scheduled for the ten o'clock slot, between Mr. Stanisewski's dressing change and Mrs. Grover's antibiotic infusion.

The next message was from Terrell Grover. His mother had been admitted to the medical center on Wednesday with a high fever and mental confusion. I copied down the phone number in her hospital room, trying to picture Mrs. Grover's incision. Did I miss signs of infection at my last visit?

Nan Malloy had called late Wednesday afternoon. "Give me a buzz when you hear this. There's been a development in the Glenning case and I want to give you a heads up." I wrote her number on the list and underlined it twice.

The last message was from Pippa. "Are you back from Maine? Please call me." Her voice sounded thin, as if the words were forced through the little holes in the telephone receiver. I wondered what was wrong, and scribbled her name at the top of my list. Did her worried voice have anything to do with the "development in the case" that Nan mentioned? I tried to imagine what Pippa's Thanksgiving had been like at Pioneer Street, with Abby dead and Tian in jail and Pippa imprisoned by a high-tech ball and chain.

I studied my schedule. Gina had inserted "Meet me at the Park" in bright green in the one o'clock slot, before my new patient intake at two. I heard the outside door open and close, and looked up from my schedule printout. Andy waved and sat down at his desk next to Marge's office without removing his coat. Checking my watch, I dialed Pippa's number. She sounded tired, like maybe I woke her up.

"Everything okay?" I asked. "I got your message."

"I wanted to make sure you're not mad at me for going to the hospital. I just wanted to meet your family, you know? I really liked them, Zoe and Sam."

"I'm not mad," I said. Well, a little, I admitted to myself. More uncomfortable than mad, really. "Sam said he was glad to have the company."

"Did he say anything else?"

So that's what she was after. I turned my back towards Andy and lowered my voice. Even then, I chose my words carefully. "He said you guys talked a little about your situation. That he had done some research."

"And?"

"He said he couldn't see any safe way to help you, not without getting caught."

Pippa was silent.

Sam probably hadn't told Pippa he wouldn't help her. At least not directly. It was easier for him to avoid a definitive answer. But he had made it perfectly clear to me on Thanksgiving, over warm pumpkin pie with vanilla ice cream. Placing his elbows on the white tablecloth speckled with food drips, he had leaned forward and said that he had liked meeting Pippa, but wasn't interested in risking his own skin for her oddball religion.

"Didn't he tell you that?" I finally asked.

"Not really." Her voice was small. "He said he would keep looking."

I slouched down in my chair, rescuing my brown knit scarf which had slid to the floor and snaked under my desk. "Then maybe he'll come up with something." I wasn't being any more honest or forthright than Sam, but it would be easier to talk about in person. I arranged to pick Pippa up Monday morning for her ultrasound, and pressed the disconnect button harder than necessary before dialing the probation office.

"Malloy." She answered on the first ring.

"This is Emily Klein. You left me a message, about Pippa Glenning?"

"Thanks for calling back. First of all, any problems with Glenning?"

No problems, except if you counted Pippa getting mixed up with my private life. It was supposed to be the other way around. I got involved with my patients and their families, but none of my patients had ever met my family before. I wasn't sure why this bothered me, but it did. "She's fine. Your message said something about a new development?"

"Maybe. You know that Glenning, along with the two other defendants, has a pre-trial hearing first thing Tuesday morning, right? And that you're expected to attend, in case the judge has any questions for you?"

"Whoa. I didn't know anything about me having to be there." Maybe I wouldn't even be working here by next Tuesday. I wouldn't be sorry to miss the hearing.

"Sorry. Your supervisor knows, but I should have told you directly. Anyway, the hearing itself is not the problem."

Maybe not for you, I thought.

"The problem is that the newspaper got wind of the hearing. There was a reporter here on Wednesday, said they got photos of the house and quotes from the neighbors. If they call, you probably don't want to talk to them."

"You're right about that. What do I do?"

"Just say No." Nan laughed at her own joke. "Really, just refuse. And one more thing."

"What's that?" I had a bad feeling about this.

"You ever heard of a hate group called the White Hats?"

"No. Should I have?"

Nan sighed. "They have recently spread into New England. They're skinheads, Neo-Nazis. They hate black people, Jews, gays, Muslims. They especially despise any ungodly combinations of the above."

I wasn't going to let myself panic. "Skinheads? Aren't they California types? Isn't New England too cold for them?"

"Don't underestimate those people," Nan said. "They have applied for a permit to rally outside the courthouse Tuesday morning."

I took a slow, deep breath, trying to imagine Pippa being led by cops through throngs of angry people who hated how she lived.

"What will you do?" I asked.

"Nothing we can do," Nan said cheerfully. "It's their right. The permit was granted. I just wanted you to know."

"Thanks." I hung up, then sat for a moment before getting up to pack my supply bag. I wondered if Nan had warned Pippa or her housemates about the White Hats.

❧

On and off during the busy morning, worries surfaced at odd times. Brief images of Pippa and the White Hats, whatever they were, alternated with sick misgivings about Marge. What did it mean to be on probation? Why hadn't I thought to ask her?

When I parked the car at Mr. S's apartment, I noticed the small city park across the street. On a whim, I left my pack in the car and walked along the leaf-strewn gravel path into a grove of maple trees. A male cardinal flew into the bare branches, the red splash of him shockingly bright against the dull brown day. I shivered and shoved my hands deep into my pockets. My fingers found the pebbles. I cupped them in the palm of my hand, warming their hardness. The tips of my fingers felt for the subtly different texture of the ring around the heart of each stone.

Maybe I should just toss them into the dirt at my feet, or into the brush. They were just pieces of rock: inert, dead. It was a silly superstition, putting them on a gravestone. As silly as dancing stoned and bare-assed in a snowstorm around a ring of flat stones in an abandoned nature trail behind a wall of rhododendron bushes. I dropped them in my pocket and turned back towards the street. I had work to do.

❧

Mr. Stanisewski's toe ulcer was almost healed, but his granddaughter's science fair plants were infected with little white bugs. Mr. S thought they sounded like aphids, and while I reviewed his glucose-testing log, he explained to me how to mash an onion and three cloves of garlic in two cups of warm water and brush the mixture on the infected leaves. His granddaughter refused to try the remedy. She just laughed and called him silly Ja Jou. "That's Grandpa in Polish," he said. "Treating the aphids isn't part of the research protocol. She said that anyway onions and garlic were for making kielbasa, and pesticides were for killing bugs."

We sat on his sofa and listened to polka tunes while I charted in the laptop and tried to control the phantasms of my sleep-deprived brain. Pippa and Mrs. Newman danced together around the tattered edges of my exhaustion. They did a lopsided foxtrot, naked in the snow, tethered together by twin ankle monitors. Their audience, two toddlers in thick blanket-sleepers, watched in delight from a small clearing, laughing and clapping their frozen hands.

22 ~ *Gina*

The duck pond at Forest Park was crowded with families recycling stale chunks of Thanksgiving bread, but Gina snagged their favorite bench. The patch of thin sunshine offered little warmth, and she tightened the fur hood of her parka. Enough of this. They would have to find an indoor lunch meeting place until spring.

Gina's gloved fingers fumbled with the cap of her thermos. When she looked up, Emily was picking her way towards their bench between the icy gray patches melting into mud. She looked exhausted, even more stiff and awkward than usual.

"I'm so sorry about your grandfather." Gina stood up to give Emily a quick hug. "How was Maine?"

"All right, I guess. We had to rush back."

"How's Zoe doing?"

Emily brushed a crinkled brown oak leaf from the wooden seat and sat, balancing her lunch bag on her lap. "She's okay. Coming home this afternoon, probably." She turned to look at Gina then, her eyes narrowing slightly. "How did you find out about Zoe anyway?"

"I called your house early Wednesday morning, hoping you'd left a forwarding number in Maine. I wanted to talk with you before I met Pippa." Gina sighed. "I guess I was nervous about the Isis cult. Sam answered, said he was in your apartment to pick up something that Zoe needed for the hospital. A purple rhino, does that make sense? They were just walking out the door for the CT scan."

Emily pulled off the corner crust of her sandwich and tossed it into the pond, choked with dead lily pads. How could they have forgotten Rufus? Zoe couldn't face surgery without him.

"Are you upset that I told Pippa?" Gina took a sip of her potato soup, savoring the comfort of cumin.

Emily didn't answer, then nodded. "A little."

Getting that girl to talk was not going to be easy. "I'm sorry. I guess it's a reverse HIPAA violation, isn't it? Don't turn me in. What did she do?"

"Skipped out on her house arrest rules and went to the hospital. She kept Sam company while Zoe was in surgery."

"That doesn't sound so awful. What's wrong with that?" Gina tipped her thermos straight up to get the last drops of soup.

Emily's voice grew stern. "I thought you were Ms. Don't-get-involved when it comes to Pippa. She disobeyed the terms of her house arrest, that's what. And I prefer keeping my home and work separate."

"I said I'm sorry, and I meant it. But, lighten up, Emily," Gina said, shaking her head. "Let your friends help you out sometimes."

"Pippa's a patient, not a friend."

Gina shook her head again, harder. "It didn't sound that way to me last week. Helping a patient escape the law to participate in some cult ritual wasn't included in the Nightingale pledge last time I looked."

"I was just thinking about it," Emily said. She pulled an apple from her lunch bag and stared at it, then put it back and rolled the fabric closure tight. "Doesn't matter anyway. There's nothing I can do to help her, even if I wanted to. Which I'm not sure I do."

"Mind you, I'm not suggesting you go breaking the law for this girl. Though now that I've met her, I think I understand why she's so hard to refuse." Gina stood up, stuffing the empty thermos back into her shoulder bag.

"Don't go yet," Emily said. "Stay a little. How are you doing? About Max, and everything?"

"I'm okay. Thanksgiving with my crazy clan was good medicine. I was too busy to brood." Gina looked at Emily's tight expression and sat down again. "What's wrong?"

"Marge placed me on probation this morning."

"What happened?"

Emily rubbed the bridge of her nose before answering. "I didn't have any other choice about Mrs. Newman. So, before I left for Maine, I called her attending doc."

Good for you, Gina thought.

"Marge was waiting for me this morning when I got in. Furious. Mrs. Newman was transferred to assisted living, so she's off our caseload entirely. Marge doesn't know what I did, but she put me on probation anyway. What does that mean?"

"Probably nothing," Gina said. "But why don't you make me copies of all your nurse's notes. Document all your conversations about her safety. Just in case. You'd be amazed how often files get lost."

Emily looked at Gina. "What do you think will happen?"

"I don't know. Marge is mostly hot air. I think this will all blow over."

"What if I lose my job? It's all I have."

Gina tried to make her voice as kind as possible. "Then, maybe it's time to look for something more."

Emily looked away, towards the half-frozen pond.

Gina touched Emily's arm. "You did what was right for Mrs. Newman. But you should probably watch your step pretty carefully with Marge for the next few weeks." She paused before continuing. "Especially with anything having to do with Pippa Glenning."

23 ~ *Emily*

Sunday mornings during the winter were cozy times at Anna's. She and Zoe would work on an art project, while I built a roaring blaze in the fireplace and wandered through the local paper and the *Globe*. The Sunday after Thanksgiving I slept late, and an anemic fire was already burning when I carried my coffee into the living room. Anna and Zoe sat at the card table, building a birdhouse from pre-cut pieces of balsa wood.

"Hey, sleepyhead," Anna said. "Good morning."

"Look," Zoe said. "We're going to paint it purple to match Rufus." She jumped the stuffed rhino from her lap to the table, then scratched at the bandage on her head.

Anna pulled Zoe's hand away, straightened the tape over the gauze, and rescued Rufus from the glistening glue nozzle.

I retrieved the newspapers from the front porch. Kneeling on the floor in front of the fireplace, I maneuvered the heavy iron tongs to expose the smoldering belly of the half-burnt log. I fed two chunks of wood to the fire and blew the embers into flame. Then, leaning back against the sofa in the renewed warmth, I spread the newspapers over my lap, the pages still radiating cold.

Staring at me from the front page from the local paper was the blank face of Pippa's house. *Danger on Pioneer Street?* the caption read. *Cult members face hearing on babies' deaths. Story on page B1.*

"Holy shit," I said, forgetting Anna's halfhearted rule about cleaning up our language around Zoe.

"What?" Anna asked, measuring the front wall of the birdhouse against the sides and picking up the sandpaper.

I passed the front page to Anna and opened the City Section to the banner headline, *Frozen Babies to Get Day in Court.*

Anna returned the front page. "What do they say?"

I skimmed the opening paragraphs. "More innuendo than news. Nasty comments from the neighbors. Mug shots of Pippa and Tian and someone named Murphy. They even list their address." I looked up from the paper. "Can they do that? What about their privacy?"

Anna shrugged and turned back to help Zoe hold the two halves of the peaked roof together while the glue set. Then she looked back at me. "You okay?"

I had to swallow hard before answering. The story didn't say anything new, but the tone was ugly and Pippa seemed so exposed. As if the facade of her life had lifted off, like the birdhouse Zoe was building, and a city of strangers could see inside.

Anna started cleaning up the wood scraps from the card table. She turned to Zoe, "This has to dry overnight. You and Sam can finish it tomorrow while I'm at work."

"And paint it purple," Zoe said. "Right?"

"Purple sounds great. Go wash the glue off. And don't touch anything on the way."

Zoe held her palms together and teetered side to side towards the bathroom, unsteady without her crutches. Anna turned to me again. "You look awful. What are you so worried about?"

I rolled the newspaper section into a thin cylinder. "Everything. I'm scared for Pippa and her family, mostly. And I'm terrified about having to testify at her hearing on Tuesday."

Anna's face was kind, but I turned away and stared into the flames, drumming the rolled-up newspaper against my thigh. "I can't stop thinking about my parents," I mumbled towards the fire. "Those dumb pebbles you gave me. I can't stop thinking about this stuff, but I can't figure it out either."

Anna came over and joined me on the rug in front of the fireplace. "Maybe you should stop running away. Like bailing out on the conversation at Laura's."

"I did it with Aunt Ruth too. She wanted to tell me something more about my parents, and I wouldn't let her." I thumped the newspaper tube against my head.

"And?"

"And now I'm curious."

"Then, that's easy," Anna said. "Call Ruth. She wanted an update on Zoe anyway."

"Now?"

Anna spread her arms in a gesture of something. Exasperation, maybe.

"Yeah." I took a sip of my coffee, now chilled, then stood up and tucked the newspaper roll under my arm. I grabbed the fleece blanket from the back of the sofa, and carried the phone onto the sun porch.

The sky was dark with squall clouds. That reminded me about the stormy painting in Nan's office and making my weekly check-in phone call to her the next day.

Stop procrastinating, I told myself. Just do it. I punched in the numbers and listened to the rings, hoping Ruth wasn't home.

Ruth sounded more cheerful than when we left. Her first thought was Zoe.

"She's fine," I said. "The surgery went beautifully and she came home Friday."

The relief was loud in Ruth's voice. "Good." She paused. "And you?"

"I'm okay. But I wanted to ask you something. Remember what you said, before Anna and I left the island? That you wanted to tell me something more, about my parents?"

"Something more?" Ruth sounded puzzled.

"Yeah, something else about them. But I wouldn't listen. I cut you off."

What if Aunt Ruth couldn't remember? What if it was a fleeting thought and now it was gone. Suddenly it seemed crucial to know this information, whatever it was. I sat down on the loveseat and waited.

Ruth was quiet for a few seconds. "I think I wanted to talk about the prison visits."

"I never went."

"I know. Your mother visited the first weekend of every month. Usually I went with her. And every single time, your parents argued about you. Jemma wanted to force you to visit. Arnie always said no. He insisted that it had to be your decision." Ruth's voice softened. "I think that's how it started. At first, Jemma would be so distraught afterwards, and she would have a scotch to help her fall asleep. She said it silenced the arguments raging in her head."

"Should I have gone with her?"

"You were just a child."

Not much of an answer. "But I'm not a child now." I should have stopped right then, but I didn't. Instead I asked one more question, "What, exactly, did Momma die of?"

Ruth was silent. Then, she sighed loud enough to travel the phone lines from Maine to Massachusetts. "They didn't really tell us much, except that they found traces of barbiturates, her sleeping pills, along with the booze."

I never knew what Momma's little pills were. She kept them locked away, so I wouldn't take them by mistake, she said. "On purpose?"

"I don't think so." She paused. "I don't know."

"So, was burning down that draft board worth it, towards stopping the war? When you balance the action against messing up three lives, four counting the janitor?"

"Like you said, Emily, you're not a child any more. Decide that for yourself."

Terrific. Another non-answer.

There didn't seem to be anything more to say. I promised to keep in touch, then disconnected. My legs ached to stretch and run, but I didn't want to leave the porch. Stooping down to pinch two dead leaves dangling from the ficus plant in front of the south windows, I saw the fat brown spider nested safe in its web.

I wrapped myself in the plaid blanket and curled up on the loveseat, facing the bare maples in the backyard, then unrolled the newspaper. I smoothed it flat on my lap and examined the photographs of Pippa and her co-defendants. I thought about Anna's question. What was I worried about?

I was worried that people would read the newspaper story and hurt Pippa.

I was worried that angry citizens would demand that Pippa be locked up, like Tian and Murphy.

I was worried that when I got in front of a judge on Tuesday, my tongue would lose control. That my mouth would fill instead with words I never spoke in defense of my father. That once I started talking, I wouldn't be able to stop, and I would spill out all those words I should have said, that might have saved my parents.

I was worried that some clever reporter would Google the name of the nurse taking care of the pregnant defendant in the frozen babies' case and discover that she was the daughter of a felon who died in prison, exposing our family guilt still glistening like the dried trail of a slug on a summer sidewalk.

24 ~ *Pippa*

"Hot damn." Marshall looked up from the newspaper as Pippa entered the kitchen. "We got lots of ink in the Sunday rag."

Pippa leaned over the table to look. "Ugly pictures. Where did they get those?"

"Mug shots aren't usually portfolio-quality prints, my sweet naïve Georgia lass." Marshall reached out to goose her bottom.

Pippa scooted out of his reach and selected a mug from the dish drainer. "What do they say about us?"

"The usual crap." Marshall ran his finger under the grimy turquoise bandana knotted around his neck. "About how those poor frozen babies will finally have their day in court. They neglect to mention that this is just a hearing, some sort of technical legal mumbo jumbo before the trial. But hey, it's a good opportunity for the local press to rant and rave about the evil cultists living in the midst of the good Yankee citizenry of Springfield, right? Ranting and raving sells newspapers."

Pippa dawdled at the counter, her back to Marshall's resentment and to the newspapers sprawled on the table. She warmed her hands around the belly of the teapot, then filled her mug. Bast rubbed against her legs, scratching her mouth on the edge of the ankle monitor, then meowed and sauntered to the back door. Pippa let her out, watching her sleek shadow run cross the yard.

"Utter crap." Marshall shook his head. "They interviewed the old geezer next door. He swears we dance naked in our back yard, every month under the full moon. His wife claims that we sacrifice innocent baby lambs to the devil, hose their spilled blood down the basement drain. She can hear the poor dears baa-ing and crying at night."

Pippa laughed, but it wasn't funny.

"Look at this." Marshall slid the newspaper across the table, his stubby finger pointing to a box outlined with a bold border: *How to protect your family from cults.*

Pippa pushed the paper back at Marshall and turned away. "Those lies have nothing to do with us." She pulled the cast iron pot onto the front burner, measured six cups of water from the faucet, and lit the stove.

"Go ahead. Make oatmeal. Stick your head in it if it will make you feel better." Marshall tugged on his bandana as he stood up. "You haven't been through this before." He slammed his fist on the newspapers strewn across the table and trudged towards the dining room. In the doorway he turned back to face Pippa. "But we have. This crap is why we had to leave Newark."

Pippa added a generous pinch of salt and covered the pot. She sat down at the table, pushed the newspapers to the far corner. It was true that she hadn't lived through any real harassment towards the cult. There was the constant minor irritation at the Tea Room from the health department. And the occasional letters stuffed into the mailbox, but their ignorant grammar and simple-minded messages made them almost laughable. Francie had once hinted at more serious troubles. But she didn't elaborate and wouldn't answer Pippa's questions.

They didn't need this aggravation three weeks before the solstice. Pippa stirred the oatmeal into the boiling water. Who would be on their side if people got nasty? The police? Her probation officer? She had no friends outside of the family. Except Emily.

Sundays were quiet and the hours passed slowly. Everyone was sleeping late. Adele and Liz would bring the twins to the Tea Room at noon, where they would take turns washing mugs at the big sink, and creating lopsided teacups at the potters' wheel, bickering happily. Pippa wished she could be there too, but the judge insisted she stay home and rest on the weekends. She reached down and scratched her ankle. She couldn't stop thinking about the Tea Room.

It must be the music. Someone was practicing the psaltery, like Murphy used to play before they hauled her off to jail. Dancing the bow over the strange triangle of the wooden psaltery, she would saturate the Tea Room with sad Celtic ballads and zippy Yiddish tunes. Concentrating so hard she wasn't aware how the tip of her tongue tapped the rhythm against her top front teeth. But whoever was playing now was making more screech than music.

Pippa stirred the thickening oatmeal, turned down the flame, and set the timer. She followed the barely recognizable notes of "The Ash Grove" to the living room. Francie sat on the yellow chair with the psaltery.

"Pretty pathetic, huh?" Francie said, looking up.

"I guess it takes practice. I didn't know you played." Pippa sat on the sofa next to Newark.

Francie grimaced. "Obviously I don't. But with Murphy gone, someone's got to learn to play this thing."

"Why?"

Francie's voice slid into the patronizing tone Pippa hated. "Because when there's live music, people sit longer at the Tea Room. And they spend more money. Then we can pay our bills."

"I guess." Pippa had never thought Francie cared so much about the money they made at the Tea Room.

"And Murphy probably isn't coming home any time soon."

What about Tian?

Francie rubbed the bow in the X pattern carved deep into the rosin cake, harder than Murphy ever did. "Our weekly income is down by more than a third. Tian's charm with the ladies increased our earnings too. We're hurting."

I'm hurting, Pippa thought. But it's not about the Tea Room revenues. Doesn't anyone else miss Tian and Murphy? Mourn Abby and Terrence?

"Francie, I'm worried. What's going to happen?"

"On Tuesday, you mean, at the hearing? Or in general?" Francie didn't look up from the instruction booklet that promised Anyone Can Play the Bowed Psaltery.

"Both."

"The lawyer says nothing much will happen at the hearing. It's just to determine whether the trials will be together or separate."

"Will Tian have to stay in jail?"

Francie placed the psaltery on the coffee table, resting the bow carefully on top before meeting Pippa's gaze. "Listen. Tian will do time. His juvy record is supposed to be sealed, but they'll somehow make it admissible. Cult leaders don't get suspended sentences. There are really two questions: how long will he get, and will you and Murphy go to prison too. The lawyer says Murphy probably, but you're younger, and might get off with just probation."

Pippa lifted Newark into her arms and rocked the cat side to side. "What will happen to us?" What will happen to my baby?

"If you believe the lawyers, and if we get a decent jury, Tian might only get a couple of years, Murphy even less. We can keep the Family of Isis going. Maybe even improve some things while Tian is gone."

Pippa didn't know how to respond. Was this a test of her loyalty? She had failed a test once before, failed to keep quiet when it really mattered. She didn't know for certain if what happened to Delmar was her fault. Maybe Ma never said a word. Maybe Stanley told Pa about the dancing. Maybe someone else saw them. Still, Pippa should never have opened her big mouth about what she saw that night at Maxy's Place.

But Francie didn't know anything about Delmar and Sally-Ann. What did she mean, that they could do a better job of running the Family of Isis? They pretty much did everything now. Except talk with Isis, and since Tian went to jail, no one was talking to Her at all. Pippa looked carefully at Francie's face, trying to read the thoughts behind her princess looks.

Francie's face softened. "Everything will work out, Pippa. Even without Tian, even with your ankle jailer, we'll figure this out."

Then Pippa remembered the newspaper story, and that Francie hadn't seen it yet. "Wait a minute, before you decide everything's hunky-dory." She collected the stack of papers from the kitchen, pointing to the front-page photograph of the house, and then to the story with its row of mug shots.

While Francie read, Pippa stood by the bay window watching Bast chase leaves across the front yard. When she glanced back, Francie looked stunned, with the same expression of worry that Marshall wore earlier. Whatever had happened to the family in Newark must have been pretty bad. Pippa closed her eyes and tried to let pretty pictures of Bast and blowing leaves dance across her brain, but the images all swirled together with dark hands on white denim and Delmar's legs all akimbo on the barn floor.

25 ~ *Emily*

I wedged the telephone receiver between my left ear and neck, scrunching up my shoulder to hold it tight. The yelling from Marge's office was loud enough to interfere with my conversation, but her closed door obscured the details of the reprimand.

Carmen was describing the stain on Josué's bandage. "It's a greenish color, and it smells bad."

The corner office door opened several inches to reveal the new nurse's hand clutching the doorknob.

"We have regulations here and they apply to everyone," Marge said, before the door closed again. I wondered what the new recruit had done, and if she would pack up the framed desk photo of her infant son and never return. Had any of us remembered to orient her to Marge's obsessions about certain procedures?

I tried to concentrate on Carmen. "Does he have a fever?"

"No, no fever. But the green, does that mean an infection?"

I could hear Josué in the background reassuring her. "No infection, Mamá. Don't worry."

We all tried to ignore the muted fury that seeped from Marge's office. Even Andy, usually the boss's stalwart defender, turned his back on the racket and rolled his eyes.

"Call the surgeon's office and let them know," I suggested to Carmen, pressing my finger against my free ear. "If they want a culture, I'll stop by after lunch and collect it."

I checked the clock. Just enough time before Pippa's ultrasound appointment for my weekly call to the probation office. A question for Nan had been nagging at the back of my brain but I couldn't quite remember it.

"Malloy." Even this early, Nan's voice had an edge of no-nonsense.

"This is Emily Klein. Checking in about Pippa Glenning?"

Ever since Momma's nightly phone calls with Daddy during his trial, I wasn't crazy about telephones. But it was better than being in Nan's office with that painting.

"How is Glenning?" Nan asked. "Any problems?"

I considered briefly the potential adverse effects of wine mixed with peyote cactus powder on a second-trimester fetus. But I doubted that Pippa planned to drink the libation. Not this year, not when she was pregnant. And what about skipping out on work last Wednesday to visit Zoe in the hospital? Strictly speaking, I only knew of that from other people, so that was hearsay. Gossip, really.

"No problems. I'm picking her up in a few minutes for her ultrasound and blood work."

"Did you see the newspaper yesterday?"

"Yeah. It makes me very nervous."

There was a pause before Nan responded. "Listen. The D.A. is putting a lot of pressure on the court to put Pippa in jail with her friends. It's complicated. Two years ago a pregnant woman miscarried in our local jail, and Judge Thomas is determined to avoid something like that again. But then last week in Cambridge, this pregnant bimbo awaiting trial for a B and E, who was under House Arrest to protect her fetus, snuck out and got an abortion and the judge is furious. For the moment, his protect-the-baby philosophy is working in Glenning's favor, but I can't promise how long that will continue."

Miscarriage. Hurt. I remembered my elusive question. "Pippa really wants this baby. She seems to be cooperating fully with the medical plan," I said. "By the way, what if there's an emergency? If Pippa starts spotting or goes into premature labor in the middle of the night? What is she supposed to do?"

"Go to the emergency room, of course. But she should call as soon as possible, and let us know where she is and what's happening. Before these damn federal privacy laws were passed, we could call around to all the E.R.'s to find out if an offender was there. But now with the HIPAA regulations, they won't say a word. Even to us." Nan's laugh sounded bitter. "Privacy laws? How do they expect us to do our job, to protect the public—don't get me started on that. No, in an emergency, of course we want her to get treatment right away. And then notify us ASAP."

I tried to choose my words carefully. "But, I mean, if she leaves the house, because she's sick or something, it's not a big deal, is it? If it's for a good reason? For her health or her baby's well-being?"

"Breaking her house arrest is breaking the law." Nan's voice was taut with certainty. "The Conditions of Bail specify that Glenning stays in the house, except when given permission to leave. In advance. By Judge Thomas, or by me. Or except in a true medical emergency. The judge doesn't give two beans for a higher moral purpose."

That's pretty clear, I thought.

"Why?" Nan asked. "Are you worried about her health?"

"No," I said, trying not to panic. I probably shouldn't have said anything. "She's fine. I'm just doing my job, trying to be prepared for anything." After promising to call again the next Monday, I pushed the disconnect button. I held the phone in my hand, listening as the dial tone changed to the oscillating sounds of the hang-up alarm.

❧

Fifteen minutes later my car was idling in front of the Pioneer Street house. I honked a second time. Gray clouds hung low and thick, threatening snow despite the forecast of dry weather. Pippa's head emerged in the doorway and she held one finger in the air before slipping back inside. I hate being late. I tried slow, cleansing breaths. Anna was taking a class in yoga and meditation. She was trying to convert me to a more serene approach to life, without any noticeable effect. Several minutes later, Pippa hurried down the sidewalk, her yellow hair sticking out every which way even more than usual.

"Sorry." Pippa fumbled with the seat belt buckle.

"Are you nervous about the ultrasound?" I put on the left turn signal and looked over my shoulder, even though there was no traffic on the narrow residential street. Glancing at Pippa, it struck me. "Or about the hearing tomorrow?"

"No, it's Bast. He didn't come home last night. I tried calling him from the back yard just now, one more time."

"He'll be back. Did you drink all the water for the ultrasound?"

"Almost done." Pippa pulled a plastic water bottle from her backpack and took a long swallow.

We arrived at the hospital ultrasound department only a few minutes late. The technician handed Pippa a faded blue hospital johnnie and pointed to the curtained changing area. She directed me to the gray metal chair next to the exam table. "You can have the daddy chair."

"This had better be quick." Pippa clutched the cotton gown around her body. "My bladder's going to burst."

"That's what everyone says," the tech said. "Never happens." She helped Pippa onto the table and squeezed gray-green gel over the slight mound of her belly. I sat close to Pippa's head. Together we looked back and forth between the probe making swoops and swirls in the gel, and the indistinct, shadowy images on the computer screen. Even with the tech's guided tour, the fuzzy shapes were hard to visualize as baby hands and head and knees.

During our regular Sunday dinner with Sam the evening before, my mind had been stuck on ultrasounds. I guess I was worried about Pippa's appointment. The whole time Anna and I made ziti with tomato sauce, the whole time Sam and Zoe built a fortress on the sun porch with chairs and blankets and construction paper turrets, I wondered what it had been like at Zoe's ultrasound.

"It's not a fort," Zoe announced as we sat down to eat. "It's a castle restaurant, and tonight's special is the oatmeal-raisin cookies. Mom and I baked them." Zoe ate three bites before rushing to the porch to prepare for customers, leaving the three of us at the table.

"Tell me about Zoe's ultrasound."

My words hovered in the empty air, shimmered in the silence over the table. I stared at Zoe's plate, red sauce splashed over white bones of pasta. Neither Sam nor Anna answered. After a few minutes, Anna stood up and started carrying half-empty plates to the sink. I looked at Sam.

"Pearls." His voice was barely a whisper. "A broken pearl necklace." Then he stood up too, pushing himself away from the table with his hands flat on the wooden surface, as if he were a much heavier man. He carried the salad bowl to the counter and rummaged in the cupboard for a plastic container for the leftovers. "Isn't the restaurant open yet?" he called out to Zoe on the porch. "I want cookies."

When Pippa's ultrasound tech pointed to the white-gray knobs lined up in a row, I understood what Sam meant by pearls.

"A flawless spine." The tech's voice was proud, as if the perfection were her personal accomplishment.

Pippa smiled back. "No spina bifida?"

"Nope." The tech shook her head and pointed again at the pearls. "See how the backbones are lined up, nice and even?"

Pippa turned her head towards me. "That's what Zoe has, right?"

I nodded.

"How's she doing?" Pippa asked. "After her operation?"

"Fine." I supposed it was good that Pippa could relax, forget for a moment that she hated all this medical intervention. But talking about Zoe was dangerous territory. I turned to the tech. "Are the other organs okay?" Pippa and I watched the technician identify her baby's beating heart, and bean-shaped kidneys. We got a glimpse of a small appendage wiggling between the baby's legs. The tech didn't say anything. She just pointed at it and grinned and gave us a thumbs-up sign. I didn't know if Pippa noticed, or if wanted to know her baby's sex, so I kept quiet.

"Now you can pee." The tech handed Pippa an ultrasound photo of her baby and helped her off the exam table. "When you're dressed, follow the red line to the lab for your blood work."

One red stripe was painted at eye-level along the wall, another on the floor. Pippa flashed me a smile and tightrope-walked down the painted line on the floor, her outstretched arms banking through the turns at corridor intersections. She appeared oblivious to the stares from passing staff and visitors. Pippa surprised me sometimes, doing childish things one minute and being so sure of herself the next. What was it the obstetrician had called her? Robust. A funny word for such a small person. But it fit and for a moment I envied her self-confidence. Still, I followed six steps behind, far enough so that it wasn't clear we were together.

"If it were up to me, I wouldn't do this triple screen," she said over her shoulder. "No matter what Dr. Zabernathy says."

I had been surprised when she agreed to the tests. I couldn't imagine Isis letting her terminate the pregnancy, even if the blood tests were positive and the amnion showed a malformation. I caught up to her. "Choose your battles, right?"

When Pippa was called into the lab, I studied the other patients in the waiting room, trying to guess their diagnosis. Some were easy, like the wheezing woman in the corner on an oxygen leash, and the bald kid playing with a hand-held computer game while his mother hovered. But the woman across from me could have stepped out of a television exercise equipment commercial. Maybe she had lost two sisters to breast cancer and wanted genetic testing? Nosy girl, I scolded myself. Get back to the business at hand. I fixed my attention on the laminated notice above the woman's shiny black curls: Please notify us if you have a latex allergy.

"You still get those itchy welts on your ankle?" I asked Pippa when she returned to the waiting room. "Under the ankle strap?"

"Not if I wear a sock between my skin and the strap. Why?"

I pointed to the notice.

"Do you think I'm allergic to my house arrest monitor?" Pippa laughed. "You won't get any arguments from me about that."

I made a mental note to examine the skin on Pippa's ankle. What if it were medically necessary to remove the monitor, for her health? I started to smile at that, until I remembered what Nan had said that morning about the D.A. looking for any excuse to lock Pippa up. But at least I should document Pippa's rash in the medical record.

Pippa was quieter than usual on the drive back to Pioneer Street. She didn't ask to stop at the park again, or bring up my testimony at the hearing tomorrow.

"Do you have time for a cup of tea?" Pippa asked as I pulled onto Pioneer Street. "I want to talk to you about something."

"A quick one," I said, opening my car door and stepping out. "Talk about what?"

Pippa leaned both elbows on the roof of the car. She looked at me across the frosty green metal.

"Are you going to help me?"

I picked a flake of rust from the roof. I should have seen that coming. Here we were just getting comfortable with each other, and now Pippa had to go and bring up the solstice again. It was a lot to ask and I didn't have an answer.

"I don't know," I said. Jiggling my car keys, I started walking toward the front door. A large brown cardboard box sat in the middle of the front porch.

"You've got a package." I pointed at it. "A present?"

Pippa shook her head. "No one sends us anything."

I climbed onto the porch and examined the box. "There's no name or address."

Pippa stood at the bottom of the steps. Her face mirrored the color of the low clouds. Had she looked that pale at the hospital? Maybe I should check her iron, even though the prenatal protocol said not until next week. Or maybe it was the box. I started to feel a little shaky myself. I squatted on the wooden porch next to the package.

"This makes me nervous," I said.

"It's not ticking, is it?"

I felt stupid, but I pressed my ear to the cardboard, and listened. "No."

"Open it."

"It's your package."

"You do it, please." Pippa said, not moving onto the porch.

Using the edge of the ignition key, I slit the crisscrossed packing tape. The flaps were slotted together, each tucked under the next, unfolding as I started to lift them up. I hesitated, glancing at Pippa again.

She stared down towards her feet, at the few remaining blades of grass. The short brown sticks, frozen erratically every which way, sparkled with ice in the stark light. Finally, Pippa climbed the steps onto the porch and stood next to me. I pulled apart the cardboard flaps.

The cat's body lay nestled on a bed of crumpled newspapers. Curled up tight to fit into the box. Her sleek black head, no longer attached, was tucked into the concavity of her body. Her eyes were open, cloudy and empty. Too late, I tried to push the flaps closed.

"Bast," Pippa said, the word a deflated sound of exhaled air and woe. She dropped to her knees and took the box into her arms, cradling it against her chest, rocking back and forth.

I took a step backwards. The air around me froze and shattered, frosty crystals plunking onto the sidewalk. I wanted to comfort Pippa, really I did, but my muscles were ice. I couldn't feel my hands and feet. It was December. It felt like snow. But this was a freezing that came from inside. I watched Pippa tremble, her shoulders hunched forward and her forehead rested on the edge of the cardboard box. The strength of her response frightened me. So fierce, so private.

I backed down from the porch, towards my car.

"Please stay." The hollowness in Pippa's voice stopped me. She was my patient.

I picked up Pippa's keys from the porch. I helped her stand and steered her, still hugging the box, into the living room. She collapsed onto the sofa.

"Anyone home?" I stood in the arched doorway between living room and dining room and called into the quiet center of the house.

A man's voice called down from the second floor. "Who's there?"

"Please. Pippa needs help."

She rocked back and forth on the sofa, cradling the cardboard box, the flaps folded down to shroud the cat's body. I turned towards the sound of footsteps on the wide staircase. A heavyset man thumped down the steps, one finger hooked onto a dark turquoise bandana knotted around his throat.

"Who are you?" he asked.

He brushed past me to Pippa without waiting for an answer. Two identical boys, perhaps three or four years older than Zoe, followed him down the stairs and into the living room. They threw themselves onto the sofa, one on each side of Pippa. The boys were striking, with startling blue eyes and coffee-colored curls several tones lighter than their skin. They stared at me. The fluffy orange cat dashed into the room. He jumped onto Pippa's legs, sniffed at the box, and darted under the sofa.

"I'm Emily Klein. From the nursing agency." I addressed my comments to the man, but watched the boys, sandwiching Pippa in a tight hug.

The man moved to the sofa and bent down to Pippa. "What's wrong? What happened?" He reached for the box.

Pippa came awake then. She pushed his hand away, placed both her hands firmly on top of the flaps. "I don't want them to see this." She turned to me. "This is Marshall. And Jeremy and Timothy." She looked back at Marshall, then patted the box on her lap.

"Bast," she said.

Marshall stood up. "Boys, get back to your math. Upstairs. Take Newark with you."

"What happened to Bast?" asked Jeremy. Timothy stared at the box.

"We'll talk about it later," Marshall said.

"Later," Pippa promised. "We'll tell you everything."

Timothy scowled but stood up and scooped up the orange cat from under the sofa. Jeremy hugged Pippa hard for a moment longer and whispered something in her ear before following his brother out of the room. The man turned to me. "Thank you for helping Pippa. You can go now. I'll take care of this."

"Okay." I started to turn away.

"Please stay," Pippa said to me, then looked at Marshall. "Do we report this to the cops?"

Marshall laughed. It was an ugly sound, containing a hint of something I almost recognized but didn't want to know.

"A lot of good that will do," he said. "We'll discuss it with the rest of the family when they get home. Let me see her."

He took the box from Pippa's lap and set it on the coffee table. His thick hands fumbled for a moment with the flaps. He stared down at the cat's body. Then he stroked the back of his fingers lightly along the quiet black fur. He touched the soft place behind the flattened ear. His hand jerked away as it touched the stiff neck hairs, coated thick with dark ooze. He struggled to maneuver the flaps back together, each one tucked under the next. Finally, he spoke. "Whoever did this is a coward. How brave is it to kill a cat? Let him come fight, man to man."

Pippa rolled her eyes, then looked at me.

Marshall's shoulders slumped. "I'll put her in the greenhouse for now."

"I'm so sorry," I said when Marshall had left. I still stood frozen in the doorway. "How can I help? Should I call Nan Malloy? She mentioned some new hate group in town. I suppose she should know about this, before the hearing tomorrow. Maybe she can do something."

She looked at me funny. "Sure. Whatever." She pointed to the telephone in the hallway. "You call. I'll make tea."

I watched Pippa spoon loose tea leaves into a small wire basket while Nan Malloy's phone rang.

"I expected something like this," Nan said when I told her about Bast.

Pippa was warming the earthenware teapot with hot water from the faucet. I turned away from her, wrapping myself in the telephone cord and facing into the hallway. Pippa should not have to hear how unconcerned her probation officer sounded about her safety.

"What do you mean, you expected it?" I lowered my voice. "If you knew it might happen, couldn't you have warned us, prevented it? Do you expect more violence? Maybe to the people in this house, next time?"

"There are thousands of hate crimes every year in this country." Nan's voice sounded defeated. "Hate crimes are message crimes. No, I'm not worried about more violence. The message has been delivered and received. Loud and clear."

"So that's all? Aren't you going to do anything?"

"What do you want me to do?" Nan asked. "I'll send a squad car out to take a report, okay? See you in court tomorrow morning. Ten sharp?"

"Yes."

"And Emily," Nan hesitated, "I hope you're not getting too involved with these people. Remember what we talked about, how manipulative they can be?"

"Don't worry." I hung up and turned to Pippa, who was holding the two cups and the teapot. A thin rope of steam rose from the spout.

"Come back in the living room," Pippa said. "You can tell me why you look ready to kill someone."

When we were settled on the sofa, Pippa started to pour the tea.

"What kind of tea?" I pointed at the teapot. "Not red raspberry?"

"What's wrong with red raspberry?" Pippa asked, holding the teapot in mid air.

I immediately regretted my words. Great time to preach about diet. Why did I have to be such a meddler? I had given Pippa the list of herbs and teas to avoid on that very first visit. Why couldn't I keep my mouth shut? Shut up, I told myself, and drink your tea so you can leave this dark place.

"What's wrong with it?" Pippa's expression was severe.

"Red raspberry isn't good for you this early in pregnancy," I said. "It can bring on premature labor."

"Not to worry. This is spearmint. House specialty." Pippa filled the cup. "But now I get it. That's what it was, the first time you were here when I made tea. You looked like something smelled bad. Why didn't you just say so, about the tea?"

"You wouldn't have listened," I said. "You didn't want me here."

"You're right about that." She tilted her head to the side and looked at me. "And now you don't want to be here."

"I'm sorry." I looked at Pippa's open face and sunburst hair. I really liked this woman. Admired her even. But a beheaded cat was more than I could stomach. I had to shift this relationship back onto professional ground, where it belonged. I stood up.

"I'm sorry," I said again. "I can't stay."

26 ~ *Pippa*

Washing the breakfast dishes the next morning, Pippa sensed she wasn't alone and turned. Francie stood in the doorway, the palms of her hands pressed against both sides of the doorframe. Like she was holding up the whole house.

"What's with the black?" Francie asked.

Getting dressed for the court hearing hadn't been simple. The public defender had instructed her to dress conservatively. "Look young and innocent," he'd said. "Wear muted colors. Pastels."

Pippa wanted to make a good impression, but couldn't figure out how to put on panty hose with the ankle monitor. She tried threading the thin fabric under the strap, but there wasn't enough space. She tried wearing the stockings on top, but a corner snagged the stocking and caused a run. Finally she gave up and wore her usual thin white sock under the monitor and pulled black knee-highs over it all, hidden by a long black skirt. Pippa couldn't believe she had been brought to the verge of tears over something that stupid. Don't waste your tears on trifles, Ma used to say. Save them for when they count.

"I don't give a rat's ass what the lawyer advised." Pippa concentrated on scrubbing the oatmeal crust on the cast iron pot. "I feel like wearing black. I am not a pastel kind of girl, number one. And number two, I'm mourning a murdered cat." And a dead daughter.

"You're attending a hearing about the murder of your child. You might want to modify your fashion statement."

"Criminal neglect," Pippa said. "I'm not charged with murder."

"Same thing, as far as a jury is concerned. If you belong to an evil religious cult." Francie pivoted and left.

Pippa dried her hands, then pressed her flushed cheek against the cold glass of the window in the back door. It had snowed again last night, and she couldn't stop thinking about the park. She pictured the flakes settling on the teardrop-shaped rhododendron leaves, muffling the winter rustlings of birds and small animals. She squeezed her eyes shut to erase the image of Abby's slight form under two layers of blanket sleeper, red against the white coverlet of snow.

It was none of their business. Not the lawyers or the judge or Nan Malloy or any of them, even Emily. It was not their concern what color clothes she wore to court. Or who she was mourning.

27 ~ *Emily*

I grew up with protests and demonstrations. Every time our president bombed a small country that we had to search for in our family atlas, we marched. Every time the state legislature tried to pass a law cutting welfare benefits or limiting gay rights, we picketed. But never in thirty-two years had I found myself in this position. Between me and the front door of the Hall of Justice marched four dozen people carrying hand-printed signs: *An Eye for an Eye. Justice for the Frozen Babies. Protect Springfield from Satan-Worshippers.*

My father's voice thundered in my head: never cross a picket line.

What would Arnie Klein say about neo-Nazis demonstrating against a cult in the neighborhood? Would he honor their picket line, engage them in political discussion about their message of hate? Who were these people, bundled up against the December cold? It was hard to identify anything about them, even their ages. They didn't look like skinheads, though how could you tell with bulky coats and ski hats and scarves? Would they mutilate a family pet to prove how much they hated people who worshipped strange gods, a deity living in a forest instead of a church?

My immediate concern was getting into the courtroom for Pippa's hearing. I stepped closer to the sidewalk. An older guy with white hair poking out around his down hood stepped out of the line of walkers to stand in front of me. His sign read *Avenge the Frozen Babies.*

"Will you join us?" he asked. "We want the judge to know that Springfield citizens will not sanction the sacrifice of innocents in our city." Wearing puffy mittens, he fumbled with the stack of bright green papers under his arm and handed me a flyer with the words of the message forming a cross.

My father spoke up again: never cross a picket line.

Mumbling thank you to the picketer, I folded the flyer into perfect quarters, and shoved it down into my jacket pocket.

Stick to unions and antiwar protests, I told my father. You don't know anything about this kind of demonstration.

My father would have welcomed an argument about the correct response to a racist picket line. Growing up, every Sunday morning was a verbal brawl between Arnie and the editorial page of the *Times*. His exuberant gestures slopped his coffee over the cup rim, stamping overlapping tan rings on the newsprint pages. Momma and I would egg him on, nudging our chairs to face him across the breakfast table like an audience, clapping at his most lucid and persuasive arguments. Arnie's eloquence shone at the table, although sometimes I wished he was like other dads. My friend Marta from next door came over for dinner one time. My father started talking about college days in Ann Arbor, when his history classes and Momma's music studies were secondary to their anti-war activism. "We majored in revolution," he shouted. Marta didn't come again.

Some of our best conversations developed as we crisscrossed the gravel trails of the city park near our Portland apartment. When I was frustrated about not being able to balance my birthday two-wheeler without training wheels, or unable to decide between the soccer team and ballet lessons, he would offer a long walk to talk it out. I had to scamper beside him, my legs pumping to keep up with his loping stride and the dipping, soaring kites of his sentences. His words wove pros and cons, reasonable possibilities and unexpected consequences. In my memory, those walks and talks were always on sunny May afternoons or glorious October mornings. Never the gloom of winter. I stamped my feet, willing blood to flow into my toes. I could use his incisive and wise brain right now. Everyone else was telling me what to do. Gina warning me to protect the career I had worked so hard to establish. Anna observing me like I was a suitcase abandoned under a seat in an airport, ready to explode.

I wished my father were walking alongside me now, his sentences somehow somersaulting my opinions into place. But he was dead. I wrapped my scarf tighter around my tingling ears and crossed the picket line to enter the Hall of Justice.

28 ~ *Pippa*

Their case had just been called, only ninety minutes late. Not bad, according to the lawyer. Turning slightly in her seat, Pippa looked back over her shoulder at the full courtroom. Mostly reporters, it looked like, which wasn't surprising after the spread in the Sunday paper. She thought she glimpsed Sam way in the back, or some guy with an eccentric mustache like his, but then a large woman shifted position and he was blocked.

Pippa turned to look at the rest of her family, sitting together two rows behind her. Francie was dressed in white, next to Marshall, who cleaned up pretty smart when he made the effort. Adele and the twins were looking down at a book. Pippa could see Timothy's lips moving as he read. Liz sat perfectly still, eyes closed, probably praying to Isis. Pippa started to wave, but Francie shook her head the slightest bit. Feeling reprimanded, Pippa flushed and turned to face the front of the courtroom.

She sat behind the defense table with her court-appointed lawyer. She had only met the guy once before today's hearing, and that was at her arraignment. He was so thin that she couldn't imagine he had room for the necessary internal organs, much less for the strength to stand up to the D.A.'s booming voice.

Arms folded across his chest, a uniformed guard stood sentry at the side door to the right of the raised stage. At their arraignment, the cops had brought all three of them through that door from the holding cells. But only Tian and Murphy returned to the jail, and Pippa had been escorted to Nan Malloy's office to hear about her house arrest rules.

The lawyer leaned close to Pippa's ear and pointed to the matching door to the left. "Judge Thomas will enter that way. When he does, stand up, and look respectful. He's the one who set the terms of your house arrest and he'll hear your case."

"Is that good?"

"So-so. He's strict, conservative. But he's very pro-motherhood, and you're pregnant, so that's in your favor. Especially if you can convince him how much you want this baby." The lawyer's mouth twisted down at the corners and he pointed down at Pippa's barely rounded middle. "When you stand up, stick out your belly. Your best chance is to persuade him that you are the innocent young mother. You're the youngest defendant, the youngest adult in the cult. That's why it's so important to separate your case from the other defendants. Our strategy will be to show you as a victim under their control. Brainwashed."

"But that's not true."

"It's your best defense. Do you want your baby born in prison?"

Pippa had no chance to answer, because things started happening. First, two men in dark suits came over to their table, leaned down to shake her lawyer's hand. Pippa recognized them as the public defenders assigned to Tian and Murphy. Then Nan Malloy and Emily walked in from the back of the courtroom and sat in the front row across the aisle, behind the table with the District Attorney. Did that mean Emily was on the other side? Pippa wanted to ask her lawyer, but he was whispering with the other lawyers, who had taken their seats behind the defense table.

She had other, bigger, questions about Emily, questions the lawyer couldn't imagine. Like, why did she run out of the house so abruptly yesterday? Was it just being squeamish about a decapitated cat? She was a nurse; she should be used to injury and death. How come she wouldn't answer about the solstice? Had Pippa been wrong to trust her?

Then the right-hand door opened and Tian and Murphy were led in, dressed neck to ankles in orange coveralls. Handcuffed and shackled. The guards had guns in leather holsters, bumping against their blue trousers with each step. They escorted Tian and Murphy to the end of Pippa's row, to chairs on the other side of the lawyers. Pippa wondered if the lawyers would change seats with her, so she could sit next to Tian. There might be a rule against defendants touching thighs on courtroom chairs. She leaned forward so she could see Tian and smiled at him, tried to capture his eyes, but he was staring at the opening door on the left. Then the bailiff announced "All rise," and they all did. Judge Thomas entered the room.

The judge's face was stony above his black gown. He seemed to scrutinize Pippa for a long moment. She stared back at the ordinary-looking man who held so much power over her. Was his life so perfect, so free of mistakes? Wasn't there anything he was ashamed of, any scene he would give anything to replay, to do it differently?

The lawyer tugged at Pippa's arm. "Pay attention. Sit down. We're starting."

It was hard to focus on the legal mumbo jumbo. Pippa tried to catch Emily's eye. She looked pretty stony-faced herself. Sometimes the lawyers talked so the courtroom could hear, but more often they gathered in a clutch of dark suits clustered around Judge Thomas' oak throne and whispered, only their arm gestures reflecting their arguments. At one point they argued loudly about whether the teachings of

Isis were admissible evidence. That was when the judge yelled "absolutely not" and smacked his hand down hard on the desk. Pippa's lawyer walked back from the huddle that time shaking his head and leaned over to Pippa.

"Bad news," he said. "Judge refuses to recognize any religion beyond the New Testament. I don't think he's going to allow any testimony about your spiritual beliefs."

A baby cried in the back of the courtroom. Pippa's breasts responded with the tingling let-down feeling, their memory strong after all these dry months. She crossed her arms tight, pressing on the nipples. How could her breasts betray her that way, ready to nurse when Abby was gone? She barely heard the rustle of someone gathering bags and walking out, shushing a hungry baby. Pippa wouldn't let herself turn around to look.

This hearing was all about Abby, but so far no one had even mentioned her name.

Then the bailiff called Emily. She walked briskly to the stand and raised her right hand, repeated some words. She had pinned up her hair, revealing her skinny neck, and she looked more gawky than usual. Even her voice was thin, and Pippa had to strain to hear her state her name and profession.

What would Emily say under oath? If she wanted to hurt Pippa, she had plenty of ammunition. Pippa could kick herself; she had supplied most of it herself. Emily could describe the details of last winter's solstice celebration, including that Pippa drank peyote in the libation. She could tell the judge that Pippa violated her house arrest conditions and snuck over to the children's hospital without permission. And worst of all, Emily could testify that Pippa planned to return to the scene of her crime. The judge would consider that was putting her unborn baby at risk, and they'd lock her up and throw away the key.

Dizzy. Like her head was filling with helium. Like when she was eight years old, sucking on the spigot from the balloon machine at the county fair because Stanley dared her and it made her voice sound funny. She began to float, a few inches into the courtroom air, looking down on Emily's arms hanging wooden in her brown cardigan. Pippa remembered to breathe. Gravity should hold her there, but it needed help. A tether, she needed a tether. She concentrated on not fainting. She grabbed onto the oak table. The defense table. Her thumb traced the rough grain. She studied the pattern of green and blue wool on the court stenographer's blazer.

Then Emily spoke and her voice was the tether.

"I know of no breach of the house arrest rules," Emily said. "Ms. Glenning has followed all the medical advice, met all of her appointments."

Pippa felt Emily's gaze flicker in her direction. Then Emily spoke directly to the judge. "In my professional opinion, Pippa Glenning is taking good care of her baby."

"Excellent," the lawyer whispered in Pippa's ear. "That will help. Now, we just have to separate your case from the losers."

Pippa smiled a private thank-you to Emily as she returned to her side of the aisle even though Emily looked straight ahead. Pippa turned back to her lawyer. "I told you, I don't want to be separated from my family."

The moment those words left her mouth, Pippa realized that she didn't know whether or not they were still true.

29 ~ *Emily*

After the hearing, I followed Nan Malloy out of the courtroom. Nan nodded in the direction of the guard stationed against the corridor wall, but her words were aimed straight at me.

"You're not getting overly involved with Glenning, are you?"

What did she mean? Nan's tone was offhand, but her words were pointed. I shrugged my shoulders, trying to match the probation officer's nonchalance. "I'm just trying to do my job."

"Good." Nan fingered through the stack of manila folders balanced in the crook of her arm. "These cult people may not be murderers, but that doesn't mean they're wholesome. They'll manipulate your emotions, convince you it's your mission to rescue them from the interference of the big bad outside world. But you're a professional, a nurse. You must know about keeping your distance."

I turned and glanced back down the corridor, looking for any members of Pippa's family. "What do you think will happen to them?"

Nan didn't answer until we reached the door to the probation department. She stopped and turned to face me. "That's up to a jury of their peers. But you want my guess? They'll be convicted. Tian will serve three to five. The woman too, probably. Your Glenning might get a year, maybe suspended. Especially if Judge Thomas agrees to separate her case from the other defendants. If it were entirely up to him, I bet he would just give Pippa probation. So the little woman could stay home and take care of her baby." Nan shook her head, like she didn't agree with the judge's priorities.

I didn't care about the judge or his priorities. During the hearing, it had been hard to look at him without thinking about the high-risk O.B. he resembled, a guy I worked with in Portland who made awful puns except when a birth wasn't going well. Then, his thin features rearranged themselves as he focused every brain cell on saving baby and mother. I hoped this stern-looking man wanted to save Pippa and her baby too.

Shifting the stack of files onto her hip, Nan opened the office door. "We'll talk next Monday. Try to control your maternal instincts with that girl, okay?"

"No problem." Buttoning my jacket, I promised myself to listen to Nan's advice and keep my professional distance with Pippa. That should be easy enough. Pippa's world was way too frightening.

That reminded me. "By the way, do the cops have any idea who killed Bast?"

"Who?"

"Bast. Pippa's cat?"

"No leads I've heard about. But come to think of it, why don't you leave by the back door to avoid the skinheads." She pointed to the Exit sign at the end of the hallway. "Take those stairs two flights down. Leads right into the parking lot."

Cracking open the door at the bottom of the back stairway, I peered outside. All clear. Once safely inside my locked car, I drove past the demonstrators still pacing back and forth in front of the Hall of Justice. Their numbers had shrunk to about a dozen and their picket line looked straggly now, with hardly enough people to cover the sidewalk.

I drove a roundabout way back to the office. Skirting the historic district, weaving in and out of residential streets to avoid Sumner Avenue and the park, I again considered Nan's advice. Okay, I promised myself. No more buddy-buddy with Pippa. Do the job; toe the line. Toeing the line made me picture Pippa, walking heel to toe along the red striped line on the hospital corridor floor, airplane-wing arms aloft on her own convictions.

Had I ever felt that confident, that certain about anything?

Marge's Oldsmobile sat in its reserved parking spot next to the brick wall of the Hampden County Home Care building. I hoped she didn't try to mess with me today. My plan was to quickly chart on Pippa's ultrasound visit, check to see if any of the lab results were available, and then pack up for my afternoon patients. Surely I could do that without having Marge in my face.

Her office door was closed. The large nurses' room was empty except for Andy, who leaned over his desk closest to the supervisor's office, unpacking his shoulder bag. I waved at him; he smiled and waved back. I had never trusted him. Gina swore that he listened to every conversation, every workplace grumble and staff complaint, and reported word for word back to Marge. But lately, rumor had it that Andy was no longer her favorite. People even said that he was working nights per diem in the emergency room, waiting for a full-time opening there. I wondered if Marge had a new spy.

I logged onto my computer. While it was loading, I dragged my rolling bag out from under the desk and opened it on the supply table in the center of the room. I gathered extra dressings and intravenous supplies. A fresh bottle of the coriander-scented oatmeal body lotion that Mrs. Grover loved. Size seven sterile latex gloves. That reminded me about Pippa; I kept meaning to document her skin reactions. Back at my desk I opened the computerized medical record labeled Glenning.

Under the Allergies tab, I typed, "Latex contact causes skin rash and hives." I dated and signed the entry, refreshed the screen, composed a quick note about the ultrasound and blood work and logged off. While slipping the laptop into its padded compartment in the rolling pack, I dialed Josué's home telephone number. I had planned to stop by his house the day before to check the drainage on his bandages, but finding Bast erased everything from my mind.

Listening to the echo of ringing on the other end of the phone line, I picked up the extra three-inch gauze dressings from my desk. Three rings. I stood two thin dressing packets upright, poised on end, leaning slightly on each other. Four rings. I added a third and then a fourth wall. Barely breathing. A wobble could destroy the delicate balance. Six rings. Steadying one hand with the other, I positioned a four-inch package across the top to complete the roof. I let my breath out, leaned back, and listened to Carmen's recorded voice. "Hóla. Leave a message."

"Hi Carmen, this is Emily. Just checking in on Josué. I'll call again later." Leaving the fragile hut on my desk, I gathered my jacket and scarf, pocketbook and rolling bag, and headed out.

The outside door opened just before I reached it, and Gina walked in.

"Hey." She smiled and slipped off her teal suede gloves. "I was hoping to see you this afternoon."

"I'm on my way out to Mrs. Grover."

Gina waved her hand back and forth. "Take a ten minute break and tell me about the hearing?" She held my elbow and led me to our corner of the office.

I made a face and flashed my eyes towards Andy.

"We'll whisper, girlfriend," she said, hanging her coat carefully on the hook next to her desk. "How did it go this morning?"

I dragged my desk chair close to hers and sat down, but didn't take off my jacket. "Okay. I only had to testify for a minute, to say that Pippa's doing everything right."

"Did you tell the judge about her visit to Zoe at the hospital?"

I shook my head. "He didn't ask."

"They say anything about someone killing the poor kitty?"

"No one seemed worried about a dead cat. The hearing was mostly about whether they should try the cases together or separate them. Nan says Pippa will do better if she has her own trial, but Pippa wants them all together. There was a lot of arguing back and forth about whether the family could talk about their religious beliefs, if that was admissible evidence. The judge said no to that, but he didn't decide anything else yet."

Gina pulled her laptop from the pack and hooked it up to the network. Then she turned to me with a serious look. "I've been thinking about this. It seems to me your client is getting a raw deal."

"What do you mean?"

"If she were Presbyterian, the judge would grant permission to turn off her ankle monitor for church. She wouldn't have to sneak around."

"Do you suppose he would give permission, if she asked?"

"That's your white skin asking," Gina said. "If you're an outsider, you try to stay out of their sight. You don't ask, when you already know their answer. They'd throw her right into jail, if they even suspected she was thinking of celebrating the solstice again. I'm no big fan of your child abuser, but it's still a raw deal."

This wasn't the direction I wanted to take. "I don't get it. You call her a child abuser. You tell me not to get involved. But now you decide she's not being treated fairly. What am I supposed to do?"

"Be careful," Gina said. "Just because Pippa is getting screwed, it doesn't mean you should risk your career."

I stood up. "Who else is going to help her?" I retrieved my rolling pack and started again towards the door.

"Nurse Klein. Hold it." Marge stood in her office doorway. "Please explain the entry you just made in Pippa Glenning's chart."

I tried to keep my voice even and calm. "The ultrasound and lab results aren't posted yet."

Marge frowned. "Not that. The latex allergy."

I stared at her eyebrows. Flying synchronized today in flawless formation.

"Latex?" Marge asked.

"Latex." I sighed. "Like rubber? She gets hives under the rubber strap of her house arrest monitor unless she protects her skin."

Marge's eyebrows soared, then plummeted. "Don't you think that's rather frivolous?"

A lot of medical people still didn't believe latex allergy was real, even though they were the biggest risk group. "Not if your OB examines the birth canal with latex gloves," I said. "Or if you need a narcotic, and it's given through a latex port. Not if one of these exposures results in anaphylactic shock. No, I wouldn't call that frivolous."

I turned away from Marge and her eyebrows and left the office.

❧

I was still smiling to myself fifteen minutes later when I rang Mrs. Grover's doorbell. Marge would pay me back with interest, but for the moment I felt gleeful. I bet Gina was still laughing. And what did Andy think of our exchange? Was he perching on the edge of his desk right now and commiserating with Marge about my unprofessional behavior? My cheeky retort would probably become the office gossip of the week.

Mrs. Grover greeted me with a wan face and bad news. "I've been so sick," she said. "There was infection in my wound and it spread to my blood. Terrell had to take me back to the hospital on Thanksgiving."

"How do you feel today?" I asked, reviewing the hospital discharge papers on her kitchen table. I thought back to the last time I changed that dressing. Had there been any sign of brewing infection?

Mrs. Grover's recliner took up most of the sunny room, but she insisted that the kitchen was her favorite place and that's where she wanted to be. I cleaned her resutured abdominal incision and taped a new dressing over it.

"How does it look now?" Mrs. Grover's eyes were unfocused and damp.

"It looks perfect." I peeled off the gloves and dropped them into the red infectious waste bag. Scrubbing my hands at the kitchen sink, I remembered Marge's inquisition. How did she know about the latex allergy entry in the computer anyway? I wondered if the witch monitored every single computer entry, or only mine.

"Are you sure?" Mrs. Grover's voice trembled. "I don't want to go through that again."

"It looks great today and we'll keep a close eye on it. These new antibiotics will help." I wondered again if infection had been smoldering under the neat row of black sutures last week. Pay attention, I scolded myself. I arranged the medication supplies on a clean paper towel, donned new gloves, and prepared the infusion.

Mrs. Grover sniffled. "My fever was so high that I saw things that weren't really there. Terrell said I was arguing with my sister, and her seventeen years gone."

I hung the medication on the wall hook with the framed scene of small painted seashells, and adjusted the clamp for a slow drip. Removing my gloves, I pulled the bottle of coriander lotion from the backpack.

"Let's make your feet happy, while the medicine infuses." I took off Mrs. Grover's bedroom slippers and massaged the scented lotion into the callus on the ball of her foot. The old woman sighed with a jagged hmmm, almost as loud as that cat of Pippa's.

"Heavenly," Mrs. Grover murmured. "Did I tell you what happened in the hospital?"

"About your infection?"

Mrs. Grover shook her head. "No, about the miracle."

"Tell me." My hands moved to the rough skin over Mrs. Grover's heel.

"I was so sick," she said. "Then I felt this presence near me, and I opened my eyes and Aleta was sitting by my bed."

"Terrell's ex?"

Mrs. Grover nodded. "Yes, ma'am. I haven't seen her in almost two years, since all the trouble with her and Terrell, when she took my grandchildren and left him. He wasn't perfect, my son, but he didn't deserve that."

"She came to see you?" I squeezed more lotion into the palm of my hand, and started on her other foot.

Mrs. Grover smiled. "I was so sick that Terrell cancelled his weekend with the kids. He never does that, so Aleta realized I was real bad, and she came to visit me in Intensive Care. She and I used to be close, before. Terrell came by, and they started talking. I don't know for certain, but it looked like maybe they were starting to forgive each other." She shook her head again. "Now that would be a miracle, with all the bad blood between them. Family's the most important thing. Maybe they're finally figuring that out."

"I hope so." I disconnected the medication tubing, then flushed the catheter with saline. "The antibiotics are finished. Anything else you need?"

Mrs. Grover patted my arm. "Are you okay, dear? You look troubled."

This old woman had been so sick. Maybe I missed the early signs and she got sicker. And she was worried about me.

"Thanks, Mrs. Grover. I'm doing okay." I bent down and kissed her cheek and let myself out of the apartment. It made me wish I had a grandmother or mother to talk to. All I had was Aunt Ruth.

Anna had after-school duty at work this week, and she arrived home just as Zoe and I put the stuffed zucchini boats on the kitchen table. After dinner, while Anna and Zoe washed the dishes, I took the telephone onto the sun porch. Wrapping myself in the old quilt, I dialed Maine.

When Aunt Ruth answered, I skipped the small talk. "For the first time in what, twenty years, I wish I could talk to my parents."

Silence. Then, "Can I help?"

I shook my head, even though Ruth couldn't see. "I don't know. I guess I need advice. I'm thinking about doing something. It's sort of against the law, but I think it's the right thing to do. I don't know. It freaks me out." I stared at the empty black squares of the sun porch windows. I imagined Ruth sitting on the plaid sofa in her living room, across from the picture window facing the island harbor. It would be dark now. "That's what they did, isn't it?"

"Your parents followed their conscience, Emily. They knew there might be consequences." Aunt Ruth paused for a long moment. "I guess you have to follow your conscience, too."

"But what do you think?"

"The times were different. We were at war and people did desperate things." Aunt Ruth paused again. "I think it's time to grow up, Emily, and make a difficult decision for yourself."

I mumbled a goodbye, pressed the disconnect button, and drew the ratty quilt over my head. Inside the cocoon, I squeezed my eyes closed, wishing I could cry. I heard footsteps and lifted the quilt to peer out.

"How can you even think about it?" Anna asked.

"You eavesdropped on my private conversation?"

"What if you get caught?"

"I haven't decided anything, Anna. I'm thinking about Pippa. Trying to figure it out."

"If you help her sneak out to that ridiculous ceremony, you could go to jail. What's so important about helping her dance naked in the woods?"

"They wear robes," I corrected her. "But it might be right, even if it's wrong. Can you see that?"

"What I see is the risk. Don't you care about that?"

"Anna, why don't you mind your own business?"

"It is my business. You're my cousin and I love you. How do you think it would feel to us if you go to jail? What about your responsibility to Zoe?"

Images flooded my brain. A little girl in the kitchen watching men in suits lead her father away in handcuffs. Sitting with Momma at the orange table in the sickening roll of the ferry, hearing about firebombing a draft board office in the middle of the night. Hiding in a tree house under a canopy of dying autumn leaves.

But that girl was me. Not Zoe.

"Zoe has you. And Sam. Anyway, I don't know what I'm going to do."

"Please don't do anything stupid."

She meant stupid like my parents. Anna towered over the sofa, her mouth twisted into an angry frown. She had inherited the same tall giraffe build as me. But inside, we might be different.

"What if what they did wasn't stupid? Just because the consequences were awful, doesn't mean it was wrong."

"I can't believe you're saying that," Anna said, stomping back into the house and pulling the door closed behind her with a loud clunk.

I couldn't believe it either.

30 ~ *Pippa*

The greenhouse was ready. Potting tables pushed against the walls to make room for the circle of pillows on the floor. The large cardboard box filled with earth. Two dozen candles, each hand-stamped with the image of Bast's paw print, burned in a spiral pattern on the cinderblock and plank shelf. Pippa and Jeremy looked at his drawings, hung between the windows. Anyone could see the kid had talent. Would the family nurture his gift?

Jeremy leaned back against Pippa's chest. "How did Bast die?"

"We don't know exactly. Someone killed her."

"No, the real Bast. The Goddess."

Pippa tried to think of a smart answer, but nothing came.

"If she was alive, she had to die, right?"

"I guess." Pippa rested her chin on his head. "I don't know."

Jeremy kneeled next to the carton, scooped out the dirt slipping back into the hole. "Why do we have to bury our Bast two days later?"

Pippa shrugged. "Francie will know. It's almost time to start. Go find Timothy."

After he left, Pippa sat cross-legged on a pillow, resting her hands on the early swell of her belly. Maybe if she could chant for a few minutes before the service, she could quiet her own questions and say a proper goodbye to Bast.

"We grow from your earth; we share your fruits," she started, but her mind was still on Jeremy's question. Why two days? If she had lived, Abby would be asking her own questions. How could Pippa be a good mother with so few answers?

"Your wings protect us." This time her concentration was interrupted by the itching under the ankle monitor strap. She chanted louder. "Strengthened by your power, we reach for the stars." She scratched her ankle through the thin white sock. After her shower, the fat red splotches had bloomed on her skin, spreading up her leg and down over the top of her foot. Pippa pulled down the sock to check. Still pink, but fading. She should tell Emily the rash was getting worse.

Emily was hard to figure out. She dealt with gravely ill people all the time, but a dead cat sent her flying. Still, if Emily had negative feelings about the family, she hid them well at the hearing. The lawyer said Judge Thomas listened to the professionals.

She couldn't blame Emily for running away; there likely weren't many beheaded cats in her own family history. But Emily seemed to like her as a person, not just a patient. She had even thought Emily might take a chance and help her with the solstice. Now that didn't look so good. She closed her eyes and tried again. "Strengthened by your power, we reach for the stars."

❧

The spiral of candle flames blazed. The square window reflected and magnified the flickering lights against the charcoal gray world outside. The wind rattled the loose corner pane, the one Marshall kept promising to fix. The seven of them sat cross-legged on a circle of sofa pillows, the tips of their knees just touching.

Nestled in the box of earth at the center of the circle, Bast's small form lay wrapped in a white sheet. Tall white candles planted at the four corners of the box represented air, earth, fire and water. The twins sat shoulder to shoulder, Newark draped across their laps. To their left sat Marshall, with Adele and Liz on his other side. Francie was already in meditation position with eyes closed and an angelic expression on her face. Pippa envied how she could open herself to Isis so quickly.

When they joined hands, the empty pillows between Pippa and Liz broke the ring. "Tian and Murphy are sitting with us in spirit," Francie said.

"How can a spirit sit without a butt?" Timothy asked, but his brother elbowed him and Francie didn't answer.

How could they have a ceremony this important without Tian to lead them? When they honored Abby and Terrence, Tian knew what to do, even though the bodies had not been released for burial.

Francie started quietly. "We grow from the earth; we share your fruits," she chanted alone. "Your wings protect us. Strengthened by your power, we reach for the stars." She let the soft sizzle of the "s" whisper into silence.

Then she turned to Jeremy on her left side, smiled, and lifted their clasped hands high like a mountain peak. She squeezed his hand and Jeremy joined her in the next round of the familiar words. With each repetition, with each smile and lift and squeeze, the prayer passed from person to person, growing in strength, mournful and joyful at the same time.

When it was Pippa's turn, Liz had to stretch across the gulf of the empty pillows. Pippa reached out to grab her hand halfway. When her voice joined the rest of her family, Pippa felt an echo of the connection that had been missing for months. When they sang together, their voices filled the greenhouse.

Their song faded into silence.

"Bast was more than a pet, wasn't she?" Francie looked around the circle. "More than a member of the family. She connected us to Isis. Her spirit will live on with us, in our home. Just like Abby and Terrence are with us."

They were all quiet until Francie spoke again. "What I remember most is how Bast liked to burrow under the blankets. Her fur was softer than a cloud." She looked at Jeremy.

"Sometimes when I draw, it's like Bast is walking on my paper. Like she pushes my pencil with her nose, like she's telling me how to make the line right." Jeremy gulped. "I mean, she used to do that."

Timothy shook his head, buried his face in Marshall's chest.

Marshall pulled the boy close. "What I remember most about Bast is how much she hated a closed door."

Timothy's voice was muffled by Marshall's sweater. "We're not supposed to have closed doors."

"Yeah, well, when I closed the bathroom door for a little privacy, she would yowl and scream."

"That wasn't about privacy," Jeremy said. "That was to warn us about the stink."

"Can't we forget the toilet talk for one hour?" Adele asked. "What I'll miss most is Bast waking me every morning with her nose in my ear."

Liz grinned. "Do you guys remember how she used to like to walk in the damp clay?"

"Before the Health Department said no cats at the Tea Room," Adele added.

"Right," Liz said. "And she would leave her paw prints in the clay, and that's how we got the idea for our logo."

Pippa hadn't known that story.

Jeremy sniffled. "That's another way she's still with us, isn't it?"

Pippa was last. She whispered, "I imagine Bast snuggled up with Abby."

For a minute, no one spoke. Then Timothy and Jeremy covered Bast's body with earth, hands patting the small mound. Their fingers left a pattern like ferns in the dirt.

Francie stood up. "Blow out the candles, so we don't torch our greenhouse, and let's have lunch." She leaned over to wipe a smudge of soil and tears from Jeremy's cheek.

❧

Jeremy licked a crumb of tofu-burger from his finger. "Okay, Francie. Pippa said you'd answer my questions."

Francie glanced at Pippa. "I'll try."

"Why do we have to bury someone within forty-eight hours? Marshall says that's what the Jews do."

Francie shrugged her shoulders. "We have to make this up as we go along. I don't think any religion has established rituals for how to bury a murdered cat. What else?"

Jeremy looked down at his lap. "Is Pippa going to have to wear an orange suit?"

Timothy broke the silence. "He means will Pippa go to jail?"

"And how long will our papa have to stay there?" Jeremy added.

Marshall answered that one. "We don't know. But even with Tian and Murphy away, you guys have the rest of us. We're your family." He stood up. "Clear the table, kiddos, and let's get back to decimals."

Pippa carried a stack of plates to the sink, grateful for something to do. She felt an arm around her shoulders.

"You okay?" Francie whispered.

Pippa shook her head.

Francie hugged her. "I've been thinking about our argument last week, after you snuck out to the hospital."

"You were so mad at me."

Francie nodded. "I think we were both partly right. Some changes need to be made in this family. If we had done it sooner, maybe we wouldn't have lost Meg and Enoch."

"Why did they leave?"

"They said that Tian was too bossy. A dictator, Enoch called him. They wanted to share a bedroom, and Tian said that was against the rules, and Enoch said then let's change the rules and Tian said absolutely not. After Ari was born, they got even more insular, the five of them. The more they withdrew, the more rigid Tian got. Finally, they moved out."

"Where'd they go?"

"I don't know."

"Why wouldn't anyone tell me what was going on?"

"Tian said not to, you were too new. Looking back, he was wrong. He should have compromised. Maybe we should have voted. Instead, he saw it all as a challenge to his authority. Maybe it was, but when they left, we all lost."

Pippa rinsed the frying pan and put it upside down in the drainer. She turned to Francie and crossed her arms. "Okay, what was I right about?"

"About how we weren't being good to each other." Francie reached for the frying pan. "And how you had to go outside the family for friendship."

"Emily hasn't been such a good friend either." Her visit that morning had been quick and businesslike, but maybe she was still worried about Zoe.

Francie put down the dishtowel. "I think we need new leadership around here."

"What about Tian?"

"He's going to be away for a while. We can make decisions as a group."

Pippa sat and pointed to the chair next to her. "If we're going to make decisions as a group, there's some information I need."

"Such as?" Francie looked uncomfortable. But if Pippa was ever going to get answers, this was the time.

"Basic stuff, like what happened in Newark and why Marshall wears that dirty rag around his neck like it's sacred."

Francie leaned both elbows on the table, cupped her chin in her hands.

"Okay. Tian and Marshall grew up in Newark. They were in opposing gangs. Tian's little sister was raped, then killed. She was twelve. Tian was pretty sure she was fooling around with a guy in Marshall's gang, and that her murder was related to that. So he fired his gang up to get revenge. There was a big fight and Marshall's neck was cut. He almost died."

Francie rubbed her face with her hands and paused for a moment before continuing. "At the funeral for Tian's sister, Marshall showed up with this big bandage around his neck. That took balls, you know? Tian's gang could have finished him off. Instead, Tian and Marshall shook hands. They had both had enough. They decided to quit the gangs and find a different way."

"And the bandanna?"

"Tian gave it to Marshall, in some kind of forgiveness ceremony."

That made Pippa smile. Tian loved making up new ceremonies. At first she thought their rituals were handed down from Isis, until she realized that Tian wrote the manual. The bandanna was a nice touch.

"That's when they started the family?"

"Not right away. Tian did all this library research about utopias, and that's when he figured out he was descended from Isis. Both guys had to ease out of the gangs. You couldn't just quit."

"How do you know all this?"

"I was working in Newark that summer, at the library. I met Tian when he was doing the research." She looked away for a moment. "His name was Earl then."

"Why did you have to leave Newark?"

"Because the citizens of Newark were uncomfortable with a cult in their fair city. First it was nasty notes, then rocks through the window. Editorials. It wasn't too bad until the mayor's daughter decided the Family of Isis was a perfect adolescent rebellion, and started hanging out with us. Then the vandalism got worse, and we suspected the cops. Tian consulted Isis and she said to leave." Francie stood up. "That's it. We came here."

Pippa stood to face Francie across the kitchen table. "Do you really think we can keep the family together?"

"We have to try. I love this family, Liz and the twins and all of you. Tian got that part right." Francie's voice turned softer. "Are you going to stick around?"

"What else would I do?"

"Go home?"
"This is my home," Pippa said.

31 ~ *Sam*

At the slam of a car door, Sam looked up from the computer and rolled his desk chair to the window. Emily was home before Zoe's school bus.

He had to admit she hadn't reneged on her responsibilities to Zoe, even if she had let pretty much everything else slide during the two weeks since Pippa's court hearing. The Sunday before, she served herself a two-inch square of Anna's lasagna and carried it to her room. A headache, she mumbled on the way out of the kitchen, navigating as if the air had become ocean.

When Emily brought her plate back to the kitchen, Sam asked what was wrong. He didn't tell her that he had observed the hearing from the back corner of the courtroom. Emily would have reminded him what he already knew: it was none of his business. But Pippa showed up when Zoe was in surgery and Sam wanted to return the favor. Besides, he was curious.

He didn't tell Emily any of that. And she didn't answer his question either.

"I'm fine," she had insisted.

"Are you scared?" he asked. "Because of the cat?"

Emily just gave him a look. It meant scorn and regret that she ever told Sam and Anna about the murdered cat. But Sam could see behind the scorn and through the regret. Emily was drowning.

Sam knew that feeling. Thick, sunken, underwater. His drowning had started the day Zoe's ultrasound showed the hole in her spine. After work the day after, he had waited for Anna in Forest Park. They were supposed to talk.

The park that afternoon had been a carnival of families. A guy in a Red Sox cap chased a toddler in and out of patches of sunlight. The boy glanced back and lost his balance, toppling sideways onto the grass. The dad scooped him up, babyfat legs still bicycling the air. Sam watched father and son, and his lungs began filling with seawater.

Sam stood alone in the shadow of the trees at the edge of the playground and watched Anna, alone, the wicker basket untouched on the picnic table. He wanted to sit close to her and share a beer. He had never been very good at figuring out what she was thinking, but that wasn't true this time. Anna wanted to have this baby and he didn't. Anna wouldn't change her mind. The ocean surged between them and he couldn't swim.

When he couldn't think of any more excuses to wait, he waded through the face-painted children and parents chasing toddlers, through a tsunami of misgivings.

"Sorry I'm late," he had whispered into her ear, nuzzling her hair. He used to love the smell of her scalp. He wondered what their baby's scalp would smell like, and how he could be a good father when he couldn't swim.

❧

At the toot of Zoe's school bus, Sam scooted back to the window. The bus driver helped Zoe down the stairs and handed Emily the backpack. Emily and Zoe disappeared under the roof of the front porch. Sam wanted to be downstairs, helping Zoe with her afternoon stretches. He tried to concentrate on his project, but building a website for two sisters from Ludlow selling hair-removal gel mixed in their garage couldn't compete with his daughter.

He knocked twice on the kitchen door before walking in. Zoe sat at the table dipping carrot sticks into peanut butter.

"Okay if I spend some time with my Poose this afternoon?" he asked Emily.

"Look, Papa." Zoe handed him a card. "I'm invited to Jessie's birthday party Saturday. Ice cream and cake, and real clowns who make animals out of balloons."

"Great." He lifted Zoe onto his lap. "The eighteenth. Almost the solstice," he said.

Emily ignored him, handed Zoe a glass of milk. "Don't get your hopes up. You're allergic to balloons."

Zoe started to argue, but Sam interrupted. "Don't worry. If your mother calls Jessie's mom and explains, they'll skip the balloons and you can go." He flashed an annoyed look in Emily's direction, but she had already turned back to the stove.

His solstice comment must have irritated her. But he forgot all about it and made up counting rhymes to accompany Zoe's stretching exercises, then played Knock Knock jokes on the bathroom door while she did her catheterization.

Anna came home with a new story about the boy in her Family Life class. He left his cranky computerized baby doll strapped in the car seat in his sister's car and she had an accident and totaled the car. The rescue squad used the Jaws of Life to extract the car seat and were furious it was just a doll. It put Anna in such a giddy mood that she invited Sam to stay for dinner, even though it wasn't Sunday. Over dinner, they argued about whether the boy should be charged with something, or just flunk Family Life.

When Anna started scooping ice cream into bowls for dessert, Zoe remembered the invitation. "My first ever birthday party. Clowns and everything."

"Clowns with balloons," Emily said.

Sam knew this was a moment when he should shut up, but he couldn't. "I'm sure if you call Jessie's mom, she'll nix the balloons, Anna."

"Call right now, Momma." Zoe bounced up and down on her chair.

"Okay. But you two keep quiet." She pointed at Sam and Emily.

From the beginning the conversation didn't sound promising. At first, Jessie's mother didn't seem to understand Anna's explanations about latex allergy. Then she apparently didn't agree that other games would be as much fun as balloon animals.

"I'm sorry." She leaned over to hug Zoe. "She said no. She's already put down a deposit for the clown."

"Just this once?" Zoe's voice was on the verge of crumbling. "After this party, I'll never go near a balloon again."

"It's just a precaution, isn't it?" Sam asked. "I mean, Zoe's never had a reaction."

"Doesn't matter. Do you remember what happened to Marilee from clinic? How she ended up in the emergency room with her throat swollen shut? From balloons at her prom."

Sam couldn't believe it. "You'd keep her home from her prom because of the decorations?"

"We don't have to worry about her prom yet. But we do have to worry about balloons on Saturday." Anna crouched in front of Zoe. "Even if they've never bothered you before, you could have a bad reaction. You could die. I'm sorry."

Anna turned to face Sam. "And I asked you to butt out." Then she carried the howling Zoe out of the room.

As he washed dishes, Sam realized that Emily had been silent. Usually she was right in the middle of any health-related conversation. She sat at the kitchen table, staring intently at the wall, as if her mind were a trillion miles away. No, Sam decided, that's not quite right. She looked like she had found something that had been missing. Emily looked like she had come up for air.

32 ~ *Emily*

I couldn't stop thinking about hives.

Sitting at the kitchen table, in the eye of Zoe and Anna's stormy argument about the birthday party and balloons and life's not fair, my mind was stuck fast on hives.

I hadn't actually seen Pippa's hives, but I could picture them. After her shower, they blossomed like mutant scarlet cauliflower on her ankle, itching fiercely. Once she slipped a sock next to her skin, they slowly faded. When Anna explained to Zoe about balloons and latex allergy and anaphylaxis, when Zoe wept about missing the first birthday party she had ever been invited to outside of her family, that's when I knew how to outsmart Pippa's house arrest.

So it barely registered when Anna dragged our wailing child from the kitchen and carried her to her bedroom, promising that they would do something special on Saturday, just the two of them. I barely noticed the swish and clunk of Sam washing the dishes. I even forgot that I hadn't actually come to a decision yet about whether or not to help Pippa.

I forgot all my promises. To Nan and Gina, to maintain a professional distance with Pippa Glenning and her oddly shaped family. To Anna, to think long and hard about actions that might be right, but had consequences I had never been willing to consider, had never wanted to face. To my other patients, to give them the care they needed, before someone else had a relapse.

I forgot that Sam had backed out on trying to help Pippa escape house arrest. Regretfully, he said, because he really liked Pippa. But it was just too dangerous.

I even forgot about Zoe, who would dearly miss me if I weren't around.

"You okay?" Sam held a dishtowel and an upside down glass, which dribbled rinse water in a splotchy zigzag down the front of his jeans.

"I'm fine, but you're leaking." I pointed at his pants. "When Anna comes back, would you tell her I'm going out?

"Out where?"

I hesitated a moment. "To see Pippa."

"You're not going to . . ."

"This is none of your business."

"I'm the guy who tried to help, remember? I'm on your side. I like Pippa."

"Sorry, Sam. Just tell Anna, okay?"

Sam nodded. "Okay. I was wondering though. I can't imagine where in the park they can find a place that is private enough, remote enough, for their ceremonies."

I scrutinized his face, but it was relaxed and open. He'd never find their sacred dingle. I didn't think I could find it again, by myself. Still, better not say too much. "I don't know exactly where it was. There were rhododendrons."

The car stalled twice in the icy night. How would Pippa react when I showed up? I had never been there in the evening, when her family was home. I had never ever visited a patient without an appointment.

But I was certain about what I was going to do.

33 ~ *Pippa*

Isis flickered in the candlelight. On the sofa across the room, Pippa resettled her tired feet on the pillows stacked on the coffee table, careful not to bump the teapot or disturb Newark's raspy purring on her lap. The Tea Room had been insanely busy when they opened after Bast's service.

"Almost," Liz had suggested, "as if the Forest Park community knew we just had a funeral and folks stopped by to offer condolences."

"But instead of bringing food," Pippa said, "they come to buy cookies and drink tea?"

"Are you complaining?" Liz asked. "Because we really need the business."

No complaints. Except that there hadn't been a moment all afternoon to sit down. Pippa's legs ached. Even after elevating her feet above the level of her heart for twenty minutes like Emily said, she could barely squeeze her pinky finger under the monitor strap. Did her ankles swell this early with Abby?

Everything about this pregnancy felt different. According to Emily's pamphlet, the baby was only about five inches long. But this kid felt immense, a whale in her womb. Abby had been light, her movements like butterfly kisses from the inside. Even in deep toddler sleep, sprawled across Pippa's chest and radiating that intense baby dampness, Abby had never been too heavy.

Pippa closed her eyes, imagined the heat of Abby's red blanket sleeper on her chest, felt herself pacing her own breathing to her daughter's rhythm. In four months, when this baby was born, Abby would have been two and a half. A good age for a big sister.

But Abby was gone, and Bast was gone, and Pippa wasn't so sure about Tian. He said he loved her and her feelings hadn't changed, not exactly. He just felt so awfully far away, wasting their phone calls talking about legal stuff. About the bald guard he was teaching to love Isis and wouldn't it be neat if a prison guard could change his way of thinking?

And what did he mean on the phone last night?

"You've really got to be at the solstice celebration Tuesday night, babe," he had said, his voice as gravelly as Newark's.

Pippa didn't know how to answer. "I'll try."

"Are you practicing the Mother Dance?"

"Adele's helping me."

"We'll all do our best," Tian had said, "to not let Isis down."

What did he mean? How could he attend when he was in jail? When Pippa asked Francie, she said to ignore Tian's grandiose ideas. Pippa wasn't so sure.

Besides, what about not letting each other down? Wasn't that more important?

He was right about one thing, though. She had better ask Adele to work with her some more on the choreography. Because one way or another, Pippa planned to dance.

When the bell rang, Pippa heard Jeremy and Timothy race to the door, jostling each other against the hallway. Then Marshall's deep voice ordered them back to the kitchen, he'd take care of it.

They were all jumpy. There'd been a string of hang-up phone calls and a sedan with dark windows parked in front of their house at odd times. The old couple next door was acting even weirder than usual, posing on talk radio as the cult experts of Western Massachusetts. But the murmured sounds of the conversation at the front door rose and fell, merging with Pippa's exhaustion, too calm and musical to be the neighbors. Then she recognized Emily's voice.

"For you," Marshall said from the arched doorway.

Emily looked insubstantial next to Marshall's bulk, her skin a soft gold in the candlelight.

"Hi, Emily. Marshall, would you bring another mug?"

He walked toward the back of the house, careful not to touch Emily. Standing framed under the arch, she looked different, less starchy.

"Have a seat." Pippa patted the cushion next to her.

"Are your legs bothering you?" Emily asked.

"Is that why you're here? To check on my legs?"

Emily shook her head and sat down on the edge of the sofa. "No. I came to apologize. I'm sorry I told you to trust Nan. I thought that she would help about Bast. I trusted her and I was wrong."

Pippa shrugged and turned to take the mug from Marshall.

"Thanks," she said to him. When he didn't leave she added, "It's okay."

The two women watched Marshall leave the living room. Pippa leaned forward and poured tea, then held a cup out to Emily.

"Thanks. Not raspberry leaf, is it?"

Pippa looked at her sharply.

"Joke," Emily said, holding both hands up in a parody of surrender. "Sorry."

Pippa smiled then. “Guess my sense of humor is a bit rusty.”

Emily took the tea cup. “I’m really sorry that Nan let us down.”

“Cops don’t help people like us. What did you expect?”

“Some measure of justice?”

“Right.” Pippa blew on the tea, sending a small cloud of steam into the air between them.

“I don’t know why I should expect justice. My father didn’t get justice.”

“What happened to your father?”

Emily rubbed the bridge of her nose. “I didn’t mean to say that. I came here to talk about you.”

“About me? Does that mean you’ll help?”

“First, explain a couple of things to me. Nan said something about gang violence, about prostitution?”

Pippa turned her face away. “I don’t know anything about gang violence. I heard there were problems in Newark, before Tian started the family. That’s part of worshipping Isis, to get away from that.”

Emily nodded. “Okay.”

“And the other? That was me, for a short time. I was a runaway. I had to eat.”

Emily’s face stiffened, like when they first met, then relaxed. She sipped her tea, then set the cup down carefully on the table.

“Listen, the only way I can think of for you to leave the house without prior approval is some kind of emergency. I’ll help you fake a medical crisis. That will give you a few hours for the ceremony. The monitor alarm will still register that you’re out of the house, but you’ll have a valid excuse.”

“How can I thank you?”

Emily held up her hand. “Not yet. There are three conditions.”

Big surprise, Pippa thought. “What are they?”

“One, you don’t tell anyone our plan,” Emily said. “Not even Tian.”

“That’s fair. I can do that.”

“Two, that you don’t drink the wine and drugs mixture. They could hurt your baby.”

“I don’t want that either. Number three?”

Emily looked square into Pippa’s face. “I go with you.”

34 ~ *Sam*

When Emily left for Pippa's, Sam sat down in her chair. He had to figure out a logical plan of action. He'd better not screw up this time.

Sam knew Forest Park. High school summers he worked on the park crew, clearing brush and cutting trees marked by the parks management guys from Boston. He had a vague memory of planting rhododendron bushes. The superintendent insisted they wouldn't survive on that cold, windy hillside, but the lady with the bucks argued that the acid soil from the pine needles was perfect. He could easily hack into the park management network. He could find the solstice ritual site.

What good was that? Even if he knew where the ceremony would take place, he had no clue what Pippa and Emily were planning, or how he could help them avoid a disaster.

He didn't realize Zoe had stopped crying until Anna returned to the kitchen.

"Thanks for cleaning up," she said. "Where's Emily?"

"She said to tell you she was going out."

"Out where?"

"To see Pippa."

Anna sat down and faced Sam across the table. "What's going on?"

He stood up. "She didn't say. She told me to mind my own business, just like you did half an hour ago. So, I'm going home to do that."

As he closed the kitchen door behind him, Sam glanced at Anna. Her back was taut with worry.

Outside, Sam leaned on the porch railing. The night was clear. Orion balanced on the tips of the frozen branches of the swamp maple tree in the back yard.

He hated to keep secrets from Anna, but she was suspicious already. Anna was a black and white kind of person. Something was right, or it was wrong. Funny, Sam didn't remember her being that way when they were first together. Things changed when she found out about Zoe's spine. She wouldn't listen when he tried to say how scared he was, how full of self-doubt. Maybe being tough went with that new territory, where he hadn't been able to follow her. Anna might feel compelled to call the cops, or the probation officer, that Nan woman Emily mentioned. He couldn't take that chance.

He climbed the wooden stairs to his apartment. He had to handle this alone. He didn't consider himself a brave guy. But Emily was family.

35 ~ *Pippa*

Francie said it always snowed on December 21, but the softening of the backyard contours was still a surprise. Pippa stood at the kitchen door watching the snowflakes ease the bleak winter shapes, then returned to the dining room table, to the strings of cranberries and small clay beads stamped with Isis symbols. She was grateful for the last-minute tasks. Maybe everyone else was thinking about the anniversary too, and that was why they were so cross. Francie strode around the house, telling everyone what to do, until even Jeremy snapped at her. "Who made you boss of the world?"

Liz just pursed her lips at Pippa, said the ceremony wouldn't work without a pregnant woman. Marshall said he had been doing his best to get Francie pregnant. Francie said maybe his best wasn't good enough.

Pippa had to leave the room then, her mouth bursting with secrets she had promised Emily not to tell. In her mind, she rehearsed the steps of the Mother Dance that she had studied with Adele and practiced every day, alone in the attic. She felt worst about not being truthful with Jeremy and Timothy, who hovered around her all evening.

"I wish you could come, Pippa." Timothy buried his face in her neck.

"We'll tell you all about it," Jeremy promised.

Pippa hugged them both. "I'll be okay. Nothing bad will happen this year."

Francie set her armful of heavy white cotton robes down on the dining room table, so she could hug Pippa too. "I'm sorry you have to stay home. Tonight's got to be the worst night for you to be alone. I wish there were some way." She paused, and Pippa thought she caught an edge of a smile. Did Francie suspect something?

"I'll be all right," Pippa said. "Make my apologies to Isis."

Francie leaned back and stared at Pippa, and Pippa felt her face flushing. Maybe she'd better act more upset. "Please. I can't talk about it."

At nine p.m., Pippa helped load the van—tarps and sleeping bags and extra blankets, the Yule log and candles and jugs. Last the family, dressed in long white robes over fleece pants and extra wool socks and insulated boots and thermal underwear. Pippa waved at the twins in the back window of the van until the red taillights disappeared.

When they were finally gone, Pippa stood in front of the painting.

"I won't let you down." She spoke out loud, her voice sounding silly in the empty house. "I'm not so sure what I think about you, but I'll be there tonight."

Pippa showered. She left her skin bare under the ankle strap so the hives would start to grow. She dressed carefully in warm layers of black clothes. When Emily knocked at the front door, Pippa was ready.

"Are you dressed really warmly?" Emily asked. "Lots of layers?"

"Yup, and I have the thermos of hot tea and the extra sock for later. And, I'm growing a good crop of hives." She pulled up the leg of her sweatpants, slipped down the thick wool sock, lifted the thermal long johns and stuck her foot out for Emily's inspection. "Lookie here."

Emily squatted to examine Pippa's ankle. "Pretty impressive. Not itching too badly?"

"Nothing I can't stand. What next?"

"Next, we call Nan's office. To establish the time and that we're still at your house. To set up your alibi."

Our alibi, Pippa thought, listening to Emily leave her name on Nan's voicemail.

"It's 10:30," Emily said into the phone. "Pippa Glenning called me. Her ankle is swollen and splotchy and itching under the monitor. I've been worried about her rash, so I came over to check."

Pippa thought Emily's voice sounded convincingly nervous and tense.

"The hives are spreading up her leg. It looks like latex allergy. This could become a systemic reaction, possibly anaphylaxis. I'm taking her to the E.R. for evaluation. She might need a shot of epinephrine."

Pippa watched how Emily's thin neck curved into the telephone receiver, how her voice strained for authority. She must hate lying about medical stuff. What would happen if they got caught? She would probably lose her job. Did Emily see tonight as part of her job, or outside of it?

Maybe Emily's decision had something to do with her father, who she wouldn't talk about, who didn't get any justice. Well, Pippa's own father probably didn't get what he deserved, either. She wondered what was happening at the farm in Georgia, how her Ma was doing. She wondered if she would have the courage to do what Emily was doing right now. To take such a massive chance, for someone who wasn't even related.

"I'll check in later." Emily's voice was winding down. "And let you know what happens at the E.R."

Pippa felt the fluttering in her belly. She slipped her hand under her sweatshirt and caressed her belly through the heavy material of her warm layers. I'm here, little fellow. She would do anything to protect this baby. But she'd felt that way about Abby too. Had she been irresponsible, to bring Abby to the Solstice last year, even when that's what mothers were expected to do in her family? A whole year had passed, and she still didn't quite know the answer to that question. But she knew that she had failed Abby.

"You okay?" Emily stood in the arched doorway.

"Yeah. What now?"

"The emergency room."

36 ~ *Gina*

Four days until Christmas, and she was stuck with late duty. If she had the time and energy, Gina thought, she would file a grievance about Marge's racism skewing the staffing schedule. But tonight all she wanted to do was finish her charting, check voicemail one last time for anything that couldn't wait for morning, and connect the phones to the night answering service. She still had to stop by the party store. Hopefully some red and green plates and napkins were left.

No balloons. She chuckled. Zoe had made that very clear on the telephone last week when Gina called to remind Emily about her Christmas Eve party.

"All of you," Gina had said. "Sam too."

Emily had sounded vague. "We'll try," she promised. "There's other stuff going on."

Chanukah was already over, so what conflicting celebrations could Emily have?

Oh. Solstice.

The slam of the office door made Gina jump. What was the boss doing here on a holiday? Marge stopped short when she noticed Gina at her desk.

"Is anything wrong?" Marge asked.

"I'm just finishing up. Then I'll put the phones on service and go home."

"Go ahead," Marge said. "I have to make a couple of calls, so I'll deal with the phones. The work will still be here in the morning."

Gina logged off her computer, and stood up. "Thanks."

"One thing before you go. You and Emily Klein are friends, right?"

"Yes."

"Is everything okay with her? She's seemed distracted lately. That cult case, you know the frozen babies, is it going okay?"

Terrific. Gina picked a bit of fluff off her burgundy sweater. If Marge asks me a direct question, am I ready to lie for Emily?

Marge didn't seem to notice that Gina didn't answer. "It's not just her. What's going on with staff here? Did you know Andy is working per diem in the E.R.?" Marge shook her head. "He's out of here. He knows the rule about moonlighting. It's damn hard to find male nurses to work home care. And the accreditation folks are big this year on staff diversity. You wouldn't believe what those bandits charge me to put us through bureaucratic hell and then point out our weaknesses and failings."

Gina checked her watch. She didn't want to hear this stuff. Diversity, was that the reason Marge didn't fire Emily? She needed the Jew, along with the black nurse and the guy, to round out her staff profile?

"So, what about Emily and the Glenning woman? Any problems?"

Do I cover for my friend, or cover my butt? Gina pursed her lips, as if she was thinking hard about Marge's question.

"I'm not trying to make trouble for her," Marge said. "I'm no ogre. You know, I had highfalutin principles too, once upon a time before I owned a business. You wouldn't believe how pitiful the new insurance reimbursements are, and nine, ten months late. This agency is barely surviving." She sighed loudly. "But, that's not your concern, is it?"

Damn straight, Gina thought, scooping up her pocketbook. "Not to worry," she told Marge. "Emily's okay. And she says that Pippa Glenning's pregnancy is going nicely. No problem."

37 ~ *Sam*

All solstice evening, Sam kept an ear attuned for the sound of Emily's car. When he heard the engine start, cough and miss, then finally catch, he scooted to the window and watched her pull away from the curb. He had been expecting this. Over the past few days, he had tried out several scenarios in his head. Various ways to monitor whatever scheme Emily and Pippa had dreamed up, so he could be available as their back up. He still didn't have a plan.

If only he had the guts to hack into the house arrest system, or tackle the electricity grid. He still didn't think it would work, but at least then he would be working with Emily and Pippa and not be left behind. He might not have the nerve to do what Emily asked, to break the law so openly, but he wasn't going to let them down. Even if Emily said she didn't want his help.

Grabbing his jacket, warm gloves, and car keys, he headed downstairs. He stood outside Anna's door, torn about what to do. She would worry, but Emily might need them all before the night was over.

Anna answered his knock.

"Where did Emily go?" he asked.

"Out for milk. Why?"

"At ten p.m.? On the solstice?"

Anna stepped back. "You don't think . . . ?"

"I do. I'm going to find her," he said. "Please don't do anything. I wanted you to know. I'll call later."

Driving towards the park, Sam waffled about which park entrance gave better access to the rhododendron grove. He had located it on the maintenance website, but there was no easy way to get there. The main gate was closer, but it was locked at dark, and his truck would be conspicuous so close to Sumner Ave and the park police station. The archway entrance was farther, but parking on a residential street was definitely safer. In either case, it wasn't going to be easy to find the place in the dark, and it was snowing again. He parked, then reached across the cab to the glove compartment for a flashlight. The bulb lit up. A good omen.

Zipping his jacket, Sam wrapped a wool scarf around his head and neck and pulled on his gloves. He shoved the flashlight into his pocket, then walked under the arch and turned to the left. Was it the cold, the storm, the night, that made him feel so awake and alive? Maybe he'd been spending too much time at the computer.

Pippa's group must have taken this path, but there were no footprints. The snow must have covered them up already. When the path ended at a wall of rhododendron, he was stymied. He walked up and down along the dense barrier before his hands found the narrow corridor sliced into the thick branches. He sidestepped into the tight passage. Sharp branches grabbed his scarf, pulled at his mustache.

When he emerged on the other side of the hedge, Sam heard chanting. Hugging the shadows at the edge of the path, he reached a spot where he could see down into a gully, to a circle of stones each illuminated with a candle. In the center, bonfire flames rose into the sky. White robed shapes whirled around it, singing or chanting. He couldn't make out the words. Hesitating, he inched down the hill, staying away from the light. How would the cult members react to seeing a strange man walking into their ceremony? A small clearing opened in the trees to his left, and he stepped back into it, to watch.

Pippa and Emily weren't there. Sam recognized the blond woman from the hearing, and the big guy with the bandanna. There were two other women. A smaller group than he expected. Just the few of them, dancing in a circle, seemed kind of pathetic. On a log by the fire, two boys sat wrapped in a white blanket. Their backs were toward him, so he couldn't see their faces. What did all this mumbo jumbo mean to them?

A rapid crunching of footsteps along the frozen path behind him broke into the smooth rhythm of the singing. Sam froze for a moment, then hunched back further into his hiding place. A tall figure burst through the thicket and down the steep slope into the circle, holding his thick, bare arms in a victory V above his head.

"Tian," the dancers shouted, enveloping the man in spinning white fabric. "Tian's here."

Sam recognized him from the courtroom. How did he get out of jail? Sam soon forgot to speculate, because Tian transformed the scene. He stood in the center of the circle of white robes. He bowed to each person in turn, motioned the boys into the group. Then he started chanting. Sam still couldn't make out the words, but the lyrics and music repeated. With each repetition, another person joined in the song, so the volume ratcheted up and the harmony too. Tian gestured exuberant circles in the air and they started dancing. The singing grew louder and the dancing intensified—faster and harder, whirling and spinning. A pottery jug was passed from person to person, each one balancing it with the same shrug of the shoulder, then pressing lips to the mouth of the jug and drinking deeply.

The boys stepped back from the fire again and sat on a log directly in front of Sam's hiding place. They leaned against each other in the shadows thrown by the dancing and the flames. They didn't look that much older than Zoe. Sam wondered if they would fall asleep there. The dancing grew wilder and the white robes of the dancers merged with the swirling snow into a maelstrom of motion. Tian's voice was thunderous and deep. He was the only dancer without a white robe. When he moved onto the large flat stone near the bonfire, the dancers all turned to watch him.

"Isis." His voice boomed into the white-swirled treetops. "Isis, your people are here to honor you. Bring back the sun. Bring us the light and the spring." Snow crowned his thick hair.

Sam had never seen anything like him. The strength and power of this guy, like he ruled the trees as well as the people who whirled and danced around him. Tian stopped singing for a long moment while he pulled the blond woman onto the flat stone, kissed her, and held her pressed against his body as he continued the song.

Wait a minute. Tian was supposed to be Pippa's guy. Did Emily know about this?

Sam couldn't stop watching. He had never seen maleness revealed so raw, the unadorned power of being in charge. He was fascinated and repulsed, at the same time.

More noises came from the woods. Voices. Fragments of sentences echoed back and forth among trees and snow, louder and closer. Thumping footsteps, many of them, blasting along the path, reverberating against the dense wall of bushes. This time several shapes exploded through the rhododendron bushes and down the hill. Flashlight beams crisscrossed the trees, ignited the snow.

A bullhorn blared. "Police. Police."

And loud voices. "Stand still. Hands up."

"Police. Do not run. Hold it there."

"We're armed, you fuckers. Stand still."

The blond woman turned her back on the invasion and stepped away from the center of the circle. She looked straight at the two boys, sitting beyond the bright lights. She extended both arms, palms outward, telling them to stay put. The woman must be their mother. She must be terrified for them.

Sam rubbed his mustache, stiff with ice. The last thing he wanted was to be implicated in this mess. But this was Pippa's family. These kids were not much older than Zoe. They were almost Pippa's sons. Sam stepped out of the shadows until he was just behind the boys. How could he reassure their mother that he would keep her sons safe? He placed one hand lightly on each boy's head, on their curls crisp with snow.

"I'm Sam," he whispered. "I'll take your boys to Pippa."

The blond woman stepped out of the lighted circle and stared at him. Then she nodded, slightly. She rubbed her finger along her upper lip, then mimed twirling an imaginary mustache. She looked back at the boys and pointed into the woods, then spun around to face the scuffle around the circle.

The boys stood up together, still draped in their blanket. With Sam, they melted back, away from the circle of flames, safely into the deep shadow of Sam's dark alcove. The three of them watched the activity in the circle. It could have been a well-choreographed ballet war scene. The army of dark dancers leapt into the swirling fake snow and vanquished the white ones, pulling them offstage. But this was no performance.

"It's okay," Sam whispered. "I know Pippa. I'll help you get home to her."

The twins spoke softly to each other before turning to face Sam. "Who are you?"

"I'm a friend of Emily's. The nurse who comes to help Pippa?"

They both nodded. They didn't look convinced, but what choice did they have? The path up the hill was crowded with cops. Sam steered the boys to the back of the clearing, helped them rewrap themselves in the blanket. Then he hunkered down in the snow in front of them, hoping that his dark jacket would shield them if anyone looked closely into the clearing.

No one did. The blond woman danced to the other side of the circle, spinning away from the invaders, then falling. A white swan creating a diversion to shift danger away from her offspring. Two cops grabbed her. Others quickly surrounded Tian, and the dancers. Their pistols dark against white robed backs. One policeman had an astonishingly bald head that reflected the flickering light of the fire. He seemed to be directing the others, barking orders and pointing.

Then Tian seemed to recognize the bald man. With a war whoop, Tian put his head down and charged, breaking away from the two officers who had been holding his arms. He landed a punch to the bald man's nose before two cops tackled him and threw him hard onto the snowy ground, held him down with boots on his back.

There was more shouting when one of the officers found two large jugs. He held them up, one in each hand, and called the others over. He sniffed, then tasted the contents, then spat the liquid out onto the snow. Holding his hand over his nose, dripping blood on snow, the bald guy yelled more orders. The cops started cuffing arms behind white robes with orange straps that looked like trash bag fasteners.

One by one the candles were sizzled out with a gloveful of snow. The cops kicked snow onto the flames of the bonfire and marched the white-robed figures up the slippery hill. The shouting faded, then the echo of voices was gone. Smoke hung over the stone circle. Sam was alone with the twins.

38 ~ *Emily*

The emergency room was overflowing with people, a crush of hacking, bleeding, moaning, wheezing, miserable citizens crowded on rows of chairs, spilling onto the floor.

"It's a full moon," the triage nurse said by way of explanation. Or apology. "Otherwise, it's never like this on a Tuesday night."

Lunar effect. We learned about that in nursing school. There's no evidence that more people get into accidents, have babies, or commit crimes when there's a full moon, but people believe it anyway. Even doctors and nurses in the E.R.

The nurse scanned the intake questionnaire, glanced at the rash on Pippa's ankle, then back at her face. "Any trouble breathing?"

Pippa shook her head.

The nurse pointed to the rows of chairs. "It's going to be a wait."

"Any idea how long?" I asked.

"An hour, easy. Come see me if the hives get worse or you have trouble breathing." The nurse turned to the next person in line, a squat man clutching a blood-stained kitchen towel printed with tulips tight against his shoulder.

I checked my watch. Almost eleven.

"We should be back by midnight," I told Pippa. "But I bet it'll be closer to one before they call you." We walked through the rows of chairs towards the red exit sign, stepping over bundles and bags and outstretched legs.

"Hey, Emily," a man's voice called out.

I looked around, but didn't see anyone I knew.

"Over here." Andy pushed through the crowd, wearing rumpled scrubs splattered with the leftovers of a long E.R. shift. "What's wrong?"

Terrific. Marge's spy just as I was breaking the law and every rule in the book.

"Hi, Andy. This is our client, Pippa. I'm here with her."

"I'm just going off shift, but I can get you in quick."

"Don't bother. The triage nurse said it wouldn't be long," I lied. "Pippa's having an allergic reaction to latex, but it's mild. I'm probably being overcautious. Because of the pregnancy, you know." Stop blithering, I told myself. Shut up before you make him more suspicious.

"It's no bother," he said.

"No thanks." Pippa smiled up at Andy. "But that's really sweet of you."

Smart girl. I smiled at Andy too, adding, "I didn't know you worked here."

"Just per diem. For now. Got to go." He hurried through the staff-only door.

"We're out of here," I said. I can't believe I'm doing this, I thought.

Outside, we waited on the sidewalk while three ambulances, sirens screaming, flew up the road and screeched into the emergency bay. I turned to Pippa, who was staring open-mouthed at the flashing lights and rushing figures pushing gurneys into the frigid night. "That gives us an extra hour."

That is, if Andy doesn't turn us in, doesn't call Marge and snitch that I'm overreacting again about this latex allergy stuff. If Nan doesn't get suspicious and call out the squad cars. Not being truthful with Andy and Marge was one thing, but lying to Nan had been harder than I expected.

We drove to the park in silence. Thick snowflakes fell heavily into the oval pools of streetlight. The drive took forever on slippery pavement, but finally I turned onto the residential road leading to the bronze arch entrance. The dark was sliced by the warning strobes of lights from three police cars, pulled up in front of the gate.

"Shit." Pippa slipped out of her seat belt and curled on the floor.

"Should I turn around?"

"No. Keep going. Pretend this has nothing to do with you."

I wished it had nothing to do with me. Though there was something almost enjoyable about the tingle of excitement, the pulse palpable in my fingertips. I wondered if my parents felt that mix of thrill and fear when they spread kerosene on military registration folders on the floor of the draft board office. When they struck the match.

The cruisers were empty, both in front and in the wire-caged back seats. No sign of any folks in white robes. Funny coincidence though, a pickup truck just like Sam's was parked near the entrance. Once the flashing lights withered behind us. I pulled the car over on a dark stretch of road between two cones of streetlight. I peeled my fingers from their tight grasp on the steering wheel, then held my hand in front of me and I watched it tremble.

"Maybe we should give up on this," I said.

Pippa wiggled back up onto the front seat of the car. "No. The cops might be here for something else. Drive into Longmeadow. I'm pretty sure I can find the way from the south. But I can't just abandon my family. I can't let Abby down again."

"It's too dangerous." I opened the thermos and poured steaming tea into the plastic cover. I took a sip. It was strong and sweet and burned my tongue. I handed the cup to Pippa.

She drank. "If I get busted, sell those yellow chairs to post my bail."

How could she joke like that?

"Listen," Pippa said. "I get it that the Family of Isis is flawed. I see the silly parts, the ridiculous parts, even. But there are good parts too, kind parts, and these are my people. I don't know what I'm going to do once this is all over. But tonight, I owe them this. I need to be there, even for a few minutes. I'm the one who's pregnant this year and I have to dance. No one else can do it. If you don't want to come with me, I'll understand."

I leaned my forehead on the icy glass of the window, looking out into the swirling snow. If only the night were clear. If only I could see Orion, find some sign or omen or something. Things seemed so clear to Pippa.

"Even if your family is flawed, you'll still risk your freedom?"

"It's not just them. It's me, too. I'm not stupid. I know that Abby's death was my fault." She paused, then added, "We've come this far."

Maybe she had come pretty far, but what about me? I still couldn't even talk about what happened to my family more than twenty years ago. All of a sudden, that seemed important.

"Before we do this," I said, "I want to tell you something. My father almost killed someone. He set a fire in a draft board office. It was a protest, against the Vietnam War. A janitor was working late and he was horribly burned." I stared at the lonely snowflakes. Funny how you knew they were white, but when you looked up at them, tumbling down in slow motion against the gray sky, they fooled your brain into thinking they were black. "It was an accident," I continued, "but it was his fault. Momma's too."

There. The words were out. I didn't feel any lighter. I was just as scared. Just as ashamed, no matter what anyone said about higher purpose or lofty ideals. And just as confused.

"What happened to him?"

"He went to prison. He died there."

"How?"

"Bad asthma. Worse medical care."

"I'm sorry," Pippa said.

I spoke into the snowy sky. "I never visited him in prison. Never tried to understand. Never forgave him." I turned to her and added, "I wish I had."

Pippa didn't say anything right away. She stared at the whitening windshield. "My father did kill someone. He meant to. My father killed Delmar on purpose."

Pippa leaned her head against my shoulder. We sat that way for a few minutes, sharing the cooling spearmint tea, passing the cup back and forth.

"We've come this far," I said. "We might as well finish the job. That monitor system downtown has probably already started its conniption fit, so the damage is done. But first, please put that sock on under the strap, so you don't really go into anaphylactic shock."

"Thank you," Pippa said, leaning over to take off her boot.

"Don't thank me. You're the one who has to find the trail."

39 ~ *Pippa*

"This doesn't look familiar." Emily peered into the trees. "Are we lost?"

Pippa thwacked through the bushes. "Not exactly. Coming in from the south, it all looks different," she said.

She had lost her bearings almost immediately, although she thought they were heading in the right direction. Visibility wasn't great, but the snow was lighter and the wind had died down. She thought she saw a star. "I think the trail is up here on the left."

Emily was silent for a moment. "I'm worried about the time."

"We'll head back by midnight. I promise." Hopefully, she could keep that promise.

The trail didn't appear on the left, but soon Pippa spotted a bush with shiny teardrop leaves. "Okay, I know where we are. This is the southern end of the rhododendron grove."

They walked side by side along the generous path, designed for people who needed extra room to maneuver. Pippa had to look away from the small openings in the hedge, openings leading to private clearings big enough for several people to lie down. Big enough for a red blanketed baby to sleep on white snow.

"We were totally lost, weren't we?" Emily asked.

"Thought I fooled you."

"Nope. But now we're okay?"

Pippa tried to smile. "We're not lost anymore, but I'm still terrified."

"Me too."

Things didn't feel right. The forest was too quiet. By now, they should be able to hear the singing, the familiar cadence and yearning melodies. They should be able to see the pinpoint lights of the candles through the trees. If nothing else, they should smell the smoke and see the sparks from the bonfire leaping into the sky. Pippa's mind shifted to a flaming night sky in Georgia, her father's tall shadow outlined dark against the glow in the pasture below. Snowflakes melted on her face, dripping down her cheeks.

"Something's wrong," Emily said. "It smells like wet campfire. Like steaming coals. Like someone dumped water on the fire."

"Or snow," Pippa said, as they scrambled down the slope to the sacred dingle. "We're here, but they're gone."

Broken branches littered the flat rock in the center of the circle. Discarded blankets were strewn like twisted corpses on the torn-up snow. The circle was gap-toothed, where stones had been kicked aside. Wisps of steam rose from the dead fire.

"We're still here." A whisper and the rustle of leaves announced Jeremy's presence just before his arms wrapped around Pippa's chest. Sam held Timothy's sleeping form draped over his shoulder. The boy's feet dangled against the man's knees.

"Please don't be angry," Sam said. "I wanted to help."

"Sam saved us from the cops," Jeremy said. "We've been waiting for you."

"How did you know we were coming?" Emily asked.

"Sam said you would," Jeremy said.

Sam shrugged. "I guessed."

Pippa looked back and forth between Sam and Jeremy. "What happened?"

Timothy's sleepy voice joined the conversation. "Tian came," he said, sliding down from Sam's arms. "He was so cool."

"He was pretty impressive," Sam agreed. "Really took over the celebration." He looked at Pippa intently, like he wanted to say more. Maybe she'd have time to ask him some questions later.

"But then the cops burst in and took them all away." Jeremy's voice wavered.

"In handcuffs," Timothy added.

"It looked like the cops had been following Tian," Sam said. "Like a trap."

"Why did they take everyone?" Emily asked.

Sam shook his head. "I don't know, but after they found some jugs, the cops got rougher, nastier. They handcuffed everyone and led them away."

Pippa pulled both boys close to her. "How'd you two manage to get away?"

"Sam helped us," Timothy said.

"The blond woman seemed to recognize me," Sam said. "My mustache."

"That would be Francie." Pippa smiled at him. "Thank you."

Emily looked at the stones and candles, disappearing into the snow. "Sam, you take the boys home. Pippa and I have to go back to the E.R."

Pippa dug in her pocket for a key. "Take them to Pioneer Street. I'll be home in a couple of hours. The Family of Isis may not be perfect, but we take good care of our children." Pippa heard her own words. That's what they always said. Was it true?

Sam shook his head. "I'd rather take them to my place."

Pippa looked slowly from Sam to Emily to Timothy to Jeremy. "Okay. But first, I have to do what I came here for." Her gaze remained on the twins. "Can you boys do the mother-chant?"

Jeremy and Timothy nodded in unison. They wrapped the blanket tighter around their shoulders and followed Pippa into the circle. She brushed the broken twigs from the large flat stone and stepped up onto it. Tian would have stood there an hour earlier, in the center of it all. Had he really been careless enough to lead the cops right to their sacred place? She pushed that thought away and nodded at the twins.

Their voices shaky at first, Timothy and Jeremy sang the words that offered new life for the family and the earth. With each verse, their voices gained strength and assurance and conviction. Pippa started slowly too, her boots shuffling on the slippery stone, her shoulders swaying to the beat of the familiar chanting. Her arms opened and her body found the rhythm of the twirling, twisting steps. She closed her eyes then, and it was her private prayer to Isis and her baby. Her undulating arms spun sorrow and regret, sang goodbye to Abby. Then Pippa shifted into the dance of gestation and birth and hope.

The soft sounds of the final repetition faded into the snow. Pippa stood motionless for a moment. Then she opened her arms for the twins' embrace. She turned to Emily and Sam, standing just outside the ring of stones. "Okay," she said. "I'm ready."

"I'm not."

Emily's voice surprised Pippa.

Sam looked strangely at her too. "What?"

Emily didn't answer. She pulled the glove off her right hand and reached deep into her jacket pocket. Her hand made a tight fist, extended in front of her chest like a weapon. She walked slowly, marched almost, into the dancing circle. Already the snow was beginning to erase Pippa's footprints.

Emily squatted, brushed the snow from the granite stone, and placed two small pebbles there. She whispered something, but Pippa couldn't hear the words. Standing up, she looked for a second like she might want to say more. Instead she walked to Pippa and took her arm. Pippa didn't understand what had just happened, what those pebbles meant to Emily, but she could see the relief in her friend's face.

"Let's go home," Emily said.

40 ~ *Emily*

Well, not exactly home. I tried to find a comfortable position on the molded plastic chair. The waiting room was less crowded and Pippa stretched out across three chairs and went to sleep.

I passed the time painting mental pictures of all the things that could still go wrong, listing them, and prioritizing them in order of awfulness. Nan could have gotten the message and sent a squad car to the hospital. When he got home, Andy could have called back to the E.R. to check on Pippa, found out that she was gone, then notified Marge. Some civic-minded busybody living near the park might report my license plate number. The cops could already be on their way to Anna's house.

My beeper buzzed. I pressed the button and read Nan's phone number on the digital display. I shook Pippa's shoulder.

"Is it my turn?"

"No, Nan paged me. I'll call her back. Wait here, in case they call you."

"Good luck."

The phone booth was on the far side of the waiting room, next to the glass doors. The storm was over except for a few solitary flakes. I punched in Nan's phone number and she answered immediately.

"What's going on? Where's Glenning?"

"We're at the E.R. Waiting. She hasn't been seen yet." I was relieved to tell a small truth.

"It's after one a.m."

"It's been insanely busy here tonight." I could answer that question truthfully too. "Just as we got here, three ambulances arrived. Major accident, I guess."

"Which hospital?"

"The Medical Center."

"How's she doing?"

"The hives are halfway up her leg. They're getting worse."

There was a deep sigh on the other end of the phone. I could imagine Nan's bullshit meter setting off alarms.

"And why'd you leave me a message on my work phone, instead of calling my cell?"

"Sorry," I said. "I didn't think about it, just dialed the first number on your card. Hopefully she'll be seen soon. I imagine they'll give her some medicine to stop the reaction, and then I'll take her home."

"By the way." Nan's voice changed in tone, became more distant. "Judge Thomas decided late this afternoon to sever the cases, to try Glenning separately from the others. He asked me if I thought she would agree to move out of the Pioneer Street house and live somewhere more wholesome."

"That's great. I don't know what she'll say about moving out though."

"Tell her I'll call her in the morning," Nan said. "Later in the morning. Call my cell when you get her back to her house, so I can reset the monitor, okay?"

"What if they have to cut it off?"

"Then I'll send a squad car out, and they'll replace the strap."

"Not with another rubber one. That's what she's allergic to."

"I'll figure something out. One more thing." Now Nan's voice turned sly. Almost like she was teasing me. "Did you hear what went down tonight in Forest Park?"

"No. What?" I held my breath.

"The cult leader, the one they call Tian? He escaped from jail and hightailed it to the park. The cops had set him up, were ready. Can you believe he fell for the sympathetic guard trick? Anyway, they brought in the whole gang, except your Glenning. She wasn't there."

"She was here with me." Each word felt leaden, mined from someplace deep, hard to locate and hard to extract. "I'd better go see what's happening with her. I'll call you later." I hung up the phone and steadied myself against the wall. My ears buzzed with exhaustion and fear. Maybe a jolt of cold would help the airless tingling in my lips. I stepped outside for a moment, into the frigid air, and searched the sky.

I used to joke with Daddy that I could see Orion in his eyes. They were so dark, almost black. He loved the night sky and the stories behind the constellations. He taught me the myths and legends, never limiting his words to what people thought a little girl could understand. His favorite was Orion, the skillful hunter who thought himself indestructible. But a scorpion was sent to sting and kill him. His mourners placed him in the sky, where they could always see him.

The night sky was clearing, but I couldn't find Orion.

41 ~ *Pippa*

Pippa watched the back of Emily's brown jacket weave between rows of chairs towards the phone booth. Watched her long legs step over outstretched boots, mounds of heaped winter coats, crumpled bags of take-out fries. When Emily was inside the booth, Pippa leaned down to check her ankle where the red raised marks were fading. Emily had insisted that Pippa keep the sock between her skin and the rubber ankle strap. It was too dangerous to fool around with an allergy, she said. You couldn't manipulate the immune system without consequences.

Maybe Emily couldn't, but Pippa could.

If the hives were gone by the time the doctors got around to seeing her, she and Emily would both be in big trouble. Emily could lose her job for lying to Nan. Pippa looked at the closed door of the telephone booth, then at the Ladies Room sign on the other end of the waiting area.

At the bathroom sink, Pippa took off her boot and sock, pushed the fleece cuff and long johns as far up her leg as possible, put her bare foot into the sink. She turned on the faucet full blast, splashing water on the ankle monitor and her skin. The sink filled, and she let her ankle and foot soak as long as she dared. What if someone else walked into the bathroom? She dried herself with paper towels, except around the monitor strap. The rash would look worse if her skin stayed damp. She left the sock off, imagining the rubber molecules burrowing through her skin. Walking back, her right foot squished with each step.

She slumped down in the chair, let her head rest against the seat back and closed her eyes. Her ankle started to itch, but she could take a little discomfort. Maybe she could nap.

The tingling started in her hands and feet. It spiraled around each finger, each toe, then tightened. It circled her ankles and wrists. Spiraling then squeezing. The zinging sensation climbed to her knees and thighs, her elbows and armpits. By then her lips and tongue and earlobes were thick and sleepy and prickly. Hornets buzzed in her ears, whirred until they roared. They raced against her heartbeat, stinging and squeezing. The tingling became bursts of impossible light, sparkles marching through her stomach, burning up all the air. There was something wrong with her eyes too. A dreadful shimmering. Electric sparks that illuminated armies of dying embers in rows. Strobe flashes of radiance.

The oscillating dazzles rode her blood and nerve highways. They gathered in her chest, where they ricocheted against each other, sucked up every bit of air, squirreled along her ribs, crawled behind her breastbone. Finally they imploded into a solid mass, a furry animal caught in a blind trap, scratching and clawing and biting to get out, get air.

Get air.

Pippa sat upright, leaned forward to grab her knees. Her hands clenched. They were heavy and cold. But electric too, still tingling with the sparkles circling her muscles up and down her body and squeezing to the unbearable pace of her pulse. She tried to breathe around the thick animal wool blocking her airways, igniting her heartbeats, avalanching her ears and eyes up into her brain which wouldn't help her, wouldn't tell her mouth to call for help, to call Emily or the nurse or even the woman still sitting two seats down cradling a red faced infant. She turned to the woman, tried to reach out, felt herself falling.

42 ~ *Emily*

I gave up on Orion and stepped back into the E.R. I doubted that Nan believed a word of my explanation. I walked slowly back towards the chairs until I noticed the crush of people in blue scrubs in the second row. Then I ran.

Two men were lifting Pippa onto a stretcher. A gray-haired woman held a stethoscope to Pippa's chest, a thin nurse held a black mask over her mouth and nose with one hand, pulling her jaw forward to open her airway, and squeezing the Ambu bag with the other. They all wore rubber gloves.

"Take off those gloves," I yelled. "She's allergic to latex. She's in anaphylaxis."

The thin nurse squeezing the Ambu bag turned to me. "What?"

I pulled the woman's gloved hands away from Pippa's face. "Latex allergy. You're making it worse. Take off the gloves and give her Epi."

"Let's go." The orderly at the foot of the stretcher pushed past me through the row.

"Look at her right ankle." I was screaming now, running after the stretcher. "Cut off the monitor strap. And she's pregnant."

"We'll take good care of your friend." The skinny nurse shoved past me.

"I'm a nurse," I pleaded. "Let me help."

"Wait here." She peeled the latex gloves from her hands, threw them on the floor, and ran to catch up with the stretcher as it pushed through the double doors.

I stood alone in the row of chairs, their metal arms linked together like one of my father's picket lines. This was my fault. I had wanted to help, but I made a horrible mistake.

43 ~ *Sam*

The phone rang. Sam had just tucked Zoe's checkered blanket around Timothy's shoulders and returned to help Jeremy recolor digital images on the computer.

Sam grabbed for the receiver. "Emily?"

"Pippa's collapsed. They're working on her now."

"What happened?"

"Anaphylactic shock, probably. From the rubber strap of her ankle monitor."

"Will she be okay?" He pictured Pippa's sunshine face, the surprise of her occasional southern accent. Her grin when she had danced the turquoise finger puppet.

"I don't know."

"What's going on, Emily? She was fine."

"It's a long story. And it's my fault."

"No, I'm sure it's not your fault."

Emily interrupted him. "Don't argue with me now. Are the boys okay?"

Sam looked at Jeremy's head bent in concentration at the computer. "They're fine."

"I'll call when there's news."

"One more thing, Emily." Sam spoke softly. "At the park tonight, Tian was kissing the blond woman. Seriously kissing. Isn't he Pippa's boyfriend?"

There was a long pause. "Yeah. I guess. We'll worry about that later, okay?"

"Okay," Sam said, but it didn't feel right. He understood that Emily didn't want Pippa to be hurt. But she had a right to know if her guy was cheating, didn't she?

44 ~ *Emily*

After I watched them rush Pippa through the double doors, after I spoke on the phone with Sam, after I stood outside gulping cold air and letting my tears freeze on my cheeks, I stretched out on Pippa's three chairs, using her coat as a mattress and mine as a blanket. I tried to reassure myself. A shot of epinephrine would suppress the allergic reaction, but I didn't know how long Pippa's breathing had been affected, whether her baby's oxygen supply was compromised. I should have been there with her, not outside searching for Orion. I wondered what the story was with Tian and Francie, and why Sam was so concerned. I worried about Nan, and would she let Pippa stay at home if she couldn't safely wear the monitor any more. Even with these questions swirling around my brain I must have fallen asleep because I woke up to the skinny nurse shaking my shoulder.

"Your friend is a fighter," the nurse said. "She's going to be okay."

"And the baby?"

"So far so good. You can see your patient now. Then we'll transfer her upstairs."

My patient. I noticed that word. They knew about Pippa and me. I gathered our coats and followed the nurse. "Thank you."

"By the way," the nurse said over her shoulder. "You should have told us she's under house arrest. We notified the probation department."

I had a moment of panic, but I had notified Nan, even if I had left out some crucial details. Let that go, I told myself. Pippa and her baby were okay.

Pippa didn't look so great. She was even more pale than usual, even with the supplemental oxygen through a plastic cannula under her nose and two IVs. But the cardiac monitor showed a normal pattern and the smaller unit above it showed a strong fetal heartbeat. The nurse moved a chair close to the bed for me.

At the scraping sound, Pippa opened her eyes. "Hi," she said.

The nurse adjusted her oxygen and wagged a finger at Pippa. "You need to rest."

Pippa nodded then turned to me. "The twins?"

"Sam says they're fine." I checked my watch; almost five a.m. "We'll call him later and let him know you're okay. Maybe he can bring the boys here to visit, after you rest." I thought again about Tian and Francie. Maybe I should warn Pippa, before Sam said anything.

Pippa closed her eyes. "Are we in big trouble?"

"I don't know. The last time I talked to Nan, while you were going into shock, she sounded pretty suspicious. The hospital called her too." I pointed at Pippa's ankle. "What happened?"

She turned her face away, toward the beige curtain divider. "I was afraid the hives would be gone by the time they saw me," she whispered. "I helped them along."

"You could have died."

She turned back to me. "You could have lost your job."

I couldn't decide if her actions were brave or stupid. Both, I guess, just like mine. When I had a moment, I would have to figure out what I thought about my own actions, about using my knowledge of medicine to subvert the rules, even to a good end. Somehow, I didn't think that's what Florence had in mind in the nursing pledge when she wrote the bit about devoting ourselves to the welfare of those committed to our care.

I pondered that conundrum while they disconnected Pippa from the E.R. equipment and wheeled her upstairs to a medical unit for twenty-four-hour observation. "Mostly for the baby's sake," the nurse explained, but I figured it was more likely at the request of the probation department. Settled in her new room, Pippa promptly fell asleep and I put my head down on the edge of her bed, close enough so I'd wake up if she moved. I dozed.

Pippa's visitors started arriving just after 7:00 a.m. First Sam brought the twins, who climbed over the guard rails right onto the high hospital bed, book-ending Pippa with their hugs. Jeremy stayed snuggled up against her, while Timothy leaned over to peer at the wiggly green lines skipping across the monitor screen and inspected the dials and alarms. Pippa smiled at Sam. "Thank you for taking care of them."

"They're great kids," Sam said.

Pippa hesitated a moment, then asked, "Tell me again what happened at the park."

"When I got there, your friends were dancing. I hid in a small clearing, near these guys. Then Tian came and it got pretty wild."

I tried to catch Sam's eye, to avert what I knew he was going to say. Pippa shouldn't have to deal with Tian and Francie now, when she'd been so sick. Sam refused to look at me.

"Tian was kissing Francie. Isn't he your guy, Pippa?" he asked.

Pippa blinked a couple of times. She looked out the window towards the dawn's salmon flush. After a moment she turned back to Sam. "What happened with the cops?"

Sam shrugged. "The weird part was how the cops seemed to know what to expect. They just ran in and started grabbing people. Especially this bald guy. Tian looked really pissed at him, charged him in rage."

Pippa turned her face to the pillow. I wanted to comfort her, but I had no idea how to explain Tian's behavior, with Francie or the bald cop. Or Sam's rudeness either, blurting that out, after Pippa almost died last night. I didn't have long to think about it, because Gina knocked on the half-open door and entered, followed by Nan. I shuddered to imagine the two of them riding up together in the elevator, discovering they were visiting the same patient and comparing notes.

Gina walked right to the bed and bent down to kiss Pippa's cheek. "Heard you had a close call, girl. How're you feeling?"

"Not too bad now, Gina. Thanks for coming." She turned to Nan. "I'm sorry I left the house without permission, Officer Malloy. I hope I haven't caused too much mess for you all." Her accent was more pronounced than I'd ever heard before, but her manners seemed to sit just right with Nan, who waved her hand in the air between them, brushing away Pippa's apologies.

"It's okay, Ms. Glenning. It was an emergency and you had to take care of yourself and that baby." She rested her slender hand on the back of my chair and I stood up. She faced me and spoke softly. "I'm not sure the extent of your role in last night's activities, Emily Klein." She held up her hand, palm towards me. "But you apparently saved Pippa's life and her baby's too. That's all I want to know."

Nan turned back to Pippa, pulled her chair close to the bed. "I'm still responsible for enforcing the court orders in your case, and for your baby's welfare," she said softly. "Maybe Emily didn't get around to telling you with all the excitement last night, but yesterday, the judge ruled to separate your trial from the others."

"What's going to happen to them? Tian and everyone?"

Nan shook her head. "After last night, Tian's charges got a lot worse; he'll spend some serious time in prison. The rest of them will be charged with drug possession, probably just get probation for a first offense." She looked at her watch. "They'll most likely be arraigned and released this morning. I'm not sure about the mother of the twins, though."

"Francie."

"Yes. The DSS worker was concerned about the boys." Nan looked from Timothy to Jeremy, both resting their cheeks against Pippa's shoulders. "Francie insisted they were with a responsible babysitter."

Sam crossed his hands over his heart. "That would be me." He motioned to the twins, who followed him to the far corner of the room. He took a laptop from his backpack and settled them on the floor before sitting on the foot of Pippa's bed.

Nan turned back to Pippa. "I spoke with the D.A. about you. We clearly can't put you back in a house arrest monitor. But if you admit neglect, you can finish your pregnancy in a supervised women's shelter. After your baby is born, you'd be on parole for three years, meeting with a nurse and a social worker every week."

"So I keep my baby?"

"As long as you comply with their instructions. I could probably arrange for Emily to be your nurse."

Which I guess was Nan's way of saying things were okay between us, whatever she suspected.

Pippa smiled. "That sounds pretty good. I could raise my little guy."

I raised my eyebrows.

Pippa looked at me and wiggled her finger, mimicking the ultrasound technologist's gesture. I guess she understood more than I gave her credit for. "Gabriel Tian Glenning," she said. "Gabe."

"You're going to name him after Tian?" Sam's voice was a combination of disbelief and disappointment.

Pippa's smile was kind. "He's the father."

Sam's mouth curled down in disgust and he pointed at Jeremy and Timothy. "He's their father too. Tian fathered all the kids."

"That's the way they do things, in the Family of Isis." Pippa looked at the twins. Jeremy held up his drawing for her to admire. Winged Isis danced with giant snowflakes. "Tian was a good father."

I noticed she said they, not we. She said was, not is.

Nan interrupted. "If you want this deal, you'd have to stay away from Pioneer Street."

"That's okay," Pippa said. "I don't think I'll be going back."

I wasn't sure what she meant. She wasn't going back to Tian, or to the Family of Isis? Sam looked puzzled too, stroking the pointy end of his mustache and not taking his eyes from Pippa's face.

"But," Pippa continued, "they're still my family. Francie and Liz and the twins and everyone. Even Tian."

Gina looked at me pointedly, but I didn't need her encouragement.

"We're your family too, Pippa," I said. I wasn't sure how that would work out, but Anna and I had an extra bedroom, and Zoe would love a baby brother. Sam smiled hugely and gave me the thumbs up. Pippa looked at him and mirrored his grin.

My beeper interrupted my daydreaming. "Anna," I whispered to Sam, raising my eyebrows.

"She knows," he said. "I had to tell her."

"Don't worry," Anna answered the phone. "I'm not angry. Can Zoe and I come visit Pippa?" She paused. "Zoe really wants to."

My beeper went off again, this time displaying the number of the Hampden County Home Care Agency. I told Anna to come on over. Then I took a deep breath and called Marge.

She answered the phone with two words, "You're fired."

How could Marge have found out about last night, unless Andy told her we were at the hospital? Maybe I broke some protocol by not calling her first.

"Did you hear me?" she yelled. "I will not tolerate insubordination. You know the rules. My staff does not go over my head and talk to a patient's attending. Not ever, do you understand, Emily Klein? Come in today and clear out your desk."

Everyone in the room could hear the slam of her phone in its cradle. I placed my receiver down softly, letting the irony sink in. Marge had no clue about last night. This was all about Mrs. Newman, and I had no reservations at all about what I did for her. I felt a twinge of worry about paying my share of the mortgage and regret about no longer working with Gina. I would miss Mr. S. and Mrs. Glover and Josué.

Gina put her arm around my shoulders. "Don't worry about it. I'll file a grievance this afternoon," she said. "You've got good documentation. Patient safety definitely trumps her stupid rules."

I could find another job, maybe return to Labor and Delivery. I might even look into that midwife program. Helping Pippa and Gabe would keep me busy, figuring out how to circumvent the parole rules once in a while. I looked at Pippa, the oxygen cannula crooked across her sunny face. I pictured her dancing in the snowy forest to honor her family. I remembered placing the pebbles on the stone to honor mine.

I shook my head and smiled at my friends. No grievance.

BIOGRAPHICAL NOTE

A literary late bloomer, Ellen Meeropol began writing fiction in her fifties when she was working as a nurse practitioner in a pediatric hospital. Since leaving her nursing practice in 2005, Ellen has worked as the publicist and book group coordinator for an independent bookstore and taught fiction workshops. She is a founding member of the Rosenberg Fund for Children and author of the script for their dramatic program "Celebrate," which has been produced in four cities, most recently in 2007 starring Eve Ensler, David Strathairn and Angela Davis. Drawing material from her twin passions of medical ethics and political activism, her fiction explores characters at the intersection of political turmoil and family life.

Ellen holds an MFA in creative writing from the Stonecoast program at the University of Southern Maine. Her stories have appeared in *Bridges*, *The Drum*, *Portland Magazine*, *Pedestal*, *Patchwork Journal*, and *The Women's Times*. *House Arrest* is her first novel. She lives in Western Massachusetts.